Praise for

Mar...

This engaging novel (*In Search of Felicity*) gives voice to those of us who find inspiration and insight into our own lives through great works of literature. Rizzo's work will resonate with Rawlings fans and even those who will take up her books for the first time.

Florence M. Turcotte
literary manuscripts archivist
George A. Smathers Libraries
University of Florida, Gainesville

Marian Rizzo explores the parallels a young writer uncovers between her own life and that of Marjorie Kinnan Rawlings, whose own focus on rural Florida cracker life earned her a Pulitzer Prize. As she uncovers layer upon layer of Marjorie's unconventional lifestyle, she discovers those parallels may also hold the key to her own social angst in a satisfying climax that will leave you yearning for more.

Emory R. Schley,
Star-Banner columnist for 30-plus years

Once again, Marian Rizzo captures the heart of her readers. In this second book in her, "In Search Of" series, Rizzo beautifully interweaves the life of Pulitzer Prize winning author, Marjorie Kinnan Rawlings, with the continuing tender love story of Julie Peters and Mark Bensen. The result is pure pleasure.

Delores Kight
co-author, *Manny the Lamb*

For the reader interested in a Florida of years gone by and Pulitzer Prize winner Marjorie Kinnan Rawlings specifically, this is a must-read story. Often spiritual but never preaching, Ms. Rizzo deftly handles the juxtapositional narrative from early 20th-century Cracker life to the contemporary lifestyle and the complications her characters encounter. Historically speaking, her book is spot-on and readers will find the story not only a delight to read, but insightful as well.

Fred Mullen
actor/director/artist

Truth be told, I am not a novel guy. But I have to admit, Marian Rizzo's *In Search of the Beloved* drew me in from the first page. I love how she weaved her characters in and out of the search for the Apostle John. Great read.

Dr. Woodrow Kroll
Creator of *The HELIOS Project*

A gripping and engaging exploration of what it would be like if John, the beloved Apostle, were still alive and living in the island of Patmos. Marian Rizzo takes us on a delightful journey through the eyes and experiences of two thought-provoking and inquisitive characters, Mark, a professor, and Julie, a newspaper reporter.

Tom Mabie, Ordained United Methodist Pastor

Marian Rizzo is a gifted storyteller, whether it be for news reporting or fiction. She has a keen eye and ear for the intricacies of a story, which translates into very powerful narratives. Marian can turn the mundane into the magnificent through the masterful weaving of character, context, and scene-setting.

Susan Smiley-Height
Longtime journalist and editor in the newspaper industry

In Search of Felicity

Also available from

Marian Rizzo

Angela's Treasures
Muldovah
In Search of the Beloved

In Search of

Felicity

In the Footsteps of Marjorie Kinnan Rawlings

a novel

Marian Rizzo

WordCrafts

The Private Marjorie, The Love Letters of Marjorie Kinnan Rawlings to Norton S. Baskin, by Rodger L. Tarr. Gainesville: University Press of Florida, 2004, selected quotations. Used by permission.

Max and Marjorie: The Correspondence between Maxwell E. Perkins and Marjorie Kinnan Rawlings, edited by Rodger L. Tarr. Gainesville: University Press of Florida, 1999, selected quotations. Used by permission.

Marjorie Kinnan Rawlings, Special and Area Studies Collections, George A. Smathers Libraries, University of Florida, Gainesville, Florida, selected quotation. Used by permission.

In Search of Felicity, although a work of fiction, includes information based on actual events. The author has endeavored to be respectful to all persons, places, and events presented in this novel, and has attempted to be as accurate as possible. Still, this is a novel, and all references to persons, places and events are fictitious or used fictitiously.

Published by WordCrafts Press
Cody, Wyoming 82414
www.wordcrafts.net

Dedicated to
the East Rochester High School Class of 1960
and dear friends who encouraged me
in all my writing endeavors.

In memory of Miss Lois Bird,
an elementary school teacher
and the first person who said
I should be a writer when I grew up.

JULIE

Grampa's farm was more than a piece of land, more than 40 acres of vegetable rows and cow pastures, more than a watering hole for family reunions, when uncles cleared the front lawn of animal droppings and propped sheets of plywood on sawhorses, and aunts spread red-and-white checkered tablecloths on top, and brought out an array of covered-dish casseroles, berry pies, fried chicken, and pitchers of lemonade and iced tea.

For Julie Peters, Grampa's farm was a lot more than that. It was a place to escape from the daily routine of school work and household chores, a place where she could run barefoot across the meadow and leap fearlessly, ahead of her cousins, into the icy waters of the creek. And most of all, a visit to Grampa's farm meant for at least five hours she'd be the center of attention to the wrinkle-faced patriarch who made her feel like she was the most important person in the world.

From the time she was five years old, Julie followed after her Grampa in the fields behind the old farmhouse. Grampa would bend over with a groan and pull weeds from his row of cabbages or spinach or green beans, and she'd do the same, digging her little fingers into the rich warm soil. Then, he'd turn his head in her direction and say something like, "You've gotta get the bad stuff out of your life if you want to grow into a healthy plant. Learn to recognize the weeds, Juliekins. Pull 'em out and toss 'em away."

She was in training for life, though she didn't know it at the time. She just thought she was helping her grampa rid his garden of the bad stuff and maybe saving his vegetables for another day. Nevertheless, Grampa's mini lectures stuck with her and often popped into her head at unexpected times in years to come. They began to make sense long after the family reunions stopped.

Most of all, Julie remembered their last Thanksgiving together, when, after dinner, she sat beside Grampa on the living room sofa while Gramma and the other ladies washed the dishes in the kitchen. With the spray of the faucet and the tinkle of china and silverware playing like a distant melody, the old sage bobbed his graying head and grunted as he shifted his bones into a soft spot on the lumpy sofa. The lines on his weathered face had deepened over the last year, and the stubble of a beard clung to his chin, even after he finished shaving. He looked old, and it frightened Julie, because even as a teenager she knew what aging meant. But the flicker of youth in Grampa's pale blue eyes belied his outer shell, and they glistened like he was looking off at something that pleased him a whole lot more than the big, red barn outside the window.

That evening, while the sun lay a golden ribbon across the horizon, he turned away from the scene and gazed at Julie in that special way when he was about to pass on another slice of wisdom. Sure enough, like always, he cleared his throat and expelled a little grunt before launching into another mini lecture.

"Sometime in life, you're gonna reach a crossroad—a

fork—and you'll have to make a decision," he said. "Mark my words, Juliekins, if you choose wisely, blessings will come. Then, move ahead with confidence and keep an eye out for the next crossroad, because as sure as the sun comes up every morning, so will another fork in the road."

She peered back at him innocently. "How will I know which road to take, Grampa?"

"Oh, you'll know. Someone will be standing behind you saying, 'This is the way, walk in it,' whether you turn to the right or to the left."

"Huh?"

He chuckled, then fell into a coughing fit. When he surfaced, his eyes had glazed over with moisture. "Just wait. You'll know. And if you choose the right path, blessings will come."

Julie left the farm that day feeling special. Grampa had taken her aside from the rest of the cousins and even from her little sister, and had imparted another gem of advice meant solely for her. Like always, she tucked Grampa's admonition in the back of her mind, went back to her life in the suburbs, and plunged into her school work, her soccer games, and Saturday night parties at the homes of friends. And she looked forward to Christmas and another family gathering at Grampa's farm. But it never came. He died December 3rd from complications of pneumonia.

Grampa's death hit like a bombshell. Overnight, everything changed. Immediately after his funeral, Julie's father and his two brothers sold the old farmhouse, the forty acres, and all the cows and sheep. They put Gramma in a nursing home, and they went back to their jobs in the city, without so much as a backward glance at the place where they'd grown up and now had left behind.

But Julie couldn't just walk away from Grampa's farm or from the old man who worked it. Nor would she soon forget the lessons she learned from him. In tiny sprinkles, they all came back to her, one after another, and eventually formed a giant pool of wisdom.

From that time, no one impacted her life the way Grampa had, until years later when she traveled to the isle of Patmos while working as a newspaper reporter for the *Springfield Daily Press*. Her editor had sent her in search of Yanno Theologos, an elderly man who'd been ministering in miraculous ways to the people who lived there. For Julie, it was a case of déjà vu. She'd gone there to take photographs and do interviews, and instead she'd ended up sitting at the old man's feet soaking up his insights about life.

What was it about the wisdom of gray-headed men and women who could open up fresh doors of understanding for a young person? While some people view the aged as bores to be merely tolerated, she'd come to appreciate them as ministers of instruction beyond the traditional classroom.

Surprisingly, the visit with Yanno brought her face-to-face with one of Grampa's "crossroads." Like the old man had predicted, she faced a decision. She'd been sent there to publicly expose Yanno in a newspaper article that would dispel or prove the rumor that John the apostle was alive and well on Patmos. But after getting to know the old man, she had second thoughts. The story would very likely subject him to a tremendous media invasion and possibly threaten the peaceful atmosphere of the tiny island. If she didn't run the story and merely offered her boss a travel piece, she risked losing her job. She was at a crossroads. In the back of her mind came that little voice Grampa had mentioned telling her to do the right thing. In the end, she wrote the travel piece, and as expected, she got fired.

But like Grampa had promised, blessings came. Immediately after Julie's article ran in the newspaper's travel section, another opportunity dropped in her lap. Ian Fairchild, senior editor at *Great Destinations Magazine,* emailed her with an offer she couldn't refuse.

Ms. Peters, his message read. *I wonder if you might consider doing a series of articles based on the same premise you used in your story, 'In Search of the Beloved, A Traveler's Pursuit of John the Apostle.'*

There it was. The blessing. In a way, she felt a little like the main character in *Pilgrim's Progress.* During Christian's walk to the Celestial City, he sometimes reached a place of decision, a crossroads, so to speak. But someone always came along at the last minute and rescued him. Perhaps she had encountered her own Faithful and Hopeful and Mr. Great Heart—only for her they were Grampa and Yanno, and now Ian Fairchild.

In any case, she was on a different path than the one she'd started on. The transition from newspaper reporter to magazine writer, though daunting, also brought some positive challenges. Her writing needed to change from factual jargon to a more relaxed feature-type presentation, and she'd have to use a different manual of style. Ian had told her she could work from home but that she should expect to do some traveling, possibly even to other countries.

For now, she needed to be in San Diego for the next couple of days visiting with her new editor. Excitement boiled up inside her. A new job with an unlimited travel budget. A higher salary, nearly three times what she'd earned at the newspaper. If she wanted to make it work, she was going to have to plunge in and start running.

A wave of discomfort interrupted her euphoria. She glanced at the ring on her left hand. Mark wanted to get married in two months, in September. She needed more time to adjust to her new job. Another crossroads; another decision. She was on her own now. No Grampa to guide her. No Yanno to offer words of wisdom. All she could do was draw on what they'd already given her and, somehow, choose the right fork in the road.

2

CALIFORNIA

Julie set her suitcase by the front door. She pretended she didn't see the worried look on Mark's face. She turned away and started toward her desk in the corner where she'd left her briefcase.

He stepped in front of her and blocked her path. "I'm gonna miss you," he said. "I wish you didn't have to go away right now."

She gazed into his crystal blue eyes. The guy made her feel like she mattered. He was handsome, a young Tom Hanks type with a crop of blond hair, a dream for any young woman. But he wanted *her*. She wavered for only a second. If she didn't follow up with this job, she'd be giving up the career of a lifetime.

She forced a smile. "You knew I had to do some traveling, Mark. I have to meet my editor and get my assignments. This is important to me, to my career. I'll be in California for just a couple of days."

He frowned. "What about the wedding?"

She swallowed and turned away from him. "We'll have plenty of time to make arrangements when I get back."

"Right," he said, a hint of sarcasm in his voice.

She dropped onto the sofa and crossed her arms. He stepped in front of her, his eyes clouded with disappointment.

"What's the matter, Julie? Have you changed your mind? Don't you want to get married?"

She managed another weak smile. "Of course, I do. But working for that magazine is a dream come true. I'm gonna be busy for the next couple of months."

"So, what do we do?"

She shrugged. "I don't know. I've spent every waking hour getting ready for this new job. I've stepped into unfamiliar waters, Mark. I've been reading online issues of *Great Destinations,* and I've searched out other magazines to see how their writers put together a good travel piece. I haven't had time to think about anything else." She bit her lip, then plunged ahead. "Do you think maybe we should postpone the ceremony until say—December? A Christmas wedding might be nice."

He breathed a loud sigh and settled onto the sofa beside her leaving a noticeable gap between them.

They sat in silence for a few minutes with Julie fidgeting and Mark clenching and unclenching his hands. She didn't dare look at his face. If she did, she'd be reminded of the day only a month ago when he dropped to his knee and proposed. She'd probably crumble then.

She loved Mark and wanted to be his wife. Eventually. But there was another problem. The monster from her past kept trying to surface. Despite Yanno's words of encouragement, she hadn't killed it after all, had merely stunned it for a while. The old man had led her back to her faith in God. And he'd helped her to forgive the people who'd turned their backs on her. Then, he'd sent her off with an admonition to deal wisely with the rest of the debris in her heart. The problem was, the memory of the trauma she'd suffered was still alive and well. Now it was clawing its way out again.

She willed the monster back inside and dared to glance in Mark's direction. His face was like stone.

"I do love you, Mark. You must know that by now."

He nodded but continued looking straight ahead. "If it's a lot to handle, I can help with the wedding plans," he said, his voice soft. "We should be doing this together anyway."

She nodded. "I know. My mother offered, too."

"That's nice."

"So did Lakisha."

"She should. She's your matron of honor, isn't she?"

"Yes, but don't forget she's six months pregnant. I don't think she'll like the idea of waddling down the aisle in a tent of a dress."

Her comment brought a smile to his lips.

"My dad wants to come up from Florida," he said. "Believe it or not, he's bringing a lady friend with him."

The image of Mark's father dating someone at his age brought a smile to Julie's lips. "Isn't he close to 70?"

"Sixty-eight to be exact," Mark said with a nod. "Ever since my mom died, my father hasn't dated at all—not until he moved to Florida, last year."

She chuckled, relieved that their conversation had turned light. "I read something about the Fountain of Youth. Maybe it's for real."

The tension had eased for the moment. Stress seemed to be Julie's constant companion these days. There wasn't a time in the last six years when she didn't buckle under the slightest pressure. Perhaps having Mark in her life was a good thing. He walked around like he didn't have a care in the world. Only matters of the heart seemed to bother him lately. Nothing else riled him, not even when problems came up at work or when his car broke down or that time he misplaced his cell phone. He always bounced back, or seemed to. Meanwhile, she fell apart over the slightest incident. She had to admit, Mark's personality balanced hers quite well.

"Okay," she said. "For the next week or so, why don't I concentrate on my first assignment? Afterward, we'll focus on the wedding, and we'll set a definite date."

Mark settled back, like he was relaxing for the first time since the subject came up. "Okay," he said. "We'll take things one step at a time. Everything will fall into place, Julie. You'll see."

He'd said something like that before, after she lost her newspaper job. He'd been proven right then, so why not now? Mark was like a young version of Grampa—calm, laid-back, and filled with godly wisdom. And, thank the Lord, he was flexible enough to give her more time.

Somehow, Julie had avoided the fork. For the time being, she was traveling straight ahead. Now she merely needed to wait and see what lay beyond the next bend in the road.

The trip to California proved fruitful. The moment Julie entered Ian Fairchild's office she felt an immediate connection with her new boss. She scanned the room and picked up several clues, not only about Ian, but perhaps the entire firm. The polished wood floor, a plush sofa, the top level of a bookshelf home to several *Ellie* awards. The rest of the shelves crammed with magazines—the company's own blue-and-green bound publications, plus the familiar yellow spines of *National Geographic* and several other periodicals Julie didn't recognize.

Behind Ian's broad, mahogany desk, a wall of glass provided a view of a treed city park four stories below. Three cozy armchairs made a half-circle in front of Ian's desk. Before him were a neat stack of magazines, an in-and-out letter tray, a laptop computer, and what appeared to be a trio of family photos, plus a plate of vegetables and crackers, a sign Ian was still finishing his lunch.

He rose from behind his desk, greeted her with a handshake, and produced a wide smile, setting off a row of sparkling white teeth. His eyes, a blend of brown and green flecks, captured the overhead lights in an animated sparkle. Suntanned and casually dressed in khaki slacks and a green polo shirt, he appeared to be content with his California lifestyle. And from the way his upper arms filled out the sleeves of his shirt, he probably worked out on a regular basis. His bronzed skin and sun-streaked crop of hair spoke of outdoor activities—boating, perhaps, or maybe surfing.

There was enough left on his plate—carrot and celery sticks, a dip that looked like hummus, and some rye crackers—for Julie to figure her new boss preferred a healthy diet. He reached for a piece of celery and scooped up some dip.

He paused before putting it in his mouth. "Would you care for a lunch plate?"

Julie shook her head. "No thanks. They served sandwiches on the plane."

There was nothing pretentious about this man. Possibly the same was true about the company he worked for. Julie could only hope. She wasn't impressed with the *New Yorker* socially elite writers who used six-syllable words, or the *People Magazine* writers who tore into celebrities' personal lives. She'd been wanting a comfortable, non-threatening job and didn't want to be called "paparazzi" or any of those other negative terms that sent sources fleeing for their lives.

She'd endured more than enough of that negativity in the newspaper business.

Unlike her former editor at the *Springfield Daily Press*, Ian exuded a mild demeanor and immediately set her at ease. Andy Jacobs never would have offered her lunch. Like the rest of the staff, Julie could expect a visit to Andy's office would involve a lot of shouting and very few pats on the back.

Smiling, Ian gestured toward one of the chairs. Julie expected him to plunge into her assignments and then dismiss her so he could tackle other business. *Isn't that the way most editors do their jobs?* she thought.

Instead, he settled into his desk chair, crossed his leg, and surprised her with a lengthy dialogue about his personal life. He produced pictures of his wife, Heather, and their three children, Joey, Jenny, and Cal. He talked about his tenure at *Great Destinations.*

"Thirteen years and still going strong," he said. "I quit work at five every day. I don't come in on weekends, except in emergencies, so I can spend my free time at the beach with my family. I've been teaching my oldest son to surf, and it's been a real trip."

The beach. She'd guessed right. What a great icebreaker for him to share his personal life before getting down to business. A good sign he'd be easy to work for. Maybe even fun.

He then turned things around and asked her about *her* personal life, which caught her off guard. If he'd asked her the same question seven years ago, she'd have rambled on like the little schoolgirl she was, talking about all the fun activities in her life and maybe mentioning the terrific grampa she had. But six years ago, the fun came crashing to an end, and Julie descended into a protective shell from which she hadn't yet surfaced. Now, this stranger was asking her to open up her life to him. Her heart began to pound. She shrank back in her chair. Ian was watching her, but he said nothing.

While he waited, he reached for a carrot stick, finished it off, and followed with a sip of water from the bottle on his desk. "Why don't you start by telling me about your family?"

Julie eased out of her shell and began slowly. "Well, my parents still live in the house I grew up in. My dad's in management, and my mom does charity work and volunteers at our church. I have one sister, Rita. She's in nursing school." She smiled. "Rita's more than a sister, though, she's been a friend to me. We get along great." She cocked her head. "No sibling rivalry between us."

Ian's eyes sparkled with mirth. "I'd like to know your secret. Our house overflows with sibling rivalry."

He cleaned his lunch plate, scraped up the last of the hummus with a cracker, then dropped back in his chair, his eyes on Julie. "What about a boyfriend? Surely, there must be a young man in your life."

A chill raced through Julie. The last time a man asked her that question she ended up fighting for her life on the floor of the church fellowship hall. She looked again into Ian's eyes. They were non-threatening, not at all like the lustful eyes of her attacker.

She squashed her discomfort and took a deep breath. "I'm engaged to a wonderful man," she said, producing a smile. "Mark is a professor at a Bible school. He's kind, generous to a fault, and considerate. I can't live without him."

Somehow, saying those words out loud made her more aware of how much she needed Mark in her life. Memories started flowing back, as if they'd only been in storage for a while.

"Mark and I dated a couple of years ago," she said. "We enjoyed a lot of outdoors activities—took long walks, went for a ten-mile bike ride on Saturday mornings, played paint ball a couple of times, and we got together for the usual movies, picnics, and dinners with friends." She lowered her gaze, then raised her head again. "We broke up last year and recently got back together."

Silence so loud she wanted to cover her ears. Ian was staring at her, like he was evaluating everything she'd said. He smiled.

"So, when's the wedding?" he said. "Do we need to postpone your first assignment?"

Julie quickly shook her head. "No, no. We haven't made definite plans yet." She couldn't tell him she'd been dragging her feet, didn't want him to think she couldn't handle the job and also plan something as simple as a wedding.

"Fine," he said. "Now, let's talk about your assignments." He folded his hands on top of his desk. "To get you started, I'd like to run your Patmos travel piece in the September issue. Of course, I'll credit the newspaper for having run it first, and I'll pay any fee they might have for reprinting it. Let's see what kind of reaction we get from our readers. I have a good feeling it will be well-received. Of course, I'll need a few more photos from your cache. We like to choose our own photo spread."

"I'll email a dozen or so when I get home."

"Great. Your story is gonna get lots more play with us. The newspaper has a limited coverage area. Our circulation numbers are in the six digits. People come from all over the world to visit places we write about. You're gonna be famous, Julie." He said it with a wink, but the idea nearly floored her.

"Our product is different from other travel magazines," Ian went on. "In addition to the usual briefs with photos, we run a four-page spread—a big cover story—plus a feature article on a key personality from the location. That's where you come in. Your finished work also should include an information box listing hotels, restaurants, interesting sites, and special tips for the traveler."

Without missing a beat, Ian reached for a large folder, opened the flap, and pulled out a pile of documents.

"These are your upcoming assignments," he said. "You can do them in any order, but I'd like you to start with the one at the top of the pile. That is, if you agree."

This guy was a refreshing change from her last boss. There were no harsh demands, no red-faced shouting, no raising of his voice. He actually wanted her opinion. He was clear, though, about the layout. Like her final newspaper piece, every story needed to focus on a famous individual, a chronicle of his or her life, and a colorful description of where he or she lived.

Ian handed her the documents. She looked at the one on top. *Marjorie Kinnan Rawlings*. She smiled. One of her favorite authors.

Julie recalled the day she first read *The Secret River*, a gift from her parents on her 13th birthday. It was Rawlings' only children's book. Over the next few years, she built up a nice collection of the woman's novels. She read *The Yearling* three times before seeing the film, and came away with a greater understanding of the kind of world Marjorie lived in when she moved to Cross Creek.

She checked the rest of her assignments, pleased at Ian's choices. When she finished, she looked up at him and smiled. "I love this," she said. "I can't wait to get started."

"Your deadline for story number one is August 20. We'll run it in the October issue. You'll need to get a move on and visit Florida before the end of July. The park will be closed to visitors in August and September for maintenance. Now for your other duties." He leaned back in his chair. "Aside from the travel piece, I want you to write a 'How-to' column for every issue. Focus on travel tips and ideas, and any little vignettes you might come up with during your travels. Keep it personal. You know, 'How to travel with one suitcase.' 'How to handle the last-minute rush.' 'How to plan a low-cost weekend get-away.' 'Planes, trains, or automobiles?' You get the picture."

Julie nodded. This could be fun. She wouldn't just be throwing out a bunch of facts and figures. She could draw from her own experiences, and she could get advice from travel agents and people she knew who'd gone on cruises and long-distance trips.

"One thing more," Ian said. "Every month we get letters and emails from our readers. I'd like you to answer them in the same way we receive them. You'll write written replies to those that come via U.S. mail, and you'll send emails to writers who send their comments electronically. Choose a few of the best ones for publication—both positive and negative. We want our readers to know we care about their opinions. Do you think you can handle those jobs in addition to your monthly assignment?"

The task sounded easy enough. "I look forward to it," she said.

The rest of their visit was equally amiable. Ian showed Julie around the fourth floor offices of the company. He introduced her to a dozen smiling faces with names she'd probably forget by the time she arrived home. Inside, she was bubbling with excitement, and it was all she could do to keep from screaming for joy.

She came away with a company credit card, a pack of airline and hotel vouchers, and three assignments tucked inside a leather-bound folder with her name etched in gold lettering on the front. Everything about *Great Destinations Magazine* exuded class without affectation. She was going to like working for this company.

During the flight back to Springfield, she ran over her first assignment. The top sheet held a complete list of Rawlings' writing projects from the time she sold her first story to a newspaper, to the posthumous publication of *The Secret River*. The next page held a chronological list of places where Rawlings lived. Ian had drawn a double line under Cross Creek, a north central Florida community where Rawlings got the inspiration for her finest works. He'd also underlined Crescent Beach, Florida, with a side note stating that Marjorie spent the majority of her relaxation time there with her husband, Norton, and their friends. In another scribbled notation Ian requested a couple of backwoods recipes from Rawlings' cookbook.

Julie shut her eyes and savored the moment. Ian had handed her a slice of heaven. It was like taking a bite out of her mother's warm apple pie, fresh out of the oven. Nothing else could have tasted as rich or as satisfying. She had the job of a lifetime, and she was going to devour every part of it. She'd stuff herself with it until she couldn't take another bite.

Then, she opened her eyes and reality struck. She was heading home, back to Mark, back to unfinished wedding plans, back to a decision that could alter the path of her life. People referred to marriage as an institution. The word conjured up images of confinement, iron bars, a loss of freedom. But this was the 21st century. The glass ceiling didn't exist anymore. Women could have marriage, children, and a career these days. If she wanted, she could have it all.

3

TIME WITH MARK

The moment Julie walked into Mark's apartment, she took one look at his smiling face and forgot all about women's equality. She'd come a long way over the past few weeks. Since renewing her relationship with Mark, her childhood dream of being a wife and mother one day had resurfaced. For the first time in years, she believed she'd actually found love and security in one man, a man she'd come to trust and admire.

Her life had changed for the better under Yanno's gentle guidance. And after arriving home, she'd made plans to receive further counseling from the therapist she'd met on the plane to the Middle East. Doctor Martin Balser had spent an hour with her somewhere over the Atlantic and then offered her his card.

"You don't have to be stuck in the past," he'd said. "Learn from what happened and move on. You know what the Bible says about someone who puts his hand to the plow, don't you?"

She'd nodded. "If he looks back, he's not fit for the kingdom of God."

Balser produced an encouraging smile and set her at ease. If she was going to schedule therapy with anyone, it had to be with him. Since returning to Springfield, she'd had one session with the kind doctor. And, she was planning to fit in another.

Even now, caught up in Mark's welcome home embrace,

the dregs of her former ordeal dissolved like chaff in a burn pile. Perhaps she could move ahead with their wedding plans after all.

She tilted her head and eagerly received Mark's kiss. Two months? Why not next Saturday? Why not elope? Or how about a quick civil ceremony at City Hall? All kinds of scenarios ran through her head.

"So," he said, breaking her trance. "Tell me about San Diego. Did you get your assignments?"

She nodded, still surfacing from the onslaught of ridiculous options. Of course, she shouldn't rush into anything. What on earth was she thinking?

"Hungry?" He said.

"Famished."

He took her hand and led her into the kitchen. A pot of water simmered on the stove. Mark tied a towel around his waist and lifted a long, thin box off the counter. "Spaghetti tonight," he announced.

He dropped a handful of noodles in the kettle, grabbed another pan and poured in a drizzle of olive oil. He glanced over his shoulder at her. "Where's the Ragu?"

Julie stifled a chuckle. She walked across the kitchen and grabbed the jar of sauce off the counter. She handed it to him and stepped back. What fun to watch the man of her dreams playing chef. Gramma once told her when a man gets in the kitchen amazing things can happen. She was right. Whenever Grampa took over the stove, he whipped up the best pot of homemade chili she'd ever tasted. Now a similar scene was unfolding before her eyes. It was as if Emeril Lagasse had stepped off the TV and into Mark's body.

The oil began to sizzle. Mark added a spoonful of

pre-minced garlic from a little jar. A warm aroma surfaced. He crumbled up some ground beef, added a splash of red wine, and dumped in the entire jar of tomato sauce.

"Bolognese..." he proclaimed, like he'd just come back from a cooking class in Tuscany.

He grabbed a wooden spoon, stirred his concoction, and winked at Julie.

"And, you thought you were gonna have to do all the cooking in our house," he said. "Think again, sister."

Julie giggled, came up behind him, and wrapped her arms around his waist. "What can I do to help?"

"Not a thing," Mark motioned with one hand toward a place at the table where a small vase of cut daisies welcomed her. "I've got this tonight," he said. "You relax and tell me about your trip."

She grabbed a chair, briefly admired the daisies, then sat back and watched Mark bounce around the kitchen. He looked like he was enjoying himself.

What had she done right to deserve such a guy? Mark was considerate, thoughtful, and now a blossoming chef? What other surprises were in store for her over the next 50 or 60 years? At that moment, life as the wife of Mark Bensen didn't seem quite as daunting as it did a couple of days ago.

"Well?" Mark said.

Julie acknowledged his subtle reminder and began to recount the events of her trip to San Diego. She gave her impressions of the office, the man who would be her editor, and the stack of assignments she'd brought home with her.

"I can hardly wait to get started." she said.

"That's great, Julie." Mark continued to dash about the

kitchen, but glanced at her every now and then, letting her know he was interested in what she was saying.

This was as good a time as any to hit him with the next big joy killer.

"It looks like I'll have to leave town again in a few days."

He stopped dead, a basket of garlic bread in his hand. He blinked at her, as though trying to make sense of what she'd said. "You're leaving again? Already?" He set the bread in the center of the table.

She nodded slowly, and raised her eyebrows in a hopeful plea. "It's my job," she said with a shrug. "You knew there'd be some travel involved."

He frowned. "But so soon?"

"Of course."

He clenched his jaw and went back to putting the meal on the table—slower this time—the bowl of spaghetti, a dish of parmesan cheese, two plates of pre-made salad he'd dumped out of a plastic bag. He dropped into the chair across from her. He stared at her for a moment, like he was trying to figure out who she was. Slowly, he reached across the table for her hands, blessed their meal, and stared at her again.

"I guess I thought you'd be working from home more than you'd be on the road. You just got home, and now you're leaving again."

She gave in to her frustration. "Mark, I can't write a travel piece without going to these places first. How would I be able to describe anything with accuracy? Plus, I have to do interviews. And I need to shoot photos."

He nodded and scowled at his food. "I see."

Her attention settled on the spread of food on the table.

Mark had put a lot of thought and effort into making this meal for her. She wanted to enjoy this time together.

"I'll be in Florida for only a few days," she said, with a lilt in her voice. "I'll be tackling my first assignment—Marjorie Kinnan Rawlings, one of my favorite authors."

"Didn't she write *The Yearling*?" Mark said. He picked up his fork and twirled a few strands of spaghetti. "And didn't she win a Pulitzer Prize?"

Encouraged, Julie nodded. "She sure did. But she did a lot more than that. She wrote several novels, plus magazine and newspaper articles, a children's storybook, poetry, and—" She cleared her throat. "She even wrote a cookbook filled with recipes she'd learned while living with backwoods people in the forest. Apparently, Marjorie loved to cook, and she loved to share what she made with her guests."

Mark continued eating, more heartily now. The guy could put away three plates of spaghetti and not gain an ounce. She sipped from her water glass and eyed him over the rim. He didn't seem to notice that she hadn't taken a bite yet.

It appeared she'd reached another of Grampa's crossroads. Mark wanted her home with him, married and bearing children. She wanted to excel at her new job. She had a strong urge to travel, to remain independent, to succeed in the world of publishing, whether in newspapers or magazines, or—God willing—in novel writing. She'd hardly realized her childhood goal of becoming a popular writer. Newspaper reporting didn't count. Too many people wanted to throw rocks at her. Now, she'd embarked on the kind of writing that would draw praises and admiring fans, maybe even a few awards.

She was back in that place of confusion again, torn between

a life with Mark and the kind of job that could consume her. Did a middle ground even exist?

She toyed with her salad, took a few bites, then tackled the plate of spaghetti, surprised to find Mark's creation as tasty as any she'd had in a restaurant.

"This is good," she said. "Really good." She dug in more heartily.

Mark raised his head and grinned. "Glad you like it."

Then he lost his smile. "I'm sorry," he said.

"For what?"

"For not understanding what your job involves. I knew you'd have to travel. I just hadn't adjusted to the idea yet. But don't worry, I will."

She nodded and kept eating.

Mark shoveled another forkful of spaghetti into his mouth. She watched him, and a sadness swept over her that she couldn't understand. She finished her meal in silence.

When dinner ended, Julie rose from the table and insisted on helping Mark wash the dishes. She stepped up beside him at the sink. A warm atmosphere settled on the kitchen and instantly brought up a memory from her past. Friday night dishwashing was one of the family rituals Julie missed after she left home. Mom usually washed. Dad put on an apron and grabbed a dishtowel. Julie and Rita raced back and forth to see who could put the most dishes and utensils away. The evening usually ended in laughter, pats on the back, then a bowl of popcorn, four sodas, and an evening in front of the TV. She'd made up her mind back then to carry that ritual into her own family, if she ever had one.

She quickly shed the bitter-sweet memory and turned her attention to Mark. "So, what have you been up to while I've been away?"

His arms up to the elbows in soapy water, Mark ran through the details of the past few days—the classes he taught, funny interactions with his students, and his efforts to complete his PowerPoint presentation.

"Melanie hired a new assistant," he said with a smirk. "I guess the work has piled up on her now that the summer classes are coming to an end. Twice as many students have signed up for the fall term."

"Will your work double?" She was almost hoping it would. Then she'd have more time to work on her own project.

He nodded. "I got a look at the list of students' requests. I won't have an empty seat in any of my classes."

She frowned in concern. "When will you be able to work on your PowerPoint?"

"I'll have to make time after hours. It's gonna be tough trying to teach, grade papers, coach basketball, and finish the thing—but I'm up for it. The information I gathered during our trip to Patmos is still running around in my head. I'm getting really close to finishing."

A bubble of sadness eased into Julie's heart. For the past few weeks, Mark had talked of little else except his PowerPoint project. Now, he was overwhelmed, and though it meant she'd have a little more freedom, she was concerned that he'd taken on too much.

She reached into the soapy water and touched his hand. "You can do it," she said. "I have complete confidence in you."

He smiled at her. "Thanks, honey. That means a lot to me." He slipped his hand away and ran another plate under the spray of water. "But I have to be practical. I'm gonna be responsible for teaching about 200 students, which should be my primary goal."

"What about all the photos I gave you from our trip?"

"They're already in. Now I have to create a narrative and select the right background music. Weaving it all together takes time. Plus, I'll need to test it out on a few people before I show it to students."

Her heart wept for him. She wanted him to succeed. Wanted nothing but the best for him. "I'm here for you," she said. "I'll support you in your work, and I'm hoping you'll support me in mine. We can make it, Mark, but you'll need to remember that I have an independent streak, and I can't let it go. Please, say you'll try."

Seconds later Mark dried his hands, and they were in each other's arms. He rested his chin on top of her head. She breathed deeply of the cologne on his cheek.

"How can I help?" she murmured. "Just tell me."

"I can handle the workload and the influx of new students and my half-finished project," he said. "What I need you to do is stick with our wedding plans. We can keep it small, if you like. Make it easy on yourself." He backed away and looked her in the eye. "Let us help. Your mom. Lakisha. And me."

"Lakisha and Greg had a *huge* wedding. Of course, her father *did* foot the bill. A Boston lawyer can afford the best, right?" She paused for another thought. "But all he did was provide the money. Lakisha and her mom did all the work. Maybe her sisters helped a little. I don't have all those resources. I have one sister, and she's busy with school. Lakisha can fill me in on what I need to do. I'll be meeting her for a jog in the park tomorrow morning." She let out a laugh. "Can you picture it? Lakisha jogging? She's six months pregnant and—"

Mark's cell phone rang and cut her off. He pulled it from his pocket, checked the screen and frowned.

"What's the matter?" she said.

"I don't know. It looks like a work call. It's 8 o'clock at night. Everyone should have gone home by now."

"Aren't you gonna answer it?"

He made a face and hit the receive button. "Hello?" His frown deepened. "Why are you calling me at this hour? What's going on?"

He looked at Julie. "It's Melanie's new assistant," he whispered.

Julie stepped away from him so he could talk.

After a series of "Uh-huhs," he said, "No, I can't come there right now. I'm busy. Look in the bottom drawer of Melanie's desk. I've gotta go." He hung up and turned toward Julie, a puzzled look on his face. "That was strange," he said. "Melanie's assistant is still at the office. She was looking for a list of classroom supplies."

"It couldn't wait until tomorrow?"

He gave her a half-smile. "Guess not."

A twinge of curiosity struck Julie. "Why did she want you to come to the college at this hour?"

He shrugged. "Don't know. She's still getting acclimated to her job. Must be a little overwhelming."

A rise of heat rushed to Julie's cheeks. "Why did she call you instead of Melanie?"

He shrugged. "How do *I* know?"

"What's her name?"

"Her name? Fiona something."

"What's she like?"

He looked into her eyes. "She's—I don't know—early 20's I guess."

Julie straightened. "No, Mark. What does she *look* like?"

He grinned with a sudden awareness. "Don't tell me you're jealous."

She raised her chin. "I just want to know what she looks like." Blushing, she let out a sigh. "It seems strange. A new girl in the office calls my fiancé at home in the middle of the night and asks him to come out. Don't you think it's odd?"

He gave her a cockeyed grin. "You have nothing to worry about, Julie. I hardly noticed the woman."

She crossed her arms in front of her and stood firm.

"Okay," he said. "Let's see—long, black hair, dark eyes, and she uses far too much makeup for a day job."

"And?" Julie said.

He shrugged. "And... today she wore a purpley-red dress."

"Do you mean mauve?" Julie said with a giggle.

"Yeah, I guess so." Mark moved about the kitchen, wiping down the table, the counter, and the stove top. "And, oh yeah, she wore those spike heels that click when a woman walks—or tries to. I can't imagine how you females get around on those stilts."

"We manage," Julie said, though she didn't have a single pair of them in her closet. "Is she—pretty?"

He hung the dish towel and washcloth on the rack in front of the stove. "Jimmy Nolan thinks she is. He hung around Melanie's office yesterday for nearly an hour."

Julie huffed. "Why didn't she call Jimmy Nolan, then?"

"I don't know, honey." He slid his arm around her. "I'm not the least bit interested in her or in Jimmy Nolan."

She pulled away. He gave her a crooked smile. "Have those green eyes of yours gotten a little greener?"

She shook her head in protest. She could thank her

mother's Irish ancestry for her fiery red hair and the rise of heat rushing to her cheeks at times like this. Then there was that stubborn gene she'd inherited from her father, the one that caused her to lash out at anyone at almost anytime.

"C'mon, Julie," Mark's tone had softened. "You can trust me. I have no interest in anyone else. You're the only woman I've ever wanted to spend the rest of my life with. Now, can we stop letting Fiona spoil our evening?"

She released a sigh and collapsed in his arms. "I'm sorry, Mark. I don't know what's the matter with me or why I react the way I do."

He held her at arm's length and stared into her eyes.

"You've had a lot on your mind. Of course, you're gonna react like you did." He backed away and smiled. "Don't torture yourself. We're gonna be married before you know it."

She gazed into his sky-blue eyes. For a split second, she saw her future there. It was warm, safe, even joyful. Just as quickly, it was gone.

"Let's just try to enjoy the rest of our evening together," she said. "No more talk about work or weddings or other people. Tomorrow, I'll begin my research, and you'll go back to your classes and your PowerPoint project. For now, I want to forget about everything else and just relax with you."

Once again, she'd been able to get their conversation off the wedding. And why not? She'd been avoiding the subject for weeks. At some point, however, she was going to come face-to-face with the real issue. Did she really want to get married, or did she just want to be engaged for the rest of her life?

4

TIME WITH LAKISHA

Julie looked forward to her morning jogs with Lakisha. Their friendship went beyond the casual lunches and shopping trips women usually did together. From the day they met in Lakisha's real estate office more than three years ago, they'd watched each other's back, through good times and bad times, like the Bible said, rejoicing together and weeping together. This was supposed to be one of those good times, wasn't it? Lakisha was having a baby, and Julie was starting a new job. If things went as originally planned, by next year she'd also be married. The thought both thrilled and frightened her.

She arrived at the park ahead of Lakisha and was retying her shoe laces when her best friend came toward her from the parking lot. Her dark eyes sparkled, and her face glowed like a kid's on Christmas morning. She wore a red-and-purple jogging outfit that contrasted with her black hair and her bronze skin. There was a happy spring in her step.

Julie smiled with understanding. "I knew it. You're having a girl."

Lakisha's smile broadened. "We went for our second ultrasound yesterday," she said, nodding. "The first one wasn't clear. This one was definite. We can start buying everything in pink."

Julie slid off the bench and gave her friend a hug. "Okay, so what are you going to name her?"

Lakisha lost her smile and shrugged. "Probably after one

of the grandmothers—or maybe both of them, if we can figure out how to combine the names without offending one of them."

Tears formed along the rims of Lakisha's eyes.

"I'm sorry," Julie said. "Maybe I shouldn't have asked." She tilted her head. "What's going on?" She blinked back her own rise of tears. "Come on, Lakisha. You know you can tell me." She peered closer into those dark pools. "Something to do with the grandmothers?"

Lakisha could only nod. She pulled a couple of tissues from her pocket, one for herself and one for Julie. "You mean, the two bubble-heads, don't you."

Her remark brought a giggle to Julie's throat. "Bubble-heads, huh?" Julie laughed out loud. "Bubble-heads." Seconds later, Lakisha was laughing with her.

"Bubble-heads," Lakisha blurted out.

Julie laughed so hard she ended up holding her side and gasping for air. A young guy wearing shorts and a tank top jogged past them and cast an inquisitive glance in their direction. He hurried off shaking his head, which set off another round of tearful laughter.

Lakisha took a deep breath. "I needed that," she said, giggling.

They stared at each other for a few seconds. "So," Julie said in an attempt to turn serious. "Tell me the truth. How are the grandparents dealing with the news?"

Lakisha cocked her head. "Much the same way they dealt with the wedding. They're tolerating it without saying what they really think. I'm guessing they're not thrilled about it, but it appears they're respecting our privacy. Trouble is, privacy is the last thing I need right now. I'd love it if those two—bubble-heads—would give me some moral support."

She broke down again, half laughing and half crying. Then she took a deep breath. "With a baby about to come on the scene, I'm watching to see which set of grandparents will come out of the cobwebs first."

Julie shook her head. "It's the 21st century, for goodness' sake. Mixed marriages are commonplace."

"I know, but my parents are ultra-conservative, and Greg's folks rarely leave their farm. They don't even own a TV. They're polar opposites, but they've taken the same stand."

"Give them time, Lakisha. It's amazing what the birth of a grandchild can do to bring people together." Julie took another step back and gave her friend the once-over. "Are you sure you can jog today? You look like you're toting around a bowling ball. That's gotta be uncomfortable."

Lakisha spun away and took off. "Just try and catch me," she called over her shoulder.

Julie set out and caught up with her friend on the first turn. "You're doing great," she said, huffing. "*I'm* the one who's out of shape."

Lakisha laughed out loud.

Julie grinned. It was good to see her friend's spirit bolstered.

"It's funny," Lakisha said, still laughing. "I've gained 20 pounds, but I have more energy these days." She jogged around the next turn in the path. "You should have seen Greg at the supermarket the other day. I was pushing the grocery cart, just moving along like I normally do, and he was panting several paces behind me. Do you believe it? He asked me to slow down."

Julie chuckled at the image. "That's classic, Lakisha. I hope I can have your vitality when I get pregnant." She caught herself then. Had she just blurted out something far removed from her plans? She slowed to a walk. Lakisha fell in beside her.

"I don't know why I said that," Julie said. "I'm not ready to have children. Not yet anyway. My career is just taking off. I want to concentrate on my work for a while. Maybe for a *long* while."

Lakisha gave her a sideways glance. "And Mark's okay with that?"

She shrugged. "Sure. I guess so. Greg didn't stop you from working, did he?"

"No, but *my* job doesn't involve long-distance travel. I sit in an office most of the time and can even work from home. But you'll be running off to California, or Kentucky, or France, or who-knows-where. Your new job isn't exactly conducive to raising kids. You'd have to turn into a real supermom."

Julie stopped smiling. Though a July sun bathed her in warmth, a dark cloud had settled on her heart.

Lakisha stopped walking altogether. "Sorry, girlfriend, but you have to face reality." She frowned. "Haven't you two talked about those things?"

Julie's throat tightened. "Somewhat, but none of the important issues that come up in a marriage—finances, where to live, work schedules, when we want to have children, whether to have them at all."

Lakisha shook her head. "Oh my. If you and Mark don't settle those issues now, you might find out too late you aren't compatible, although that's hard for me to believe. You do not want to end up divorced."

Julie trembled at the thought. The idea of divorce frightened her. But right now, marriage frightened her even more.

"We're gonna start pre-marital counseling soon," she said,

though her voice sounded weak. "I'm sure we'll get an opportunity to discuss everything that matters. Including children."

Lakisha's black eyes grew darker. "You're getting married in two months." She cocked her head and eyed Julie with suspicion. "Aren't you?"

Julie ignored her question and moved back onto the trail. They started walking, side-by-side, along the paved path, across the little walking bridge, into the wooded area where the leafy maple trees blended with the sky and created a blue-and-green canopy overhead. The peaceful retreat should have soothed her. It was time to admit the truth.

"You're right, Lakisha," she said, her voice shaky. "I've been avoiding the subject of marriage and children. Getting engaged has been great, but I'm not sure I'm ready for marriage. And what about the honeymoon? Our first night together. How can I move past the attack and into the arms of a man I should trust?"

Lakisha stepped in front of her and made eye contact. She grabbed Julie's arms and held her fast. "That's the real problem, isn't it, Julie? Because of what happened to you six years ago, you're afraid to face Mark in the bedroom."

Julie choked up. She shook her head. Tears came.

"Oh, Julie." Lakisha's voice was soft, gentle. "Mark isn't that monster who attacked you. He's kind and compassionate. He'll help you through this. He wants to protect you, Julie. You simply need to trust him."

She slipped from Lakisha's grasp and pulled the used tissue from her pocket. More tears escaped. She dabbed at them, nearly shredding the tissue. Sobs erupted from deep inside her.

Without hesitating, Lakisha wrapped her arms around her. "It's gonna be alright," she murmured. "I'm here."

After returning home, Julie cleared her mind of the morning's drama and set to work on her magazine assignment. If she wanted to do a good job, she had to stop thinking about so many negatives and just concentrate.

It turned out, getting back to work had a cathartic effect. She could focus on the details, conduct some in-depth research, and keep her mind on her topic. And what a terrific topic it was. To be able to dig into the life of one of her favorite authors was the most welcome opportunity of all. She could travel back in time to the 1930s and '40s, retrace Marjorie's steps, mentally interview the people who knew her, maybe even walk in her shoes. The project offered more than a story and the promise of a paycheck. It offered an escape.

Julie's background in investigative reporting had equipped her with the right tools for this new job. She started with an internet search of Marjorie's stomping ground in Florida called Cross Creek. One site simply referred to it as *The Creek*. It was on a body of water connecting the Lochloosa and the Orange lakes.

She then focused her attention on the Marjorie Kinnan Rawlings Historic State Park. The web site offered a colorful collection of photos. The property was surround by a hammock of moss-laden oak, lofty pines, and a proliferation of sharp-leafed palmettos. A trio of spindly-trunked palm trees graced the front lawn in front of the farmhouse, which looked more like a rambling ranch than a Cracker style home.

Her interest pricked, Julie moved ahead with her search. Several virtual tours took her through the house, the barn, and around the grounds. Except for some minor renovations, everything looked like it was frozen in time. Suddenly it was 1930, and Marjorie could have appeared at any moment. Wouldn't it be nice to tour the grounds with the woman who immortalized Cross Creek?

Julie turned her search onto Marjorie herself. She recorded specific details. Date of birth: August 8, 1896 in Washington, D.C. Death: December 14, 1953 at Flagler Hospital in St. Augustine. The report said Marjorie suffered a number of debilitating accidents and illnesses. She fell off a horse and walked around with a broken neck for several days before seeing a doctor. She was bedridden with malaria, and she suffered periodic bouts of diverticulosis, a painful intestinal disorder that put her in the hospital multiple times. The woman walked the earth nearly a hundred years ago, back in a day when medical care was sparse and even less available in the heart of the Florida wilderness. Yet, despite those setbacks, she won a Pulitzer Prize and two of her best works were made into movies.

Marjorie married two husbands but had no children, having had a hysterectomy. Instead, she satisfied her motherly instinct by taking under her wing her protégé, Julia Scribner, the closest thing she ever got to having her own child. Julia, the daughter of Marjorie's publisher, later became the literary executrix of Rawlings' unpublished manuscripts and was responsible for the publication of *The Secret River*, Marjorie's one and only children's book.

Julie continued through file after file. Though early photographs depicted Marjorie as a feminine waif of a girl with soft features and wearing fine clothes, later photos showed a totally different woman. In one black-and-white picture, Rawlings looked more like a frumpy schoolmarm than a literary icon. She wore a striped housedress and her hair was tucked back from her face in a simple coif. No makeup, no jewelry, none of the frivolous reflections of the New York social scene. Just plain and simple Marjorie at work at her typewriter, pounding out the next best seller.

Nothing about the woman agreed with what the public thought a famous writer should look like. Old movies depicted such women in elegant clothes and holding a glass of wine in one hand and a long cigarette holder in the other. Similarly, male novelists were shown wearing tweed hunting jackets, seated in front of a fireplace, and puffing on a pipe. Many of them spoke with a fake indiscernable accent. And, of course, they had a Golden Retriever at their side.

But Julie imagined a different image. The real writers of yesteryear didn't submit to such frills. They pounded a typewriter from dawn until dusk, sometimes by candlelight, and they probably wore the same clothes every day until they finished a manuscript. Food and drink? If they had no one to cook for them, they just grabbed what they could from the pantry and went back to work. Coffee? Black, please, to keep the creative juices flowing until three in the morning. It wasn't the movie image. It was reality.

Another website carried bits of trivia about Rawlings' early years. Her father worked in the U.S. Patent Office in Washington, D.C. Rawlings spent the best years of her youth on the family farm in the nearby Maryland countryside. Julie could relate. She loved leaving the big city to frolic on Grampa's farm.

While Marjorie's mother pressured her into the lifestyle of the social butterflies, got her dance classes and singing lessons, and dressed her in expensive, store-bought clothes,

Marjorie confessed that she preferred the country, overalls, and swimming in the river.

Julie had to laugh at the similarity. It was during those times when her family went to Grampa's farm when she was happiest. There she could lose herself amidst the rows of corn, the unending stretch of unplowed fields, and the barnyard filled with small scurrying animals. Perhaps Marjorie experienced the same high when her family traveled to Michigan, where her mother's parents lived on a farm. That rural setting must have planted the seeds of nature in her heart, so that one day, she settled into a backwoods community in Florida and called it *home*.

Once Julie finished her preliminary research, she'd be heading off to Florida. A mini vacation with a little work thrown in, as her former newspaper editor had called such long-distance assignments. Wasn't that the way he'd described her trip to Patmos? This time, she was making her own arrangements, like a true professional.

She sucked in a satisfied breath and continued her search. The next site gave particulars about Rawlings' writing career. Julie gawked in surprise when she learned Marjorie began writing when she was six years old. But it wasn't only about writing. As a young girl, she often gathered other children on the steps of the Baptist church and told them stories she'd made up.

At the age of 11, Marjorie kicked off what ended up being a lifelong career in writing, by submitting stories to local newspapers. Her first big encouragement came when she entered and won a children's story contest in a Sunday paper under the pen name, Felicity. Julie mulled over the coined name. *Felicity*. How appropriate that a woman who found joy in her writing and in the simple libations of life, should begin her writing career with a *nom de plume* that meant *intense happiness*.

Julie continued through the file. Well into her teens, Marjorie won several contests for her submissions to newspapers and magazines. By the time she was 14, the Washington Post was publishing her letters and short stories, many of them award winners, on its children's page. Her father died when she was 17, and her family went to live in Madison, Wisconsin.

While studying English at the University of Wisconsin, Rawlings became interested in drama and even performed in a play. She'd dreamed of writing Gothic romance novels. Little did she know that, one day, she'd reach fame and fortune writing a novel about a little boy and his fawn.

During her junior year at the university, Marjorie met Charles Rawlings, who also aspired to be a writer. After graduation, she took a job with the YWCA in New York City, earning $25 a week. She and Charles married in 1919 and moved to Rochester, New York, his hometown.

Rawlings' newspaper career blossomed at the *Rochester Evening Journal* and at the *Times Union*, which also published her poetry in a daily series titled "Songs of a Housewife." The column was syndicated to 55 newspapers across the nation. Despite Marjorie's immediate success, her attempts at novel writing earned multiple rejection slips over the next few years.

Julie sat back in astonishment. If one of the most successful writers in American literature couldn't get the attention of a publisher, what hope did she have? Should she be content with the magazine assignments and forget about the half-written novel she'd shoved in a box under her bed?

Overwhelmed by a sense of discontent, Julie walked away

from her computer and went in the kitchen to fix a cup of peppermint tea. She needed to relax. To focus. To absorb all the intricate details of Marjorie's life. The woman had met with her own particular crossroads and had made choices that seemed to alter her path. What if she hadn't gone to college? What if she hadn't married Charles? What if she hadn't persisted in pursuing a writing career, especially after receiving all those rejections?

But she hadn't quit. She'd kept going, despite the forks in the road and the decisions, both good and bad. Surely, Julie could keep on going too. She knew she had to try.

5

MARK

Mark hadn't been able to concentrate all morning. He'd made it through three classes, all the while hoping his students would learn *something*. Then, he retreated to the quiet of his office. Julie smiled at him from the picture at the corner of his desk, like everything was okay. He hadn't slept well. She'd left him last night with the same sense of disappointment he'd experienced during their trip to Patmos. Like back then, she'd fallen into that secret place of hers and was cutting him out.

Her former arguments came rushing back at him. She didn't need him or anybody else. Did she still feel that way? After spending time with old Yanno, she'd finally come around. They were on the same page for a while. After coming home, she accepted his proposal of marriage.

So, what happened? He couldn't pinpoint when her demeanor changed. Maybe it had something to do with her new job. She was overwhelmed. Had too much on her plate.

Fortunately, she'd started counseling with Doctor Balser, the family therapist she'd met on the plane. She wanted Mark to go with her next time.

He turned his attention to his computer and called up the file he'd been looking at earlier that morning. Julie had shared enough details about her assignment to prick his curiosity. He wanted to show the woman he loved that he was interested in everything she did, even her work. The biography of Marjorie Kinnan Rawlings provided enough background information so he'd be able to carry on an informed conversation with Julie.

The site described Marjorie as a strong-willed woman who was intensely dedicated to her writing career, a woman who vacillated between soft-spoken sweetness and furious outbursts, who didn't hesitate to lock herself away in solitude without any concern for the people she blocked out of her life.

Sounds exactly like Julie, he mused.

He lifted her photo off the desk and held it in front of him. She was wearing the embroidered yellow blouse she'd purchased in Ephesus. The sunlight bounced off her flaming red hair. Her eyes sparkled with—what? Adoration? Surprise? Annoyance? She was staring right at him when he shot the picture.

He shook his head and laughed at himself. For some reason beyond his own understanding, this was the woman who'd caught his attention, the only one he wanted to spend the rest of his life with. His friend Greg told him he could have his choice of females. Well, he'd made his choice, and she was driving him insane.

Like the description of Marjorie, Julie was one minute soft-spoken and compassionate and the next she was a sharp-tongued spitfire, quick to retaliate against an insult, but equally hasty to defend someone in need. She put forth a complex mix of honey and venom.

A knock on his office door broke into his reverie. It was almost lunchtime. Who could be knocking now?

"Yes?" he threw his voice toward the door.

Another knock, louder this time. Maybe Jimmy Nolan was looking for a lunch buddy, or perhaps his boss was about to pile another job on him.

"Come in," he called, louder.

The knob turned, the door eased open. In the doorway stood a mirage, or it could have been. Mark stared in awe at the apparition in a flesh colored dress, cut low at the neckline and tucked at the waist. The willowy form moved into the room and glided toward Mark's desk. A strong exotic perfume came with her. As she passed under the overhead light, he recognized her immediately. Fiona, Melanie's new assistant.

She stood still and waited, as though giving him time to look her over. It was difficult to keep from doing that. She was a vision of loveliness. Her dark hair was tucked behind her ear on one side, exposing a dangling gold triangle. On the other side, long ebony curls caressed her face and swirled down to her neck.

Blinking, he tried to recover. "Can I help you?" he said, in as professional a voice as he could muster.

He set Julie's picture back on the desk and turned it slightly to one side so it would be visible to Fiona. No sense leading this woman on. He was engaged, and he wanted to stay that way.

"I need to talk to someone who's been working here a long time," she said, her voice almost a whisper. She gave a girlish one-shoulder shrug. "I haven't quite gotten the hang of things around here. Melanie's great, but I can't talk to her. After all, she's the one I'm trying to impress."

Really? Mark thought, but he said nothing. He didn't rise, didn't offer her a chair. Though his father had taught him better manners, he stayed seated and folded his arms across his chest. She rambled on for a couple more minutes, her voice breathy, her smoky dark eyes never leaving his face.

He was immediately reminded of those verses in Proverbs

warning young men to beware of seductive women. Thank God, he'd memorized some of them and had followed their wisdom for most of his life. He shot a look at the picture of Julie, the other reason he was trying to be virtuous. He wanted their relationship to start off right. Too many guys got the cart before the horse. Those relationships sometimes ended up in disaster.

The girl went on with her monologue. He hardly paid attention. She'd said something about her responsibilities and her need for guidance. "Lunch?" she said at the end.

He shook his head. "Look, Fiona. I don't think I'm the one you should be talking to. The school has a human resources person who can address your concerns."

He rose to his feet. It was time to show her the door.

But she stood firm. "No. I want *you* to help me." She came around his desk and blocked his path. "I feel comfortable with you. I've seen how you talk to your students. You guide them. You connect with them like—" Her face brightened. "Like a big brother. You make people feel like they can trust you."

The compliments nearly snared him—*big brother?*—but he shook his head. "No, Fiona. First of all, I don't have the time. Second, I believe men should counsel men, and women should counsel women." His pastor taught that principle. Now he had the opportunity to live it out.

"You need to go," he said as sternly as he could.

She tilted her head and smiled, like she hadn't heard him. Now what? This girl was beautiful. She'd chosen him to guide her. A big brother? He doubted it. At the moment, he didn't know where he stood with Julie. A flash of heat rushed to his face.

In desperation he drew again from the Scriptures. *Flee also youthful lusts...* Thank God for Timothy. Paul's young protégé must have experienced similar struggles. Paul had written a warning to the young man, a warning for *all* young men.

Mark stepped around her and walked to the door, opened it, and moved to one side.

She flashed her dark eyes at him. He turned his face away.

She brushed against him on her way out the door. "Maybe later," she said, still smiling.

He shook his head. "Sorry. Not gonna happen."

She raised an eyebrow. "We'll see." And, she walked away, her head back, a swagger in her step.

Mark shut the door firmly and set his jaw. There wasn't gonna be another time, not if he could help it. For 15 minutes, he'd wavered, even contemplated letting Julie have her way and cancel the wedding. Did she say *cancel* it? Or *postpone* it? There was a big difference. Canceling sounded final. Postponing meant there was still a chance for them.

He hurried back to his desk, plunked down in his chair and punched in Julie's number.

As soon as she answered, he plunged ahead. "Listen, honey. Take as long as you want. I'm here for you. I'll help or not help. Whatever you want. All I know is, I love you with all my heart, and if you need to hold off our wedding plans for a couple of months, it's okay by me."

He looked at her picture again, and his heart throbbed with love for her. He'd do anything to keep from losing her. The silence was deafening. Had she hung up?

"Thanks, Mark." Relief flooded over him. "But, I don't need more time," she said. "Let's start our premarital counseling with Doctor Balser. As soon as possible. I have a few issues, but we can work them out." There was a noticeable pause. "Together," she added.

Mark had been holding his breath. Now he let it out. "Let me check my schedule, and I'll give him a call," he said, a spark of hope jolting his paralyzed heart back to life.

He called Doctor Balser's number and waited for him to answer. Again he reached for Julie's picture. He'd withstood one of the toughest challenges known to man. A beautiful, alluring woman literally had thrown herself at his feet, and he'd kicked her aside. There was no doubt in his mind. It was gonna be Julie or no one.

6

TIME WITH DOCTOR BALSER

J ulie stood next to Mark before the front door to the family counseling center. A list of psychologists graced a wooden placard on the wall to their right. Half-way down the list was the name of her therapist, Dr. Martin Balser, the man she'd met on the flight to Izmir.

The man had done something most people had no hope of accomplishing. He'd gotten Julie to open up about her past. Maybe it was the fact that she'd never see him again. Maybe it was the masterful way he'd guided their conversation. In any case, she'd spilled out her pain 30,000 feet over the Atlantic.

But when Julie read his business card and learned he was an associate pastor at a church, she nearly choked.

"Wait a minute," she'd said. "This says, *Pastor* Martin Balser." A surge of heat had rushed to her cheeks. "Are you telling me I've been spilling my guts to a *minister*?"

The man merely smiled. He didn't push, didn't criticize, didn't make her feel like less of a human being. By the end of their talk, she trusted him enough to want to speak with him again. It turned out, Balser's office was just a half-hour drive from her condominium. In the end, Julie tucked his business card in her purse. Maybe she'd call him and maybe not. It was her decision.

Now, she was about to enter his office for the second time since coming home. For her first session, she'd counseled with him alone. She needed the privacy of his office and the doctor/client privilege. This time, it was going to be her and Mark taking their first step in premarital counseling.

She already had a ring on her finger. Perhaps they should have started counseling first. What if it turned out they weren't a good match? She couldn't bear the thought of handing the ring back to Mark, couldn't bear the pained expression on his face. The diamond belonged to his mother, which meant it was pretty special to him, which also meant *she* was pretty special to him.

She chewed her bottom lip and proceeded into the building ahead of Mark. Doctor Balser greeted them at the entrance to his private office. Unlike his attire on the plane, he wore no suit-coat or tie, just a pair of khaki pants and a long-sleeved dress shirt. There were those familiar wire-rimmed glasses. They made him look wise, even prophetic.

Like before, he greeted her with a welcoming smile.

After a few pleasantries, Julie and Mark settled together on a comfy sofa. Doctor Balser shut the door and grabbed a leather office chair on wheels. During her first visit, Julie had eyed the decor with interest. It was comfortable, not at all like what she'd expected from the dignified professional she'd met on the plane. In this environment and dressed as he was, he looked more like somebody's uncle.

There was almost nothing to his desk, just a glass-topped table with no drawers, a simple private work station he could have set up at home. There was a large notebook, an opaque jar filled with pens, and a box of tissues. Period.

A wooden bookshelf contained a few translations of the Bible and several books on relationships. During her first visit, she'd read the spines with amusement. *The Five Love*

Languages, The Complete Search for Significance, and *Boundaries.* Balser had noticed her interest and had offered to let her borrow any she might want to read, but she'd graciously declined. It was enough that she'd signed up for counseling. She didn't need to keep picking at those old wounds.

Her self-imposed therapy was simple. She'd learned to put on a different metaphorical hat for each aspect of her life. When she was working, her reporter hat automatically came out, and she could concentrate on her interviews. When she was out with friends, the reporter hat came off, and she wore a more casual bonnet. When she was with Mark, she wore imaginary flowers in her hair. She could be anybody to anyone, and they didn't know the difference. Whenever the trauma of the past rose up to haunt her, on went a steel helmet. Now, Balser was about take that helmet away. She wasn't sure if she was ready.

She peered past the wire-rimmed glasses into his all-knowing hazel eyes. She'd been painfully truthful in her conversations with him. If she wanted him to help her, she was going to have to continue to be honest.

"So," Balser said, his kind eyes crinkling at the corners. "You're planning a wedding."

Mark nodded. Julie sat rigid. Balser broke into a wide grin.

"Congratulations," he said. He crossed one leg over the other, opened one of his notebooks, and pulled a pen from the jar on his desk.

"Why don't we start with a series of questions, so I can find out where the two of you stand on certain issues?"

"Sounds good to me," Mark said. He slipped an arm around Julie's shoulder. She straightened, but she didn't push him away.

Personal questions meant she was going to have to open

up in front of Mark. What if he didn't like what she said? Her mind began to reel with safe answers, even before Balser asked a single question. She pressed her lips together and waited for the attack.

"First thing," Balser said. "I want each of you to look at the other person and name your favorite attribute about him or her."

Mark didn't hesitate. He gazed into her eyes and smiled. "I love your spunk, Julie. I love the way you don't let anyone push you around, not even me. And how, when you agree with me, I know it's sincere."

She swallowed and blinked hard against a rise of tears. No one had ever paid her a better compliment.

"And you, Julie?" Doctor Balser urged from behind his desk.

She didn't have to think twice. "I love your ability to keep control, Mark. You remain calm in every situation. You're my rock in a storm, my pillar of strength, my prince."

Balser scribbled something in his notebook and nodded. "That was poetic."

Julie began to relax. She leaned against Mark's strong arm and savored the moment.

"Okay, this one's going to be harder," Balser said, his tone serious. "Now, I want you to look at each other again and tell the other person what you *don't* like."

Julie's heartbeat quickened. She sought for an answer. She couldn't find any fault at all with Mark. He never faltered. She closed her eyes. If anything, he was too perfect.

"I suppose," she said at last. "The one thing I don't like might be your innocence."

She opened her eyes, surprised to see shock on his face.

"Innocence?" he said, frowning.

"That's right, Mark. You are so kind and trusting, women mistake your naiveté for an invitation." She shook her head. "I'm sure you're not even aware, but you are a chic magnet, and I don't like it one bit."

The two men burst out laughing together. Julie stiffened, certain her face must be a sizzling shade of red.

Balser was still chuckling when he spoke. "Sorry, Julie. I find your honesty quite refreshing."

Mark, however, had grown quiet. He appeared to be remembering something. "Are you serious?" he said.

She nodded at him and giggled.

"Well, I guess I'd better be careful how I come off to people, especially women," he said.

She was still giggling when Baler turned his attention on Mark. "Your turn," he said. "Tell Julie what you dislike most about her."

Mark turned his upper body toward Julie. He stared into her eyes and took a breath.

"I guess..." he said. "I guess, it's the same thing I love about you, Julie. Your spunk. Sometimes it gets you in a whole lot of trouble. And you probably aren't aware how many people you offend."

She couldn't disagree. She'd seen the pain and disappointment in people's eyes, wasn't surprised when certain individuals dropped out of her life. Over the last six years, she'd gradually turned into a bitter woman, ready to lash out over the slightest offense.

Balser scooted his chair out from behind his desk and rolled up in front of them. "Okay, let's move on," he said. Then he began to hit them with one question after another.

"Why do you want to get married? Do you want children?

How will you deal with in-law issues? How will you resolve conflict?"

Julie handled an hour of grilling without having to think twice. She'd already considered all of those issues and several others that hadn't come up. Balser didn't have to dwell on where they were going to live or what church they'd be attending. She and Mark had easily decided those two issues. Probably their biggest disagreement was when to start a family. Julie preferred to wait several years, so she could settle into her job. Mark had been honest from the start. He was tired of the dating scene, he'd found the woman he wanted to marry, and he was prepared to support a family.

In the end, Balser handed each of them a questionnaire focusing on different aspects of married life, such as finances, family relationships, and job-related issues. Julie scanned the page. At the bottom was a question on intimacy. She immediately froze up.

Her one close encounter of that kind had been forced on her. Now she was having to address the issue right there in Balser's office.

"You may take the list home," Balser said with uncanny understanding.

Unable to look either of them in the eye, she folded the paper and jammed it in her purse. She left Balser's office unsure whether they'd scheduled another session. Her mind reeled with forebodings. During the drive home, they passed through a family-style residential section of town. She stared out the side window at the passing houses, toys in the driveways, and glimpses of swimming pools and swing sets in the backyards. Inside those homes lived married couples with children. She didn't know if she could ever reach that place.

Her parents had. So had Lakisha. And her sister was already planning to marry Daniel Blankenship. Rita had told Julie she wanted to have a houseful of "little tykes," as she called them. She also had decided to specialize in pediatric nursing. She'd been caught up in the whole domestic scenario, complete with PTA meetings and grocery coupons. Until today, Julie hadn't considered any of that for herself.

She thought about the list in her purse, particularly the last notation. How many counseling sessions was it going to take for her to feel comfortable in that way with Mark? Did she dare dream of having a normal, healthy marriage relationship with anyone? Or was she going to be permanently stuck on the floor of the fellowship hall, fighting for her virginity, and losing?

7

GETTING STARTED

The premarital counseling session sent Julie back six years to the most traumatic experience of her life. She dealt with it like she usually did when confronted with those demons. She dropped Balser's list in a desk drawer. *Out of sight, out of mind,* she figured.

Now, she needed a distraction. She didn't have to look far. Her assignment. Delving into the life of one of her favorite writers would certainly help her step away from her own troubles. She could lose herself and all her problems in the life of Marjorie Kinnan Rawlings.

Ian had given her a deadline, August 20, with a goal for publication in the October issue of the magazine. She pulled Rawlings' books off her shelf and arranged them in neat, little piles on her kitchen table. Her personal collection included *The Yearling, Cross Creek, The Sojourner,* and *The Secret River.*

Julie had already read *Cross Creek* three times. With each reading, she came away with a deeper understanding of Marjorie's life in that secluded part of Florida amidst oak hammock, marshland, open range acreage, and an orange grove that needed her constant care and attention. The woman's keen eye had captured more than the physical images. Marjorie had caught the essence, not only of the people who lived there, but of nature itself.

In a way, Marjorie was unknowingly training Julie for her

own writing career. Julie didn't merely read the words in each book, she dissected every sentence, mulled over every description, studied Marjorie's style like she was in a classroom learning from the greatest literary mind on earth.

Julie smiled at the rise of a sweet memory. When she was a child, nearly everyone knew the path she wanted to take. Her English teacher had said she should be a writer when she grew up. Julie's parents also had caught the wave and had encouraged her to keep a journal. She took English and creative writing classes in college, and she majored in journalism.

After graduating, she landed a reporter job at the *Springfield Daily Press*. Her reporting position had provided the tools for conducting research and for working on deadline, so the transition to magazine writing had come easy.

She surveyed the meager assortment of books on her table. *Time to go to the library.* She grabbed her car keys and headed across town. The pickings were slim, mostly books she already owned. She came away with a few biographies and a copy of *Blood of My Blood,* an autobiographical novel about the love-hate relationship Marjorie had with her mother and the contrasting brief time of joy she shared with her father before he died. Arthur Sr. took his little girl away from the stiff social life that her mother preferred, and he introduced her to the humble pleasures of farm life, much like Julie's grampa had done for her.

Like Marjorie, Julie had gotten a taste of that rustic world, and she loved it. Even now, years later, she missed the sweet scent of mashed corn and the woodsy aroma of fresh hay, the soft chorus of moans in the milking barn, the nuzzle of a cow's nose against the back of her hand. But, Grampa was gone now and so was the farm. Never again would the old man's calloused hand lead her into the chicken coop where she would gather eggs for Gramma's chocolate cake. During the drive home she continued to mull over the way life had changed for her literally overnight. Grampa's death had left a huge void, one that couldn't easily be filled.

Back at her condo, she sat for several minutes in front of her window and gazed at the passing traffic. Most of those people were probably unaware of what amazing joys lay beyond the sterile buildings and impersonal highways.

She caught herself then. Here she was wasting her time mourning over the past, and she had a job to do. She'd already wasted an hour in Balser's office, and now she was reminiscing like a tired old woman with nothing else to do.

Snapping out of her reverie, she hustled over to her computer and immediately went to Amazon's web site. The online retailer offered a long list of books by Rawlings, plus other resource materials. Julie pulled out her company credit card and placed a large order.

But this was merely the tip of the iceberg. Julie's research needed to go beyond reading books and taking notes on the internet. She needed to travel to Florida, to experience what Marjorie experienced, to breathe the same air, to touch a palm tree, to walk the forest trail, to even sample the same foods Marjorie might have eaten.

She booked a flight to Jacksonville for next Wednesday, ordered a rental car, and arranged for a room at a small hotel in south Gainesville, a stone's throw from Cross Creek. She didn't have to endure any more counseling sessions for a while, and she could put off planning a wedding for at least another two weeks. With a clear slate and an equally clear mind, she could concentrate on her assignment.

For the next several days, she'd spend every waking hour reading Rawlings' books and the biographies people had written about her. She locked the door of her condo and turned off her phone. She was escaping again, but this time it was for a new job, and she needed to remain focused.

She gathered Rawlings' novels in a neat stack on the floor beside her reading chair. On the side table she set a plate of crackers and cheese, a bowl of red grapes, and a cup of herbal tea—enough to sustain her for the next couple of hours.

Settling into her chair, she selected *The Yearling* first. Instantly, she was outside the Cracker house in the Baxters' clearing. She could almost hear the buzz of wild bees in search of a chinaberry tree, could almost smell the whiff of smoke rising from the cabin chimney, could almost hear Ma Baxter rattling pots and pans at the hearth.

Like always, books swept her away from reality and into a safe, make-believe world. Now she was back in the early 1870's, stomping through the backwoods of central Florida, trailing a little boy named Jody on his adventure. By the time she finished the first page, Julie had blocked out the busy street outside her condo. Suddenly, she was bounding barefoot through the brush. She heard the rustle of palmetto fronds, felt the caress of a soft breeze against her cheek. Cottony clouds swept across the azure sky. Redbirds and whippoorwills sang sweet melodies, and mockingbirds added their own high-pitched imitations.

Julie took a bite of cracker. She could have sworn it tasted like Ma Baxter's cornpone. A couple of grapes turned into elderberry jelly, and a sip of herbal tea left Julie's tongue tingling like she'd downed a cup of Gramma Hutto's lemon leaf drink. She shut her eyes and let the images swirl around in her mind.

One of Julie's college professors had taught her how to immerse herself in a piece of literature. "You have to let go and become part of the book," he'd said. "Read between the lines, and let yourself experience what you find there."

The technique worked for Julie now. Marjorie's words were bringing the people of the forest back to life. She got to know them well while living among them. Got to drink moonshine with them. Got to eat roasted game at their outdoor tables. Sat on the front stoop beside their unwashed bodies, and shared a pack of cigarettes with them. They let her in on their secrets of unfettered living. Though they were a humble, honest group of individuals, they developed their own set of laws that rarely agreed with what the state levied. They fished and hunted without a license, shot deer out of season—often in the middle of the night while carrying a lantern—and dynamited the lake to catch their fish. The outside world had moved on without them. They were stuck in the early 20th century and they preferred to stay there.

Breaking only for a visit to the bathroom or to put together another bite of food, Julie remained in her reading chair until long after dark. The hours had slipped away. Like her professor had urged, she'd become so engrossed in the story she'd lost track of time.

She looked about her, surprised to find herself sitting in her own living room and not in somebody's Cracker house in the forest. She stared at the page before her. It blurred for a moment. She inserted a bookmark and set the book aside. Heaving a sigh, she stumbled off to the bedroom and barely made it into her pajamas before falling asleep.

The next two days went pretty much the same. She finished

The Yearling and completed two more of Rawlings' novels. On the third afternoon, a FedEx driver knocked at the door and delivered a large box. Her Amazon order had arrived with several more novels and a few biographies about Marjorie's life written years after she died. She'd barely made a dent in all the reading she'd have to do.

Needles of guilt instantly pierced Julie's heart. She'd have to avoid seeing Mark and Lakisha for a little while longer. The truth was, she'd gone back to her old routine and already had shut them out of her life for three days. Giving in to her conscience, she picked up her phone and checked her calls. Mark and Lakisha had left several messages and texts. She'd done the same thing when she got fired from her newspaper job. She'd locked herself away in her condo. Whether it was for a work project or to deal with personal issues, she'd made it clear. No interruptions.

She released a long sigh and listened to their messages, one after the other, asking her to call them back. The last one was from Lakisha.

Enough, girl. Mark says he hasn't heard from you either. Now, listen up. Meet me at the trailhead tomorrow morning, the usual time. I won't take no for an answer.

Julie set aside her phone and dropped into her reading chair, but she didn't reach for a book. Instead, she succumbed to several minutes of self-castigation for blocking out the two most important people in her life.

Filled with remorse, she bent over and pressed her fingers against her eyes. Tears oozed out. She sobbed with regret, dampened several tissues, and felt drained. She opened her eyes, stared at the pile of new books, and fought the impulse to call Mark and Lakisha. Instead, she reached for a book on top of the stack. The next few hours flew by. She filled a notebook with ideas and tossed each book aside to reach for another.

That night, she fell into bed, exhausted. Inside, she was still weeping. She was standing on the edge of a precipice. Before her was the pit she had created for herself. Behind her stood the people who loved her, reaching out with open hands.

She didn't know when she fell asleep, but backwoods images rambled through her brain and didn't dissipate until a dagger of sunlight slid through the blinds of her window and awakened her. Her first thoughts were of Mark and Lakisha. She'd treated them unfairly.

Pushing off the edge of the bed, she set out to repair the rift she'd caused. First thing, she called Mark and was able to reach him before he left for work. She apologized for her behavior and promised to try harder. The sweet tone in his response told her all she needed to know. Then, he invited her to go out for dinner that evening.

"You need to take a break, Julie," he said. "We can check out that new Lakeside Inn. Pick you up at seven?"

She agreed. She felt ready to walk away from her project for a while. She slipped into a pair of jogging pants and a T-shirt, laced up her Skechers, and was out the door with a bottle of water in her hand. When she got out of her car at the trailhead, Lakisha was already standing there with her arms crossed. Her dark eyes shot darts at Julie.

"I was worried about you, girlfriend," Lakisha said, her voice firm. "I was afraid you'd slipped back into that miserable place again." She opened her arms and engulfed Julie in a hug.

Julie sputtered out an apology.

Lakisha released her and beckoned her onto the trail with

a jerk of her head. "Come on, let's clear our minds with a nice easy jog." She picked up her pace.

Julie fell in beside her and inhaled deeply of the fresh morning air. As she jogged along the trail, she took in her surroundings—the golden cast to the sky as the sun began its steady climb, the cheerful greetings of the songbirds, even the stillness over the park before the day got into full swing. She'd gotten so wrapped up in Marjorie's descriptions, they made her more aware of her own Garden of Eden, a slice of nature in the center of Springfield. She glanced around and began to appreciate the pink flowering azaleas, the beds of purple and white petunias, the bright yellow forsythia trailing over the stone wall beside the stream—her own little *creek*. After sitting in her reading chair for three days, she welcomed the feel of the dirt path under her running shoes, the rattle of boards as the two of them traversed the wooden bridge, the gravel side trail leading into a more secluded section of the park.

Keeping her tone light, Julie filled Lakisha in on her activities over the past few days. She talked about the research she'd been doing and the mountain of books and files she still needed to go through. She shared details about Marjorie's unsettled life—her erratic relationships with people, her tendency to shut herself off from the rest of the world, and her unwavering passion to become a famous writer.

"Sounds a lot like you," Lakisha said with a grin.

Julie snickered. Her friend's comment was a left-handed compliment. A lot of issues that had come to light regarding Marjorie's demeanor certainly matched Julie's behavior. But, she had to admit, nothing would please her more than to be able to win some big award, or at the very least to get a book published.

"I wish I could be half the writer Marjorie Kinnan Rawlings was," she said.

Lakisha shook her head. "Don't slight yourself. I believe you're on your way, but you haven't realized it yet. So tell me, once you finish your research, what's the next step?"

"I'll be heading to Florida on Wednesday. I'll tour Marjorie's farm, take some pictures, and talk to some of the locals. There's nothing like first-hand accounts to bring a project like this to life."

Julie breathed easier now. Though a stack of unread materials still beckoned her back at her condo, she needed this time of refreshment. What did someone say said about all work and no play? She was playing now, getting a shot of adrenaline, a boost of energy to invigorate her through the rest of the day.

Lakisha slowed her pace. "It sounds like things are working out for you, Julie."

"What do you mean?"

"Well, the job, for one. And you're getting married soon."

Julie swallowed. Lakisha *would* bring up the wedding.

"The job, yes, but maybe not the wedding—at least not in two months."

Lakisha came to a sharp halt and faced Julie. "Say what?"

Julie shrugged sheepishly and turned her face away. "Things are piling up on me. This new job is taking up a lot of my time."

She looked at Lakisha, saddened by the disappointment on her face.

"I'm sorry, Lakisha, but I think Mark and I should postpone the date."

"Are you seri—" Lakisha began.

"I just need a few more months," Julie cut in. "And, don't

forget, you're six months pregnant. Imagine how you'll look in a bridesmaid's gown in two months. Deliver your baby first and get your figure back. Afterward, you can walk down the aisle looking fabulous."

Lakisha's frown remained, but she nodded in half-hearted agreement. "I wasn't concerned about standing up in your wedding while I'm pregnant. Lots of women do it. There are some really attractive maternity gowns." She paused and the lines on her face softened. "Don't fret about it, Julie. Whatever you decide will work for me."

Julie shrugged. "I need to focus. Need to make this job work."

She didn't like disappointing her friend. Lakisha and Greg had kept no secrets about their desire to see Mark and Julie married.

"Let's talk about it again when I get back from Cross Creek," she said, knowing she was merely buying more time.

Lakisha sighed and started walking again. "Whatever." She gave Julie a sideways grin. "By the way, when you decide about your color scheme, keep in mind I look my best in turquoise. It's on everybody's color wheel. Did you know that?"

"Okay, turquoise it is," Julie said with a giggle. "I'll tell my sister we've picked a color, and she can go out and start looking at dresses."

"What about *your* gown?" Lakisha said. "Won't it be fun to start trying some on?"

Julie glanced in her direction. Her friend was beaming. Her black eyes sparkled with optimism. She smiled, and her coffee-colored cheeks began to glow, like someone had added a dollop of cream.

A flicker of excitement made its way into Julie's heart. Nearly every young girl dreamed of having a wedding.

Sometimes, they also dreamed about a marriage, which, as most people might agree, could be an entirely different thing.

Try on gowns? She hadn't considered such an outing until this very moment. The thought appealed to her.

"Maybe after I get back from my trip to Florida we can go out and try on some gowns," she said, and she watched for Lakisha's reaction.

Her friend's face lit up. "I'll hold you to it," she said, narrowing her eyes. "Don't you dare back down on me. We can make a day of it, have lunch at that Asian restaurant by the square. There are a couple of nice dress shops down there."

Julie had spoken on impulse. Now she had to commit. "What about the guys?" she said. "Mark's expecting Greg to be his best man."

Lakisha smirked. "Their part is disgustingly easy," she said, frowning. "They'll rent their tuxes and show up at the altar. Period." She let out a little laugh. "Oh, yeah, and they'll throw the wildest bachelor party they can think up."

Julie giggled. "I'm not letting Mark off that easy. He *did* offer to help with the plans, so I'm expecting him to help write out the invitations, maybe go on a cake-tasting venture with me, which he'd for sure want to do, and even check out some musical groups for the reception."

"I don't know if he should," Lakisha said, shaking her head. "Sometimes they only get in the way. Men have different ideas about such things."

"Mark won't be a problem. He's so easygoing, I think he'll agree to whatever I want to do."

Lakisha raised one eyebrow in suspicion, then she walked on in silence. They'd made half of the two-mile loop and were already on their way back to the trailhead. Julie glanced at Lakisha and a pang of guilt struck her.

"You know," she said. "We've been talking about me and my work and my wedding this whole time. I'm so sorry, Lakisha. That was very self-centered of me."

"Really? Don't even think about it."

"No, I'm serious. I haven't once asked how you are—although you appear to be in fine shape. But you have plenty going on in your own life."

"Nothing I can't handle."

"What about the in-laws?"

Lakisha nodded. "Okay, I was wondering when you'd get around to asking." She took a deep breath and frowned. "Nothing's changed, Julie. My folks have called a couple of times, but they're too busy to drive down. And Greg's parents haven't budged. The last thing they said to him was they didn't want to compromise their beliefs."

"I thought Christians were supposed to accept people and love them, not judge and condemn them."

Lakisha smiled, but her eyes filled with tears and told a different story.

Julie's friend was in pain. She wanted to help but didn't know how.

"Greg's terribly hurt," Lakisha said, her voice thick with emotion. "They're not only rejecting me. They're rejecting their grandchild. He tries to hide it, but I know he's hurting."

She stroked Lakisha's arm. "I'm so sorry. I wish I could help."

"Thanks. There's nothing anyone can do. I stay positive by thinking about the baby. We're already setting up a room, stocking up on disposable diapers and wipes, a rocking chair of course, and a complete layette."

Julie gazed at her friend and marveled at the glow on her cheeks. Though she'd dried her tears, Lakisha's eyes continued to sparkle. There was something special about the look of an expectant mother that stirred Julie's heart.

They approached the exit and slowed their pace. Lakisha checked the readings on her fitness watch. "Looks good," she announced. "Got time for another go-around?"

Julie checked the time and shook her head. "I can't. I have a ton of research in front of me, and I'm leaving for Florida Wednesday."

Lakisha nodded. "Okay. Call me when you get back."

They leaned close for a goodbye hug. Lakisha had given her a brief, much-needed respite. Tonight she'd have dinner with Mark. With no more feelings of guilt to interfere with her concentration, she could wrap up her research and get ready for the next phase.

8

MORE TRIPS INTO RAWLINGS' PAST

J ulie returned home and plunged back into her reading. She wanted to fill the remaining time before Mark picked her up for dinner. She reached for *Blood of My Blood*. Marjorie had written the book in 1928, the same year she and Charles moved to Cross Creek. It wasn't published until 2002, nearly five decades after she died.

With a glass of iced tea and a ham sandwich on her side table, Julie opened the book to the Editor's Foreword, surprised to learn Rawlings had entered the manuscript in a competition sponsored by the *Atlantic Monthly Press*, only to be rejected.

Julie paused and absorbed the irony. *Marjorie Kinnan Rawlings rejected? It was hard to imagine.* In her early writing career, she'd earned a decent amount of literary prizes, mostly from magazines and newspapers. As for her novels, rejections flowed in. It wasn't until she started writing about the Cracker people that she became recognized as a literary genius. Then came her greatest accomplishment, the Pulitzer Prize for her book, *The Yearling*. Eight years later, the film came out.

What a shame Marjorie never realized the impact her books would have on readers for many decades to come.

Julie was one of those fans. Not only did she devour every word in every chapter of Rawlings' books, but she also tended to read the forewords, which helped her connect with the writer on a more intimate level.

More interesting details came to light as Julie got deeper into the story itself. She became familiar with Marjorie's early years. Her mother, Ida May Traphagen, a bitter, unattractive social climber, was unhappy with her own life and tried to live out her dreams through her only daughter, often pushing her to extremes and then plying her with new store-bought dresses and opportunities to mingle with the elite. In contrast, her father's easy-going manner brought a gentle balance to the young girl's life. Tragically, he died when she was a teenager.

Julie snickered at the all-too-familiar similarities in her own life. In her case, her father was the domineering force who'd demanded more than she could give, while her soft-spoken mother, though pathetically weak, provided the merciful balance Julie needed. It was true, a person's early years played a role in their future goals, but didn't free will play a role, too? And what about the crossroads Grampa predicted she'd meet along the way?

In a letter to Julia Scribner, Marjorie encouraged the young girl to pursue two channels for happiness. Julie paid close attention. Rawlings recommended a balance between doing the work a person had been equipped to do and maintaining a happy marriage.

Julie reread the paragraph. It was as if Marjorie had written those words specifically for herself, and maybe even for Julie. She had embarked on the career she wanted since childhood. Except for a brief period when visiting missionaries sparked her interest in foreign missions, she'd never imagined herself doing anything else except writing. She trained to be a writer in college and earned some success as a reporter over the past four years. After the incident at the church, she'd gone back to her original dream and forgot about God's calling. She wanted nothing more to do with missions or any other work of spiritual significance. She dove into her job and didn't look back.

But after she met Yanno last month, everything changed. A smile tugged at her lips. The old man managed to dig out a festering bitterness and drew her to the first step of healing—forgiveness of the people who'd turned their backs on her.

She wondered now if Marjorie also had to confront issues from her past. Did she deal with them, or did she simply take the next fork in the road and move on?

Perhaps the rest of the book might provide more insight. Already, there were too many similarities to ignore the truth. Julie's life paralleled Marjorie's to a certain degree, not only in her desire to be a writer, but also in her relationships with other people—particularly with men—she came to discover as she read on.

Though several young men showed an interest in Marjorie, few were able to earn more than a passing smile or possibly one date. Before the incident took away her innocence, Julie hung out with a mix of guys and girls from her school. Afterward, she crawled into a shell and didn't date for several years. There were a couple of persistent young men in college. She limited each of them to one date, like Marjorie had done with her beaus. And, like Marjorie, she plunged into her studies, and after graduation she concentrated on her work. The whole while she refused to let a man get close to her.

Until she met Mark at Lakisha's wedding. For the first time in her life, she felt comfortable with a young man. Mark was so sweet and patient, he quickly won her trust. But his unwavering faith in God and the Bible irritated Julie. She tolerated Mark's preaching for nearly a year, then she broke off with him in a storm of emotions. Now she was about to marry the guy. Who knew?

Julie considered the pattern in Rawlings' life, how she also avoided dating in favor of her career. Yet it took decades before everything came together to produce one of the most prolific writers of her day. Her fame didn't happen overnight. She was 41 years old when she wrote *The Yearling*. She suffered plenty of literary disappointments before then. Her success came after she traded in her life of ease in favor of Cross Creek and the humble folks who lived in the forest.

Aside from her work as a reporter, Julie had almost no interaction with people of other levels of society—not the elite nor the socially inept. Except for her interviews, she remained somewhere in between. She'd done newspaper stories about the homeless situation in her town, but she'd done so without ever soiling her hands or looking through trashcans for her next meal. Did she really understand where these people came from and what had reduced them to homelessness?

Marjorie did more than write about the backwoods people. She lived with them in a jungle wilderness called the Big Scrub. She learned how to tie a worm on a hook and how to kill a deer and gut it. She went to the bathroom in the woods, lit a kerosene lamp to read by at night, and ate possum and squirrel for dinner. As a result, she produced some of the most memorable works in literary history.

Though she shared similar aspirations, Julie hadn't come close to the kind of sacrifice that made Marjorie a literary icon. At times, she felt like taking a hammer to her computer.

If she ever wanted to reach the same proficiency, she'd have to quit her job and run off to some wilderness and do what Marjorie did—experience the land and the people. Perhaps, if she'd followed the call into missions, she'd have a few experiences akin to what Marjorie had, living apart from the modern world, where high-tech conveniences tended to stifle one's inspiration.

Except for some school-based studies, the real lessons lay beyond the classroom, beyond the comfortable lifestyle she'd enjoyed. She could hardly wait for the trip to Cross Creek. Perhaps there she can get a small taste of what Marjorie experienced.

Of course, the Cross Creek of today would be different from what Marjorie discovered when she first arrived there, nearly a century ago. The roads are paved now. There's electricity, running water, cell phone towers. Yet, Julie believed she could look past the modern improvements and envision the forest the way Marjorie described it in her books. Reading about Cross Creek was only half the battle. She would never fully understand Marjorie's life until she stepped foot in that place.

By late afternoon, she approached the last few pages of *Blood of My Blood*. She needed to freshen up for her date with Mark. If it were up to her, she'd finish the book and make him wait. A nervous tightening of her stomach took over whenever she quit a project before she was ready to stop. The constriction had already begun. But Mark would have made a reservation by now. Mr. Punctuality wouldn't stand for a delay over something as time-consuming as finishing a book.

In a way, she'd reached a mini crossroads, hesitated for only a second, then, groaning, she set the book aside and went to get ready.

9

DINNER WITH MARK

As Julie expected, Mark showed up on time for their dinner date. Punctuality was one of his finest qualities. It was also one of the things she disliked about him. His promptness put pressure on her to also be on time for everything.

Yet, she could depend on him. He usually did what he said he was going to do, even though at times his promises cost him dearly. Like the time he turned down a lucrative speaking engagement in order to keep a dinner date with his father. A special bond existed between them. Al Bensen rarely left his comfortable home in Florida, except to visit Mark. Most of their visits happened on the telephone. But once Al's travel plans were set, Mark kept their dates. If he said he was going to be somewhere, he always showed up. And on time.

Even tonight, he could have been working on his PowerPoint presentation. It was long overdue, and he'd already contacted colleges across the country. During the day, he stuck with his classes and other college duties. The summer classes kept him even busier than the regular sessions from fall through spring, which left him evenings and weekends to work on his project. It was amazing he'd been able to make time for her. Yet he'd somehow managed to squeeze in an occasional movie or dinner out. And he phoned her at least once a day—when she answered.

He'd have plenty of time for his project while she was out of town stomping around Florida. For now, they were going to spend a relaxing evening over dinner. She could fill him in on her work, and their marriage plans were sure to come up.

They walked into the Lakeside Inn at 7:30 as a large group of people left. Good timing. No waiting for a table, and they had a choice of seating. As usual, Mark requested a private table where they wouldn't be disturbed. Julie slipped her hand in the crook of his arm. She liked the sense of togetherness, if only for a little while. The single life had fit in with her need for independence, but it also left her weary at times.

The hostess led them to a table in the corner next to a window that overlooked the water, now streaked with orange from the setting of the sun. Directly outside their window, a wooden pier stretched out onto the lake. Several small boats were moored there, driven by people who lived on the other shore and had come there for dinner. One of the boats sputtered to life and left the pier.

Julie scanned the menu and chose shrimp scampi. Mark ordered linguini with clam sauce and white zinfandel for the two of them.

The wine came first, along with a basket of hot rolls and an olive oil dipping sauce.

Mark lifted his glass. "Let's celebrate," he said with a grin.

Julie held her breath. "Celebrate? What are we celebrating?" *Please don't say our wedding.*

"Your assignment, what else?"

She raised her glass and smiled with relief. "I thought we already celebrated my new job."

"Yes, but this time we're gonna send you off to Florida with a wish and a prayer."

She giggled. "Okay. What's your wish, and what's your prayer?"

They clicked glasses. Mark took a sip and set his glass on the table. She did the same, never taking her eyes off of him. He'd pricked her curiosity.

He leaned toward her and clasped her hands in his. "First my prayer," he said. "I pray you'll have a safe and profitable trip to Florida, that you'll come back armed with plenty of material for your story, and that you'll do the best job ever."

She tilted her head. "And your wish?"

He released a sigh, and his blue eyes sparkled. "My wish," he said, almost in a whisper, "is for this woman I love with all my heart to overcome her fears and trust me enough to walk down the aisle with me. I want her to keep moving forward, knowing God has placed His hand on our relationship to keep us and guide us and bring us closer to Him."

She stared at him, unsure of how to respond. Few men stooped from their macho image and opened up the way Mark had. Only guys who possessed a great deal of self-confidence could share their feelings like that. Sitting across from her was the epitome of strength under control; a man of integrity, strong, yet pliable, having firm convictions, yet able to give in when appropriate. For the moment, Doctor Balser's premarital list didn't bother her anymore.

Mark released her hands and passed her the basket of rolls. "I'm starving," he said, also letting go of the topic she often avoided. His insight was overwhelming.

As they dipped their bread in the herbed oil, the conversation turned to his work at the college and his scramble to finish the PowerPoint. She welcomed the opportunity to get her mind off of the pile of work still waiting at home. She could relax for a while and enjoy this time with Mark. Such moments provided a foreshadowing of what life might be like as his wife. They could live independently of each other during the day and come together in the evenings. They could work at their own jobs and save the weekends for fun. That was her dream—but dreams didn't always materialize.

Their food arrived and momentarily distracted her. She hadn't eaten for hours and discovered she was famished. While they ate, Mark turned the conversation to Julie's research. "So, what have you discovered so far? Have you learned anything of significance about Marjorie?"

She was about to run through a chronological history of Marjorie's life when he leaned toward her. "You know," he said. "I've been doing a little research myself."

She gave him a puzzled smile. "What do you mean?"

"Well, I called up some information on Rawlings on the internet, and I was surprised by what I found."

"Like what?" Julie lifted a piece of shrimp to her mouth and savored the taste of garlic butter.

"Are you aware of how much you have in common with Marjorie?" Mark said, and she almost choked. "It's uncanny, Julie. You're like two peas in a pod."

She took a sip of water and forced the shrimp down. "Come on, Mark. You're kidding, right?" Though she protested, she'd discovered the same thing. She just didn't want to admit it.

"No, I'm serious. Except for a few differences—"

"You mean *lots* of differences," Julie interrupted.

He shook his head. "Listen. Your backgrounds may have been slightly different, but like you, she wanted to be a writer all her life."

"And *that's* where the similarities end."

He set down his fork and sat up straight. "Not really, Julie. Your personalities are also similar. You're strong-willed, passionate, even rude at times. So was she. Marjorie was known to lash out in anger one minute and speak sweetly the next. I've seen you flare up at people only to regret it and apologize. You speak before you think. It's nothing to be ashamed of. It's your personality, and I wouldn't change you for the world."

She was stumped for words. Was that a compliment or an insult?

"Look," he said. "I read one of Marjorie's short stories, *Cocks Must Crow*. Are you familiar with it?"

She avoided answering by taking another bite of shrimp.

"The main character was a woman with a sharp tongue. Quincey Dover. In a way, I think Marjorie was describing herself. And I hate to say it, but it also sounded an awful lot like you. As hard a time as she gave her husband, the woman ended up being his saving grace. You're like that, Julie. Tough, but when the going gets rough you're loyal."

She set down her fork and glared at him. "I don't like where this conversation is going," she said.

"Think about it," he went on, as if he didn't notice the scowl on her face. "Marjorie would hole up in her house for weeks, then she'd rise from the shadows and throw a dinner party, or she'd deliver a box of food to a poor family." He grinned with pride. "You've done the same thing. Maybe not a dinner party, but you have reached out to your friends on occasion. And even though you sometimes avoid people like the plague, I've seen you reach out to the less fortunate. Didn't you take a bag of clothes to the women's shelter last week?"

Julie shrugged, too embarrassed to answer. She still didn't

want to admit that she'd also discovered the similarities. She was caught between being boastful and offended.

He leaned back and took a deep breath. "Tell me, how can you say you're not like Marjorie? You have her same mix of strength and sweetness, her same passion for adventure outside of your normal sphere of life, her same independent streak that is both endearing and frustrating to those who know you. You also have—" Mark stopped short, his eyes on the front door of the restaurant.

Julie followed his gaze. A beautiful young woman stood beside the hostess' counter. Her long, black hair fell in layers to her shoulders. She was wearing a green blouse and tan slacks. Her dark eyes scanned the restaurant and rested on Mark.

A surge of heat rushed to Julie's face. She looked back at Mark. He wasn't smiling. In fact, he looked downright angry.

"Who's that?" she said.

"That, my dear, is Fiona. Remember the phone call?"

Julie scowled with confusion. "What's going on, Mark?"

"I have no idea, but I think we're about to find out. Here she comes."

Fiona approached their table with boldness. As she drew closer, Julie got a better look. The girl wore far too much makeup. An excessive amount of blush on her cheeks and a thick coat of mascara on her lashes. Julie suppressed a chuckle. It looked like two big spiders had latched onto the girl's eyes.

Mark didn't rise, a surprise to Julie. He usually stood up in the presence of a lady. Instead, he was glaring at her.

"What do you want, Fiona?" His tone was anything but inviting.

A smile lit up the woman's face, like she hadn't heard the irritation in Mark's voice.

"I'm surprised to see you here," she said. Her black eyes shot icy darts in Julie's direction.

Julie returned the fire.

"And who's this?" Fiona said, her voice smug. "Aren't you going to introduce us?"

Mark made the introductions, but his voice sounded strained, like he was struggling to remain polite. To Julie's delight, he referred to her as his fiancée. The woman didn't flinch.

Julie raised her left hand to brush back a crimson curl from her forehead, making sure Fiona caught sight of the sparkling rock on her finger. She hated to sink to feminine wiles, didn't think she needed to in order to keep her man, but she had to make this woman understand she would fight if she had to.

Fiona looked away with obvious disdain. An air of discomfort mounted and swirled over their corner. This Fiona person was spoiling the evening for them. Julie couldn't let her get away with such a brazen interruption. But wasn't it Mark's responsibility? She stared daggers at him, willing him with a silent message to take action.

He flexed his jaw, a sign he was definitely irritated. "Look, Fiona. I'm having a nice dinner with Julie before she leaves on a work trip. Say what you've come to say, and then let us be."

Mark's rudeness shocked Julie, but she couldn't deny her appreciation for his remark. He'd been blunt with the woman, as though defending Julie's territory on her behalf.

A fleeting stab of pain crossed Fiona's eyes. She let out a breathy sigh that turned the head of a young man at a nearby table. "Oh, well," she said. "I guess it can wait. You say your friend is going away? I'll get with you then."

"Not my friend; my *fiancée*," Mark corrected her.

Fiona's smile widened. With a toss of her head, she turned from their table and left the restaurant.

Julie leaned toward Mark. "Why did you tell her I'm going away?"

He patted her hand. "You have nothing to worry about. I'm not interested in Fiona. I don't like pushy women. Even if you didn't exist, I would never go for someone like her."

She already knew that. Hadn't he walked away from a group of eager coquettes at Lakisha's reception, and hadn't he come after her, sitting alone at a table, overtly disinterested in him or any other male at the wedding?

By this time, Julie's appetite was spoiled. She shoved her plate away, unable to take another bite. Like always, when Mark was filling his stomach, he didn't pay much attention to anything else. Now she looked across the table at a man who'd committed the rest of his life to her. Someone had invaded their space, yet he'd already gone back to his linguini, like nothing had happened. Five minutes later, he was scraping up the last of her shrimp.

Though he amused her greatly, the confrontation with Fiona had left her wanting to run. She didn't need that kind of drama in her life right now. One way or another, she was going to have to get through the next couple of months. A double-edged sword had plunged into her heart. She still wanted to hold onto her independence. Maybe Mark was right. In that respect, she *was* a lot like Marjorie. Yet, the other edge of the sword kept slashing away at her self-centered defenses, and a part of her yearned for a sense of security. The truth was, life without Mark would be unbearable now that she'd let him in.

10

GETTING TO KNOW MARJORIE

Three days of research remained before Julie could leave for Florida. Most of the books and resource materials had given her a decent picture of what life was like in the Florida forest in the late 1930s. Yet, she still needed to get to know the person who'd left a legacy of reminiscences.

Julie had already gathered a ton of information from Marjorie's autobiographical writings and from accounts others wrote about her. But those records provided only a surface knowledge. She needed to delve into Marjorie's heart. She wanted to find out what had caused her to leave her pampered lifestyle in Rochester and relocate to Cross Creek? Why did she give up the conveniences of life—a toilet, a shower, a grocery store around the corner—for a roach-infested shack with no plumbing or electricity? Why did she leave friends and family in order to rub elbows with scruffy Crackers who drank rotgut liquor and eyed her with distrust?

Julie snickered over what Mark had said about her being a lot like Marjorie. She doubted she could give up the comforts of home to live in the brush. In a way, she had nothing at all in common with the woman. Marjorie had many unique character traits—resilience, strength of character, perseverance, and her ability to spark life into the people and places she wrote about. Julie could only dream she might one day possess such talent. Marjorie's knack for detailed descriptions left Julie's brain reeling with vivid images. She'd gotten a taste of Florida from Rawlings' books. Now she needed to fly down there and experience the same sights, tastes, and smells that drew Marjorie back to Cross Creek multiple times during her lifetime.

But there was still more to learn from the books. She lifted a heavy tome off the pile at her feet. *The Private Marjorie: The Love Letters of Marjorie Kinnan Rawlings to Norton S. Baskin.* Already her curiosity had been pricked.

The large book carried only a portion of the many letters Marjorie wrote to her husband. Julie scanned through the pages, winced at the occasional blasphemies, and smiled at the endearments. Most of Marjorie's letters to Norton were written during World War II when he served overseas in the military. She started every message with a loving salutation—*"Hello, darling," "Mister Honey," "Dear Honey," "My dear,"* and *"Good morning, my sweet."* She signed a few of her letters with her alter ego, *"Dora"* or *"Dora Regina."*

Julie detected a change in Marjorie's demeanor. Following her divorce from Charles in 1933, she settled into a life of isolation and could work for hours, days, and weeks without any interruptions. However, years later, after she connected with Norton, her letters revealed a different side to Marjorie. She confessed that she'd wanted marriage before he did.

"I loathe living alone," she wrote in August 1939. *"I need more solitude, more privacy, than most women, but even I can get all I want in the course of a day. My work does not satisfy me as the end and aim of my life."* She wrote those words the same year *The Yearling* won the Pulitzer Prize for fiction.

Other letters included a mix of details from her daily routine, visits with mutual friends, the trials and tribulations of juggling her writing projects, and even the different foods she'd tried. It was as if she wanted Norton to be involved in every aspect of her life.

Once they married in 1941, he easily fell into her routine and accepted the many weeks and months they were apart. He was busy too, with his hotels and restaurants. It was a good match.

Julie sat back and considered her relationship with Mark. Except for the marriage part, didn't he have many of the same characteristics as Norton? Hadn't he exercised patience when Julie needed to be alone? Hadn't he spoken words of encouragement to her, especially when she lost confidence or was about to make a life-changing decision? Even now, with another woman trying to steal his heart away, he'd remained firmly committed to Julie. He'd told her as much. Few other men would have put up with her erratic behavior for very long.

She turned back to the letters. In July of 1943, Norton left to serve as an ambulance driver with the American Field Service in the India/Burma theater. Marjorie's letters bore a more serious tone during Norton's time overseas.

"How I wish I could reach you..." she wrote in August of that year. And later the same month, *"I have made so many guesses as to where you are—N. Africa—the Middle East. I dreamed last night that you were in actual battle action."*

And in September, *"All my love. When I went to bed with a book last night, how I wished you were here!"*

It was as if Marjorie's heart was breaking. Julie shook her head in wonder. Norton must have worked some kind of magic on Marjorie. Gone were the complaints and the flare-ups. Her letters to Norton revealed a sweet, compliant paramour who was longing for her soldier to come home. It was like seeing a rerun of Shakespeare's *Taming of the Shrew.*

Through all her letters to Norton, Marjorie invited him into her life—what she was working on, the people she got together with, how his business ventures were going in his absence, the projects being done on their Crescent Beach cottage, and her work with the war efforts. And above all, her extreme loneliness without him.

But Marjorie's letters to Norton weren't all roses and honey. Some of them were filled with complaints but with a touch of comic relief.

On a bitter cold November evening in 1943 she was absorbed in Dostoyevsky's *Crime and Punishment,* when the heater quit working. This time, her letter to Norton was filled with rantings about the help not being able to fix it, her dog Moe making a fuss, and a gunshot going off in the middle of the night. *"Old Will had shot a 'possum,"* Marjorie wrote. *"So I came back to the cold bed and hated the world."* After cursing everyone who'd had a role in making her evening miserable, including herself, she said she'd felt better and had dropped off to sleep.

Julie was laughing out loud by this time. She loved this side of Marjorie. Her spunk, her outspoken honesty, her folksy sarcasm. Norton, too, must have been in stitches when he read her letters. How could he not laugh when she wrote about ringing for her servant, *Sissie,* and having the girl come in and say, *"Did you rung?"*

"No I did not rung," she went on. *"But I thought I will wring your neck some day."* She expressed a few more complaints, and then added, *"I made a fresh pot of coffee myself and it was delicious, and now I feel all right again."*

In an October 17, 1943, letter to Norton, Marjorie moaned about the *"beautiful lines and passages"* in the writing of James Joyce and in other authors' works she'd ordered from the Modern Library. *"It seems asinine to turn out my trivial tripe when the Big Boys have already said about all that needs saying,"* she pined. *"It makes me feel like a rag-picker, pawing through the cosmic dump."*

It struck Julie as absurd that a writer of Marjorie's caliber should have such a low self-esteem. To have one of her favorite authors write so humbly about herself brought a deeper sense of conviction to Julie. How, then, could her own attempts to succeed ever measure up?

With the book of letters still open on her lap, Julie flipped through a few other materials she'd pulled out of the pile. Together with the letters to Norton, they created a well-rounded picture of Marjorie and the people who played decisive roles in her life. The Cracker folks made the biggest impression of all. Through their outspoken honesty and their guilt-free mentality, they unknowingly taught Marjorie many down-to-earth lessons about life. In time, she easily adapted to their lifestyle and even appeared to enjoy it. The rest of the world was passing them by, but the forest people didn't seem to care if it did, and when Marjorie was with them, she stopped caring about it too. After all, she could return to her former life any time she wanted to, yet she chose to spend much of two decades living in the forest.

Marjorie was as comfortable sitting on the back step of her Cross Creek home guzzling moonshine out of a Mason jar as she was sipping champagne and eating caviar at a political party in Washington, D.C. She milked her own cow, plowed her own garden, dug for turtle eggs in the sand,

and went deer hunting with a lantern in the middle of the night. She even went rattlesnake hunting with Ross Allen, a herpetologist who set up a reptile exhibit at Silver Springs Park in Ocala. Although Marjorie wanted nothing to do with poisonous snakes, Ross Allen was hoping she'd write an article about his work. As it turned out, she accepted his dare, plodded into the swamps with him, and even bagged a rattlesnake of her own.

Julie couldn't have gone anywhere near a snake hunt. Yet despite her fear of snakes, Marjorie had stepped out of her comfort zone and had gone trekking through the marsh with Ross Allen, like it was part of her daily routine.

Julie flipped through another document. Marjorie moved from one place to another—Crescent Beach, Cincinnati, Louisville, a rented cabin in North Carolina, and a farmhouse outside of Van Hornesville, New York, where she spent six months of every year from 1947 until she died. But inevitably, she returned to the place she most often called home—Cross Creek. It appeared Norton simply went along with the flow. He concentrated on his work, first at the Marion Hotel in Ocala, and later at his own Castle Warden Hotel in St. Augustine. He spent lonely days and nights in the hotel suite while Marjorie traipsed about the central Florida forest. They were two people who'd formed an irrevocable bond, whether they were alone or together, showing complete trust and dedication to each other's needs. Julie hoped to get the same support from Mark. If they were ever going to marry, they had to be that committed.

In several of her final letters to Norton, Marjorie spoke about the progress she was making on her research for a biography of Ellen Glasgow, also a Pulitzer Prize winning author.

Sadly, Marjorie never completed the work. She suffered a stroke while playing Bridge with Norton and friends at their Crescent Beach home. She died the next day, December 14, 1953, at Flagler Hospital in St. Augustine.

In her last known letter to Norton, dated November 4, 1953, she included this reflection: *"I walked to Ellen's home, and entering un-noticed, sat on the back steps of the old gallery over-looking the garden which was once so beautiful. There were no ghosts there...."*

Tears rushed to Julie's eyes. That seemed to be Marjorie's natural bent. Always grasping for a few minutes of seclusion where she could lose herself amidst nature and her own musings.

Julie brushed moisture from her cheeks and read on.

Near the conclusion of the letter, Marjorie shared her plans to join a friend for a supper of *"oyster stew, thick with cream, lightly spiced, and laced with sherry."*

A terrible lump had risen to Julie's throat. Marjorie's love of Norton had come through those letters with such profound force, they brought Julie's research to a standstill. She couldn't move ahead without first mulling over what she'd just read. Her heart was breaking along with Marjorie's and probably with Norton's too. Love like theirs was rare.

Julie had witnessed her parents' example of marriage. It seemed stilted next to what Marjorie and Norton had. Her mom, the submissive housewife, catered to her dad, the domineering CEO, who'd never learned to leave his authority in the office. Yet they seemed to have made it work for them. But where was the message of undying love? Here, in these letters, was something else she was learning from Marjorie.

She shoved the book and the papers aside, and she reached

for her cell phone. It was 12 o'clock noon. Mark would be between classes right now.

He picked up on the first ring.

"I wanted to apologize, Mark."

There was a moment of silence, then he spoke. "For what?"

"For not being more enthusiastic about the wedding."

"Look. I'm not going anywhere. I'll still be here when you get back from Cross Creek and anywhere else you need to travel for your job. I have plenty of work to keep me busy."

Like Norton.

"Thanks, Mark."

"Tell you what," he said. "I know you're swamped right now, but let's have dinner again tonight. You barely touched your food at the Lakeside Inn."

She smiled, though he couldn't see her face at the moment. "You finished it for me."

"I didn't want it to go to waste," he said.

"Dinner sounds like a good idea. Should we invite Lakisha and Greg to join us?"

"Great idea, honey. It might be nice to see how things are going with them." he cleared his throat, a sure sign something was on his mind. "I may be leaving town myself in a few days."

"Leaving town? Where are you going?"

"My PowerPoint project is almost finished. One of the professors at Moody Bible Institute contacted me and asked if I'd do a presentation to the student body. I sent out a synopsis to a number of big colleges, and... well, it looks like the responses are starting to come in."

Mark had talked of little else since they came back from Patmos. "I'm happy for you, Mark. It's what you always wanted."

They concluded the call, and Julie went back to her research.

The trouble was, the deeper she delved into Marjorie's life the more she was learning about herself. At what point did Marjorie's life end and her own begin? She couldn't ignore the similarities—her need to be alone, her obsession with her work, her angry outbursts.

She'd become distressingly aware at how she'd compartmentalized everyone in her life. Rita was in a compartment called "nursing school." Lakisha was in the "best friend when needed" compartment. Mark was supposed to stay inside one labeled "dinners out, shoulder to cry on, and ego-booster." And none of them were allowed to leave their compartments without her permission.

It was like looking in a dark mirror and seeing a monster. How could she do that to people who loved her? Was she like Marjorie? Of course.

Marjorie did the same thing with Charles and Norton, every one of her society friends, the Cracker people, and even her hired help. Each person fit inside his or her own little cubby. She summoned each of them at will and put them back when she was finished with them. She was in charge, and everyone knew it.

Though her life appeared to be full and she'd enjoyed the best of two worlds, they were far removed from each other. Though she'd used the pen name, Felicity, when she was a beginning writer, Marjorie's letters to Norton revealed someone who wasn't completely happy with her life. Somewhere beneath her spontaneous rants and her vain attempts at humor lay a discontented, lonely woman who, on the surface, appeared to have everything under control but deep inside was still that little girl looking for happiness.

In making this evaluation, Julie could have been describing

herself. But it wasn't too late for her to change. She could realign her priorities, stop being so self-centered, and pay more attention to the needs of other people. She could let everyone out of their compartments and see what happened. If she didn't make some adjustments soon, she could end up a lonely, bitter woman, imprisoned by a career with a few prizes to keep her company, and destined for an early grave.

11

MARJORIE AND MAX

Julie gazed at the yet untouched pile of research materials and released a dispirited sigh. A large, heavy book caught her eye. *Max and Marjorie, the Correspondence Between Maxwell E. Perkins and Marjorie Kinnan Rawlings.* She looked inside. It contained nearly 700 letters, far more than Julie could read in one day, yet a mere drop in a bucket compared to the reams of letters Marjorie was said to have written over the years.

Most of the communication between Marjorie and her editor, from 1930 to 1934, bore a professional, impersonal tone. They referred to each other as *"Mrs. Rawlings"* and *"Mr. Perkins."* Unimpressed with the formality of those letters, she skipped ahead to those written from 1935 to 1947. Now it was *"Dear Marjorie"* and *"Dear Max."*

So, what had happened? Max's letter to *"Mrs. Rawlings"* on March 9, 1935, contained his impressions of a poem she'd written and his favorable outlook for her book, *Golden Apples.* Strictly business. Ten days later, he wrote a more personal note about people getting the flu and his desire for her good health, plus another request for *Golden Apples.* This time he referred to her as *"Marjorie."*

From that day on, it was *"Max"* and *"Marjorie,"* and their letters became more interesting. In between the necessary repertoires about her writing projects, Marjorie wrote about her friendships with other writers, her travels, her medical problems, her issues with the help, and her interactions with the people of the forest. Unlike her former correspondence with her editor, these letters were filled with vitality.

On March 30, she wrote and told him she was thrown off a horse and ended up in a neck brace. She ended the letter by saying she'd sent a revision of *Golden Apples* to Cosmopolitan. And so it went. Each letter carried a brief personal note amidst business as usual.

Despite the personal tone of her letters, Marjorie maintained an air of respect for her accomplished editor. After all, his clients were among the great writers of their day—Ernest Hemingway, Thomas Wolfe, F. Scott Fitzgerald, and a host of others.

Though Max was able to place some of Marjorie's work in magazines, he confessed he looked forward even more to the letters she wrote about her home in Cross Creek and the intriguing neighbors she'd met there. He pressed her often to write a novel based on that culture. In later correspondence he informed her he had placed two of her forest stories, "Cracker Chidlings" and "Jacob's Ladder," in magazines, and they'd been well received. Max encouraged her to work those same images into a book. The result was *South Moon Under,* a novel about the Big Scrub people on the other side of the Ocklawaha River. It was a huge success.

"The Florida Crackers have always been looked upon as a low people, and have been despised," Max wrote to her in 1930. *"You enable the reader to see them from a new point of view by which he can sympathize with them."*

Julie turned the pages, stopping now and then to capture the essence of a particular letter, especially those that revealed how the relationship had progressed.

On March 26, 1936, Max wrote, *"The oranges are beautiful and delicious, and I thank you for them... I think I should be happy with an orange grove."*

Max encouraged Marjorie to write a *"boy's book"* set in the Big Scrub of central Florida, like she'd done with *South Moon Under.* It took her five years of writing and shelving and more writing to complete *The Yearling.* Then she complained about all the cuts it took to turn the huge manuscript into a more acceptable length.

Julie could relate. How many times had she wept buckets over the huge chunks of text her newsroom editors cut for the benefit of space? Magazine writing offered a much bigger spread—possibly three or four full pages, with no ads to interfere with the flow. She could only imagine how devastating it was for Marjorie to let huge blocks of her sweat equity get obliterated from her novels.

Julie turned her attention back to the letters. As she worked her way through them, it became evident how Max, with his easy-going demeanor and tremendous literary wisdom provided a necessary balance to Marjorie's erratic personality. The woman needed someone like Max to push her in the right direction.

In the end, Max was able to groom Marjorie into one of the great American authors of the day. They were an ideal match. Though Marjorie had struggled with her writing and received multiple rejections before meeting Max, from the time she began to write for him her work blossomed.

Meanwhile, Max did more than encourage and edit. He ran ads and also wrote to the "Ocala Banner" suggesting they serialize *South Moon Under.* Julie smiled with amusement. In their day, newspapers published fiction in their entertainment sections. Perhaps it would help boost circulation if they had continued the practice, particularly today when the numbers of subscribers had dropped to an all-time low.

She returned to the book, skipped ahead, and neared the end.

On June 7, 1947, Marjorie wrote Max and complained about a lawsuit her friend Zelma Cason had filed against her. The woman was angry over the way Marjorie described her in *Cross Creek*. This was the person who'd met Marjorie and Charles when they disembarked from a steamer in Jacksonville in 1928. She also was the census taker who invited Marjorie to go along on horseback into hard-to-reach places in the brush. They started as friends. But after the book came out, they ended up in a trial, which Marjorie won, followed by Zelma's appeal through the Florida Supreme Court. In the end, Marjorie had to pay $1, plus court costs.

Shortly after, another correspondence stood out. It was a wire sent ten days later from Charles Scribner, Marjorie's publisher, addressed to Marjorie informing her that Max had died of pneumonia. He'd been ill for only two days, so there'd been little warning.

That had to be devastating for Marjorie. She'd lost one of the most important people in her life. Julie considered the works that followed. None of them compared to what Marjorie had produced under Max's guidance.

Julie closed the book, held it on her lap for a minute, and gazed out the window at the rush-hour traffic. How that wire must have troubled Marjorie. To think, one of her last letters to her friend and editor had included an angry tirade over Zelma's lawsuit. What could have been going through her mind when she read that telegram? Did she wish she'd written something lighter, more uplifting, in her last letter to Max? Julie tried to imagine how she might have felt if someone dear to her had died in the midst of one of her angry outbursts.

She took a deep breath. Unable to read any more, she checked the time. She had an hour before Mark would be picking her up. She could use some of the time to set aside a few items to take on her trip. She'd need her tablet, of course, and a couple of notebooks and pens. She decided to take along Rawlings' book, *Cross Creek*, which would help prepare her for what she would encounter in Florida. She could immerse herself in the backwoods culture before ever arriving at Cross Creek, and perhaps a little more of Marjorie might emerge from between the lines.

Satisfied, Julie went into her bedroom to get ready for dinner. How nice it will be to see Greg and Lakisha again. She stopped short of getting in the shower. A thought struck Julie like a bolt of lightning. Somehow, in the midst of everything else, she needed to plan a baby shower for her best friend. Moments ago, she'd berated herself for her self-centeredness. Now she faced a test. How she fared depended on the level of conviction she had. It was time to put someone else's interests ahead of hers.

Mark arrived home from work and checked his mailbox. Along with a bill for electric service there was an unmarked, unstamped envelope. The hairs went up on the back of his neck. He didn't have to look inside. The envelope reeked of perfume. It reminded him of the scent Fiona wore the day she came to his office.

He went into his apartment, dropped his briefcase by the

door and tossed the mail on the kitchen table. He'd been able to avoid Fiona the whole day. Now what was she up to?

He stared at the envelope, unsure if he should open it or toss it in the trash. He was supposed to pick up Julie in an hour. He left the envelope on the table and went to the bathroom to escape under a hot shower. The woman was relentless. She'd seen the ring on Julie's hand. He'd told her more than once he was engaged to be married. It hadn't discouraged her. *Too bad men don't wear engagement rings,* he pondered. *Perhaps we should.*

He stood under the oscillating spray and escaped for a moment within its gentle massage. He let the water trickle down his forehead and onto his shoulders, let it wash away every trace of Fiona, down the drain and out of sight. The woman didn't appeal to him. Even if he and Julie broke up, he'd move on alone, concentrate on his work, and forget about dating for a while.

Still fighting the irritation, he cut himself shaving. He grabbed a piece of toilet tissue and stemmed the flow of blood. He brushed his teeth, gargled with a mint-flavored mouthwash, spit and missed the drain. What was wrong with him? He'd always kept control in the most trying circumstances. But he suspected this was the beginning of his troubles.

If Fiona didn't let up, he'd have to talk to Melanie and get her to take action. Wasn't this a type of workplace harassment? Didn't it work both ways? If men could get accused of breaking the rules, so could women, right?

Mark glanced at the envelope on his way out the door. It could stay right there on the kitchen table, for all he cared. He was almost to his car when he decided to turn around and go back inside his apartment. Why not open the thing at dinner and let everybody see what the pest wrote? Greg might come up with an idea. And Julie? He didn't want to keep any secrets from her. Not when they were so close to tying the knot. If they put their heads together, the four of them could come up with a plan and send Fiona running back to wherever she came from.

12

DINNER WITH FRIENDS

Mark knocked on the door to Julie's condo, confident she'd be ready and waiting. Unlike most of the women he'd dated, she didn't spend hours in front of a mirror putting on gobs of makeup so she could make a grand entrance. Her natural beauty always shone through.

He slid his hand in his pocket and fingered the edge of the envelope. Whatever it held, he'd be as surprised as everyone else at the table that evening. If he ever needed the support of his friends, it was now.

When the door swung open she stood there looking as gorgeous as ever in a satiny blue dress. Her crimson hair hung to her shoulders. She wore dangling earrings, a silver chain around her neck, and a matching bracelet. His eyes strayed to the diamond on her left hand, and a lump came to his throat. Fiona didn't have a chance. Nor did any other woman.

"You look great," he said.

She leaned close for a quick kiss, then she grabbed her purse and went out the door with him. During the drive to the restaurant, she mentioned a TV news report she had listened to while getting ready.

"It looks like the *Daily Press* laid off a couple more people," she said.

"You got out of there in the nick of time."

"I did," she said, though her tone was solemn. "It's sad

though. I have a few friends who may get the axe—Roger Cappella, for example. And even Mary Beth Simmons."

He raised his eyebrows and glanced at her. "I thought Mary Beth was your nemesis."

Julie shook her head. "Not always. We were close friends at one time."

"Yeah," he said with disgust in his voice. "Until it came down to the big stories. Then it was every woman for herself."

"That's the newspaper business," she said with a shrug. "Let's just say I'm glad to be out of there and working on something that excites me. Mary Beth's still getting the city council meetings and stories about other people's accomplishments. The breaking news usually goes to one of the more seasoned reporters. It might be a blessing in disguise if she gets canned. Then she can find something better."

They fell into silence for a couple of blocks. Mark checked the time. "Looks like we're gonna beat Greg and Lakisha to the restaurant."

"It's okay by me. It'll give us more alone time." She turned away to look out the side window, as if something had caught her eye. When she looked back, she was smiling. "So, what's happening with your PowerPoint project?"

"I'm making progress. Your photos from Ephesus and Patmos worked in like magic. Last night, I narrated the historical information, and I added some Middle Eastern background music. I'm beginning to feel more confident, although it could stand a little tweaking before it's finished."

Julie stared out the front window. The setting sun cast a pink glow on her cheeks, giving her an almost childlike look. He savored the image. Could a man's heart rip open his chest from the inside? At that moment he believed it could.

They arrived at the Luna Bistro ahead of Greg and Lakisha. Mark asked for a table for four, and he and Julie sat where they could keep an eye on the front door. While they waited, Mark perused the menu. He was ravenous.

Julie studied her menu too, then she sat back in her chair, her eyes on Mark. He stared back at her, perplexed by the look on her face. She was pinching her lips together, like she had a secret and couldn't wait to let it out.

He set the menu aside. and gave her his full attention.

"Is something wrong, Julie?"

She shook her head. "No. Nothing's wrong." She leaned toward him, smiling. "I had a sort of epiphany today."

"Good or bad?"

"Both."

He straightened and held her gaze.

"Don't worry. I was reading through Marjorie's letters to her husband, Norton, and it struck me that maybe they were a lot like you and me."

She'd pricked his interest. "Go on."

"First the bad part. Like you said, Marjorie was known for saying whatever she thought, whether or not it offended someone. If someone pushed the right buttons, she'd flare up at them. Then she'd either apologize or make a joke about it. You said I was like that, and you were absolutely right, though it pains me to admit it."

He was laughing softly now.

"There's more," she said. "The woman was a workaholic. She spent long hours in solitude, obsessed with finishing whatever she was working on at the time, and no one had better interrupt her."

"I get the picture." He allowed a silly smirk to cross his lips.

Julie's green eyes flashed to deep emerald. "Okay, Mr. Smarty-pants. You already know what I'm driving at, don't you?"

"Yep. All of that is exactly like you, too."

She forced her lips to one side in an annoyed smirk. At that moment she looked like she was 10 years old.

Mark laughed to himself, and Julie's face turned red. She breathed a heavy sigh. "I don't know how, but it looks like I inherited Marjorie's worst character traits."

He was laughing out loud now. "Wait up, honey. You also have some of her best attributes."

She tilted her head quizzically. "What do you mean?"

"Well—" he said, grasping her hand. "You're a talented writer. You push yourself to accomplish what you set out to do. You tackle the obstacles that come up, hardly ever complain about the challenges, and you always finish the job. It's like you have a compulsion to finish whatever you start. More people should have that quality."

The blush slowly drained from her face. She was smiling now. "Quality?" she said. "Are you saying it's a good thing?"

"Of course. What's more, your quick temper could actually be a defense mechanism. While it sometimes gets you in hot water, it also provides a certain amount of protection. People can't take advantage of you. Your independence and need to be alone reveals a certain inner strength. I don't have to worry about you or constantly come to your rescue." He gave her hand a gentle squeeze. "Do you remember that little blond I used to date?"

"Katie?"

He nodded. "She wasn't anything like you, Julie. She needed someone to take care of her. All the time. There's a guy out there who's perfect for her, somebody who prefers a woman who needs him. That isn't me. You're different from Katie, more my type. I like the way you stand up for yourself and deal with whatever comes up. I like your strength of character, your no-nonsense attitude."

"That's comforting." She slid her hand from his grasp. "Okay, so I just said that Marjorie and Norton were a lot like the two of us. Did you catch that?"

"Yeah." He gazed at her, urging her to go on. "So, you think I'm like Norton Baskin?"

She giggled, and her eyes sparkled with mirth. "That's right, and it's all good. Norton was the perfect man for Marjorie. When she needed to be alone so she could work, he kept busy with his own interests. He managed hotels and restaurants. He stayed an hour away at Crescent Beach, while she mingled with the forest people and fixed up the Cross Creek property. He was there when she needed him, and he knew when to disappear. In all of her letters to him, she wrote only sweet things. Her relationship with her first husband was nothing like what she had with Norton. Charles didn't support her work like Norton did. In fact, he harshly criticized her writing. He appeared to be jealous of her success. Maybe because he also aspired to be a writer, but didn't make it like she did."

After all of that, the main thing she'd said that stayed with him was the comparison she'd made between him and Norton Baskin. "So, that's what you think of me?" he said. "I'm flattered."

Her smile fired off a sparkle in her eyes, like they were two emeralds. "Norton and Marjorie were soul mates," she said, leaning close to Mark. "I think we are too."

He was about to plant a kiss on her lips when Greg's voice sailed to him from a few feet away. "Hey, you two. Sorry to hold things up. Lakisha spends a lot more time in the bathroom these days."

Lakisha shot a dark sideways glance at her husband and jabbed his arm. "It's not all my fault," she said. "The baby's moving around a lot more. Sometimes she rests right on my bladder."

Mark rose from his seat and pulled out a chair for Lakisha. "It's okay. You're not that late," he said. "Anyway, we were just talking."

"Really?" Lakisha said, her eyes wide. "That didn't look like talking to me. It looked like you were about to kiss her." She started laughing, and the others joined in.

Mark looked at Julie. Sure enough she was fighting another embarrassed flush of red. He patted her hand and drew her attention, then gave her a comforting smile. She settled down like he'd just wiped away her discomfort. Maybe she *did* need a little protecting. That wouldn't be a bad thing.

Things quieted down while Greg and Lakisha checked out the menu. By the time their server showed up, they were ready to order. Greg also asked for a bottle of red wine for the table, and within a couple of minutes they were toasting Julie's job, Mark's PowerPoint, and the Davises' baby.

Mark immediately shifted his attention to his best friend. "So, Greg, what's it like living with a fat lady?" He flashed a grin at Lakisha. She made a face at him.

"Watch it," she said. "You'll be in the same boat one of these days."

Out of the corner of his eye, Mark caught Julie shrinking in her seat. She wasn't going to be ready for a family for a long time. Though he longed to be married to this woman, he feared tying her down would destroy her spirit. He was going to have to take things slow and easy.

In answer to Mark's question, Greg brought up their last Lamaze class. "With all the huffing and puffing, Lakisha hyperventilated, and our instructor ran out to get a paper sack for her to breath into." He got everyone laughing, which provoked him to tell more stories about his pregnant wife.

Lakisha moaned, but she didn't interrupt him.

When he'd exhausted all the tales about morning sickness and strange cravings, he quieted down, and Lakisha took over.

"That's all pretty funny," she said with a smirk. "I'd love it if you guys had sympathy pains—maybe the heartburn, the nausea, and the need to keep a bathroom within sprinting distance."

Her account raised more laughter around the table. At one point during the meal, she quickly excused herself and ran off to the ladies' room, leaving the two guys snickering and Julie running after her.

When they returned to the table, Julie berated Mark and Greg for their insensitivity.

"C'mon, Julie," Greg said, his tone light. "You can't tell me your biological clock hasn't started ticking."

Mark kept his eyes on her and waited for a response. She avoided his gaze and took a sip of water.

The server brought Mark's steak and boiled potatoes. The sizzling meat distracted him for the moment. Julie was picking at her salad. And, like they always did, Greg and Lakisha started sharing items off their plates with each other. Mark eyed the two of them with envy. They had a system. Greg sampled Lakisha's broiled fish, and she took a bite of his roast beef. He'd seen them do the same thing whenever they ate dinner together. Why didn't their parents see the obvious? They were made for each other.

Mark finished off his steak and potatoes and drained his water glass. Julie was now attacking her buttered carrots and roast chicken, her attention on her plate, like she was avoiding eye-contact with him. Like always when the conversation turned to marriage and children, she found ways to avoid it.

Greg was still joking about life with a pregnant woman. Mark laughed aloud with his friend, but he kept glancing at Julie. She appeared to have tuned him out. She didn't look up from her meal until she was done eating.

Toward the end of the meal, Lakisha switched to a female-only conversation about pre-natal vitamins and nursing versus formula. The girls laughed together over Lakisha's recent weight gain and her need for larger maternity tops. Then, Lakisha pulled an ultrasound photo out of her purse and showed it around the table. Julie oohed and aahed, and passed the black-and-white photo to him. He stared at it, amazed by the clear image of the baby.

Mark made eye contact with Greg. His friend shrugged and gave him a cockeyed grin, like he was trying to hide the sense of pride that had surged up within him.

The atmosphere around the table was as pleasant as it would ever get. It was now or never. Mark slipped his hand in his pocket and pulled the envelope out. "Guys," he announced, and drew all eyes in his direction. "This was in my mailbox when I got home from work." He held up the envelope and waved it. "I have a sneaky suspicion who put it there. I needed to open it among friends."

Julie was staring bullets at him. Her green eyes darkened. Lakisha tilted her head and gave him one of her stern, *you'd better be good*, looks. And, Greg set down his fork and gave him his full attention.

"The woman at your office?" Greg said, grinning like a fox.

Mark looked at Julie. Her cheeks had turned deep red.

"Yeah," he said with a sigh. "I'm guessing, of course. But who else would do something like this?"

"Well?" Greg urged. "Are you gonna open it?"

Mark nodded. Using his steak knife, he slit the envelope and pulled out the scented note.

"Whew!" Greg gasped. "What perfume factory did *that* come from?" He waved his hand across the table, as though trying to clear the air.

Mark shot a warning look at his friend and unfolded the note.

"Dearest Mark..." he read.

"*Dearest* Mark?" Greg fell into hysterics. "You've got to be kidding."

Mark raised his hand to silence him. *"Since you've made it clear that I shouldn't bother you during work hours, I've decided to write a note instead. I recently learned about your upcoming trip to Chicago to present your PowerPoint program. It sounds like an awesome opportunity, and I'd like to take part in it. I've asked Melanie to allow me to accompany you—"* Mark nearly gagged.

Julie looked like she was about to leap out of her chair.

Greg shook his head. "Wow, man. The girl sounds delusional."

Mark clenched his teeth. "I can't believe her nerve," he said. "I've told her I'm engaged. It doesn't phase her in the least." He slammed the note on the table. "I'm not gonna put up with this any longer. I'll have to talk with Melanie, and maybe I'll file a complaint with human resources." He looked at Julie. "I do *not* want Fiona going on my trip."

Lakisha placed a hand on Julie's arm, restraining her. "Do

you think Melanie will listen to you, Mark? What I mean is, Fiona probably has convinced her nothing's going on, or she would have stopped this nonsense a long time ago. Maybe you've kept your mouth shut too long."

Mark nodded. "I kept hoping this whole obsession would blow over, that maybe Fiona would just go away. I thought she'd given up. She hasn't bothered me for a couple of days. Of course, there was that one phone call. And now there's this blasted note."

"Are you sure you're not a little too flattered by her attention?" Julie was scowling at him.

He shook his head and was about to snap, but quickly calmed down. "Maybe at first I was flattered. But I thought it was a harmless flirtation. I didn't expect her to take it this far. It's gotten out of hand, Julie, and I want to put a stop to it." He leaned toward her, pleading. "You've got to believe me, honey. I never encouraged Fiona."

The lines on her forehead softened. The flame left her eyes, and her cheeks faded to a pale pink. "This whole thing is exhausting," she said, her voice soft. "I have way too much on my plate to have to fight with another woman. I'm afraid I won't be able to do a good job on this story if I have to worry about Fiona."

An uncomfortable silence fell over their table. He looked from one to the other. None of them could come up with a better solution beyond what Mark had proposed. He shifted in his seat and gazed at Julie. She was going away, and she didn't need this kind of pressure while she was in the middle of a major assignment.

Old Yanno had said something about giving up one's life for someone else and how it didn't always mean a person needed to die in someone's place. Sometimes it meant giving up a dream for the benefit of another. Though it would tear his heart to pieces, he might have to give up his dream of marriage and family for a little while—or maybe for good. The way Julie avoided the topic, it seemed she didn't want to get married at all. If that were true, he'd have to set her free. It was down to decision time. And he had to make up his mind tonight.

13

DECISIONS

Mark's mouth had gone dry. After they left the restaurant, he clammed up. Too many thoughts were running around in his head. Thoughts about his future with Julie, the problem with Fiona, his PowerPoint presentation. For the first time in ages, he felt overwhelmed. He usually had everything under control. He kept a tight schedule and rarely met a snag. Now his life was filled with snags.

He peeked at Julie. Her face was like stone. He couldn't guess what was tumbling around in her head, but it didn't look good. The truth was, they'd rushed into things. It was fine to be engaged, but setting the date right away was a big mistake. He'd followed his heart instead of his brain, another anomaly for him. He usually planned things better than this. Julie did too. Though extremely driven, she was a sensible person.

Perhaps this trouble with Fiona had unleashed the real problem with their relationship. They were moving too fast.

They reached Julie's door. "We need to talk," Mark said, a wave of caution enveloping him. "Will you fix us some tea?"

His heart was pounding. Should he wait until they were in Doctor Balser's office? The man could help guide their conversation. He stared at Julie. She remained quiet but unlocked the door and stepped inside her condo ahead of him. Her cool demeanor sent an imaginary knife into his heart. She turned and looked at him, then beckoned him inside with a nod. Her face was a blank canvas. She didn't utter one word. But her actions spoke volumes. A huge rift had come between them.

She went straight to the kitchen and started the tea kettle. He shut the front door and followed her, grabbed a chair at the kitchen table. A scattering of white petals lay at the base of the vase of daisies he'd given her the other night. She'd brought them home with her. Now they were dying.

"Cookies?" she said, and slid a plate of macaroons in front of him.

He smiled at a memory. "This is like Yanno's tea time, isn't it?" he said.

"Yes. He had a routine, didn't he?" she said. She was loosening up, a good sign. "He scheduled tea at 10 a.m., visitors at noon, lock the door at 2 o'clock for a ten-minute siesta."

She actually chuckled then, easing the tension even more.

Mark brushed the stray petals into a tiny pile. He reached for a cookie. The kettle sounded off. Julie went back to the stove to fix their tea. He ate another cookie. And another.

"I miss him," Julie said, a wistful smile on her lips.

"Huh?"

"Yanno. I miss him. I sure could use his wisdom right now." Her smile dissolved and her eyes darkened.

She set two cups of hot tea on the table and settled in the chair across from Mark. The scent of peppermint rose with the steam from his cup. He shut his eyes and inhaled the aroma. For an instant he was back in Yanno's living room in Patmos. With an invisible needle and thread, the old man had mended the wound in his heart. His kind words helped him deal with the pain of losing his mother.

When he opened his eyes, Julie was staring at him. The look on her face wasn't bitter. It wasn't angry. Encouraged, he carefully sipped his tea, then placed the cup back in the saucer and leaned back. "You know I love you more than life itself, don't you?" he said, keeping his voice soft. "I want to encourage you in your work."

"Even if I travel to far-off places?"

"Yes, even if you travel to far-off places. Most women won't even go the bathroom by themselves. But you're not like most women."

She laughed. He loved the melodic tinkle of her voice.

"Julie, you know I want us to be married, have wanted that since the first day I saw you at Lakisha's wedding."

She nodded, but said nothing. A wrinkle of concern creased her brow.

"But..." He kept his eyes on her and scrambled to find the right words. "Honey, we've been moving way too fast."

The troubled lines on her forehead eased.

He reached across the table and took hold of her hand. "I'm making a decision." He paused and searched her face for a clue. She'd frozen. "I'm willing to call off the wedding until after the new year."

She slid her hand out of his hold. "Mark, you—"

He shook his head and cut her off. "Hear me out, Julie. You've already pointed out more than once that you need time to settle into your new job. And here I am, getting started with my PowerPoint presentation. There's no telling how many offers I'll get once I do the program at Moody. Let's take the pressure off of both of us. And don't forget about Lakisha. You said it yourself. She's gonna get bigger. Pretty soon, she may not fit into whatever gown you two pick out for her. Let's allow her to deliver her baby and get back in shape. It's close to the end of July. I'd say six months would be more reasonable for a wedding. In the meantime, you can keep meeting with Doctor Balser."

She let out a long sigh. It was obvious he'd taken a huge weight off her shoulders. For a moment, he felt like her rescuer. But what was he rescuing her from? Marriage to him? Or simply from an overwhelming amount of commitments?

"Thank you, Mark. You can't imagine what this means to me." She moved her head from side-to-side. "It isn't that I don't want to be married to you. I simply need more time. And you're right. We were moving way too fast. Now we can slow down and do this right."

His throat had tightened. Partly from an overpowering love for this woman and partly from disappointment. But he'd made a decision, and now he had to follow through.

"You're leaving for Florida tomorrow morning. You should concentrate on your assignment for now. We'll talk again after you come home—or even after you finish writing your story—whatever—take all the time you need."

She tilted her head coyly and produced a little smirk. "I'll be home Friday evening, and then you'll leave for Chicago on Sunday, right? And if that witch, Fiona, gets her way, she'll be tagging along with you. I'm sure we're both gonna have lots to talk about when you get back."

"My flight doesn't leave until 1:30 on Sunday. How about we get breakfast and go to church together?"

"Don't we always?"

"Yes, but you'll be exhausted from your trip. I don't want to put any pressure on you."

Her smile broadened. "I look forward to spending Sunday mornings with you."

The atmosphere in Julie's kitchen had brightened. Mark locked eyes with her and was able to envision their relationship in a whole new light. He'd removed the pressure. He'd appeased Julie. And after all, six months wasn't so far off.

As he'd planned, Mark headed for Melanie's office first thing the next morning. He whizzed past Fiona's desk without speaking one word to her.

"Hold on, Mark," the girl called after him. "Melanie's on a long-distance ca—"

He slammed Melanie's door and cut her off. He was in control now.

Melanie glared at him from behind her desk, her cell phone raised to her ear. She narrowed her eyes, and her irritation seemed to melt away. Lines of concern gathered on her forehead.

"I'll call you back in a few minutes," she said into her phone. Then she hung up and placed the phone on her desk. She leaned back in her chair and tilted her head to one side. "This better be important, Mark."

"It is, and I've waited way too long to discuss it with you."

She nodded in silent encouragement.

"Melanie, you have to get that little flirt off my back." He pointed at the door. "Fiona has been coming on to me with no respect for my relationship with Julie. Now she wants to go with me to Chicago. I'm not going to have her spoiling things for us."

Melanie almost smiled. "I thought something was up," she said. "But since you never said anything about it, I figured you were handling it, or maybe you were encouraging her."

"No." He'd raised his voice. "If anything, I've been trying to *dis*courage her. She's like a runaway train. Doesn't take no for an answer. Calls me at home, sends me notes. Look at this..." He pulled Fiona's note from his pocket and thrust it on Melanie's desk.

She picked it up and read it. Frowning, she looked up at Mark. "I'm afraid we have a problem," she said, her tone solemn.

"What problem? All you have to do is tell her she can't go with me to Chicago. Oh yeah, and that she should *leave me alone*." He crossed his arms and stood firm.

"It's not so easy, Mark."

"What do you mean? You're her boss, aren't you?"

"Not exactly." Releasing a long sigh, Melanie rose from her chair and came around the side of her desk until she was face-to-face with him.

"Mark, Fiona's father is *my* boss. He's Arthur Askren. His grand- father founded this college, and now Arthur is in control over all of us."

A stark realization hit him. "Wow. Fiona Askren. It all makes sense now."

"I'm sorry, Mark. *I* didn't hire Fiona. I was doing fine without her. *Arthur* put her in this position. *He* ordered me to send her with you to Chicago. He does whatever his precious daughter wants—anything to get that little pest off his back."

"So, you agree she's a little pest?"

She laughed. "Of course I do. She doesn't do her job, forgets to keep track of my appointments, doesn't tell me when someone calls. No one likes her around here. Except for Jimmy Nolan. For a smart guy, his head turns far too easily."

Mark shook his head with disgust. "What can I do, Melanie? Should I file a complaint with human services?"

She gave a half-hearted shrug and went back to her desk. "It won't make any difference. Arthur's in charge."

"So tell Arthur. He obviously knows she's trouble. Make him understand what's been going on."

Melanie chuckled. "The thing is, he's lost control of his little girl and was looking for a way to get her on the right track. He put her in this job hoping to salvage whatever worth she might still have in her."

"That's incredible. He's depending on us to fix his daughter. Isn't that *his* job?"

She dropped in her chair with a sigh. "I'm afraid my hands are tied, Mark. You're gonna have to take Fiona with you to Chicago."

The hairs on the back of his neck bristled. "Then, we should cancel the trip."

Melanie shook her head with emphasis. "We can't cancel, Mark. The arrangements have been made. You and Fiona will go to Chicago, and you'll put on the presentation, and then you'll come home. Two days. That's how long you'll have to put up with her."

He ran a hand through his hair. It came up damp. "Melanie, you know how hard I've worked on this project. I traveled all the way to Ephesus and Patmos. I did tons of research. The PowerPoint is nearly complete. I'd hate to lose it all because of some Jezebel."

"You won't lose anything. Not if you keep your head." She leaned across her desk toward him, her expression intense. "She's gonna try to get you alone, Mark. Do everything you can to keep your distance. Don't even eat with her. The flight is two hours long. You can discuss the project on the plane. Afterward, you need to go your own way."

He nodded thoughtfully. "I'll be on my guard. Now all I have to do is explain all this to Julie. She already saw Fiona's note. I told her I'd handle it. She's not gonna like this. Not one bit."

"Look, I've been rooting for you and Julie for months. Why do you think I sent you on that trip to Patmos with her? I knew you two belonged together." Her tone had softened. "If Julie loves you, she'll understand."

He thought about his redheaded firecracker and shook his head. He'd promised her he'd get Fiona off this trip, and he'd failed. He'd seen Julie's little flare-ups before. This one was gonna be a humdinger.

14

JULIE'S TRIP

Julie was enjoying packing for the trip to Florida. Excitement coursed through every part of her body. No longer did she feel the weight on her shoulder. Mark had put their wedding on hold until next year. She could concentrate on her first few assignments. No more stress. No more anxiety. She could go to Florida, write a decent magazine article, and tackle the other jobs Ian had given her. And she could plan a baby shower for Lakisha.

She thought about the journey she took a little over a month ago. If not for that bizarre assignment putting her halfway around the world, she might still be sitting in her newsroom cubicle, pounding away on her computer, unaware of another life outside the door of the *Springfield Daily Press.* Then, she'd taken one of Grampa's crossroads, and everything had changed.

Best of all, she'd met Yanno. He helped her forgive people who had turned their backs on her. Those women at the church. Her parents. Even her friends. He also drew her back to her faith in God, and as a result, she reconnected with Mark. Didn't all of it amount to a fork in the road? Hadn't she chosen the right path?

She lifted Mark's photo from the top of her bureau, planted a kiss on his face, and returned the photo to its resting place. She finished packing a small carryon bag, checked to make sure she'd put all the essentials in her briefcase, then she was out the door.

The flight to Jacksonville took two hours. Julie munched on pretzels and a 7-Up and buried her nose in the book, *Cross Creek*. As Julie read, the complex author who wrote it was beginning to come to life. In addition to colorful images of the Florida wilderness, Marjorie also revealed a lot of hues and shadows about herself. Here was a woman who knew what she wanted and how to get it. But she also bowed to the needs of others at unexpected times. One minute, she'd holler at her servants over some minor infraction. The next minute, she'd make excuses for them. She sometimes treated her help with disdain and referred to them with the "n" word—a racial slur Julie resented, not only because of her friendship with Lakisha, but because she'd always considered the crude expression morally wrong. On the other hand, Marjorie also developed a close friendship with several black American leaders. Zora Neale Hurston was one of her closest friends, although, when the famous author visited Cross Creek, out of some sort of habit, Marjorie relegated her to staying in the tenant house with her servants.

Julie wondered that Marjorie got away with such behavior. Of course, she'd won a Pulitzer Prize, so maybe she'd earned the privilege. She was a popular writer and speaker, a friend to the rich and the poor, a pillar of strength, strong-willed but gentle of heart. She was different.

Julie thought about her own quest for fame and fortune. If they ever came to her, would she be prey to such emotional upheavals, like Marjorie had? Her autobiographical novel, *Blood of My Blood*, revealed a person who'd been rebellious and outspoken from early childhood. Because of her love/

hate relationship with her mother, she'd say horrible things, only to regret them later. Many times she ended up in humble apology. She confessed her flaws over and over again in her letters. Her temper flare-ups often ended with a switch back to joking around and sweet-talking everyone.

Julie's admiration for the woman centered more on her writing ability than on her behavior. She'd love to be able to describe her surroundings the way Marjorie did in *Cross Creek*. She created beautiful images. She connected her readers with nature in a way most writers couldn't.

The thing was, Marjorie used all her senses. Julie could almost hear the multi-voiced song of the mockingbird and the melodic trill of the redbird. She could feel the warm sun on her shoulders. Could picture the roaches and dirt daubers, the snakes, and rats that Marjorie encountered when she moved into the rundown house in the forest. She could nearly smell a freshly squeezed orange, almost taste the sweet goodness of the fruit.

Through her books, Marjorie took Julie to places she might never have imagined. Now, with a tour of Cross Creek on the horizon, she perked up like an electric current was coursing through her veins. She could hardly wait to experience firsthand the setting that had so powerfully captivated Marjorie Kinnan Rawlings.

Julie was still absorbed in the book when the plane landed. After picking up her luggage, she rented a Nissan Versa and made the drive to south Gainesville—about two hours. She chose not to stop at the hotel, but kept right on driving. She wanted to see Cross Creek.

Along the way, she marveled at the drastic change in the environment. She'd been transported from a subtle warm temperature in the north to a balmy climate and a landscape bathed in the merciless Florida sunshine. She flipped on the car's air conditioning system and donned her sunglasses. During the drive to Cross Creek, she eyed her surroundings with childlike interest.

That morning, she'd left behind in Springfield the familiar stately elms and maple trees, the blue spruce, purple rhododendrons, yellow forsythia, and flowering azaleas. Now, she'd entered a lush forest of spindly pines, oaks dripping with Spanish moss, and an assortment of palm trees—some tall and slim, some squatty and fat—standing like bold ornaments on broad stretches of emerald lawns. Rambling along the side of the road were pink, purple and white wildflowers, and beyond, scrub pines and sharp-tongued palmetto bushes. Fuzzy cattails stood like a small army at the edge of an endless marsh, its metallic surface dotted with pond lilies and swirls of algae.

Long-legged cranes waddled along the rim and dipped their beaks in the pool. One of them lifted off the ground, its broad wings scooped the air effortlessly, and the giant bird sailed beyond the treeline.

Julie had stepped into an unfamiliar environment, yet she knew the names of nearly every creature and every plant, thanks to Marjorie's vivid descriptions. Everything she had read in those books was coming to life in front of her eyes. She needed to slow down, needed to soak up this wonderful new experience. Though she'd been operating at high speed for most of her life, it was time to stop and smell the roses. Even though a deadline was hovering in the near future, and she needed to fill every minute collecting information, at this moment, she didn't feel the need to hurry. It was as if this wild and magical place was telling her, *Don't merely write about Florida's backwoods, immerse yourself in it.*

Such was Julie's welcome to central Florida. The drive on Route 441 gave her a half-hour of bright sunshine and an introduction to the place where she would live for the next couple of days. It was a good start. She reached Highway 325, turned off the broad, cold highway, and moved deeper into the woods until she came upon a big landscaped lawn and an entry sign—*Marjorie Kinnan Rawlings Historic State Park*. There was a paved parking lot, but no other cars were there. This was Wednesday, an off-day Julie had chosen for her private tour, which meant she'd have plenty of opportunities to ask questions without any interruptions.

She left her car and paused briefly at a glassed-in entry station, gathered up a handful of brochures, and began her walk along a dirt path onto the main property. She passed through a metal gate and into a lush orange grove. Dozens of trees stood in neat rows, like soldiers ready for inspection. The flowering season had passed. Tiny green globes had begun to appear on the branches. Within a couple of months, they'd ripen into those little balls of sunshine Marjorie often wrote about in her novels.

Julie moved from the cool shadows of the grove into blinding sunlight. Florida heat was different from what she experienced back home. Here the air was closer and moister. It exuded a tropical feel. Already she was mopping perspiration from the back of her neck.

She paused on the front lawn and took in her surroundings. A huge barn loomed before her, like a majestic centerpiece, its graying vertical boards and tin roof gave off a reflection of yesteryear. She checked one of the brochures. It said the

A-frame structure was an exact replica of the original barn, which either fell down or was knocked down in the 1960s. The former barn stored crates of oranges for shipping and also served as a shelter for Dora, Marjorie's milk cow, plus goats and pigs, and any other barnyard animals seeking protection from Florida's monster electrical storms.

It was hard to imagine Marjorie and her first husband, Charles, lived on this farm nearly a century ago. After their somewhat rocky marriage ended, he'd left for the north, and she'd remained in Cross Creek. What was it about the land and the people that made Marjorie want to leave the comforts of the north and stay in this place? Certainly, in the 1930s and '40s, the backwoods of Florida had little to offer a woman who'd grown up pampered and socially connected.

Julie shot a few pictures of the barn and surrounding property. Some would be used for the photo spread, others were simply another form of note-taking. A flock of ducks waddled close by, hardly concerned about this stranger who'd invaded their territory. Several chickens were confined to a wire mesh enclosure. The livestock helped to maintain the rustic feel of the farm, keeping its decades-old ambiance strong.

Grampa would have loved this place. It has all of the flavor of his old farm and more. But Grampa was a farmer, through-and-through. He'd grown up on a farm, so he didn't have to make any major adjustments to live on one. This was different. This place was a far cry from the dress shops and modern conveniences Marjorie had left behind in Washington and New York.

Straight ahead was the main house. Julie's imagination soared. What was it like to take up residence in a dilapidated Cracker home, to pump water from an outdoor well, to take showers under the rain running off a tin roof, and to dart across the lawn—no matter what the weather—and grab a seat in the gray-sided outhouse with its red "occupied" flag? What about subsisting on home-grown vegetables, fish caught from a nearby stream, and whatever could be shot and killed in the brush?

Being here, in the midst of nature and far from the modern world, Julie tried to picture herself living in this place. She'd always wondered if she could do without many of the conveniences she enjoyed. What would it be like to cook meals on a wood-burning stove, pick fresh vegetables from her own garden, and in the evening, relax on a front porch swing with nothing but the screech of crickets and the hoot of owls for entertainment? A good book and a cup of tea—that's all Julie needed.

And Mark? She snickered. He'd never leave his job at the college, his church, his Boy Scout troop, or his workouts at the gym. As much as he liked the outdoors, Mark had organized his life to his liking. She'd never be able to convince him to give it all up to live in near poverty. Charles didn't even stay, but left Marjorie to fend for herself.

She lifted her camera and shot pictures of the multi-colored flowers surrounding the base of the house. In *The Yearling* Marjorie wrote about chinaberry trees, sweet gums, and loblolly bays. Until now, Julie wasn't sure what they looked like up close. Now she'd reached Marjorie's little paradise, and everything had a name.

Spears of sunlight broke through the canopy of oak hammock and cast glittering diamonds across the lawn. Lacy tangles of Spanish moss sagged from nearby branches, and passing clouds turned the spread of grass from emerald to black and back to emerald again. A midday stillness fell on the property, like all of nature was taking a siesta.

Julie held her breath. What if Marjorie suddenly emerged from the barn with a crate of golden oranges in her hands? What if her energetic pointer, Pat, suddenly came back to life and charged across the lawn? Or perhaps Geechee, her beloved servant, might hurry from the tenant house to hang the wash on a line or to gather beans and tomatoes from the garden.

A sadness washed over Julie. Marjorie was gone now, and all that remained was the impression that someone had lived there at one time. Perhaps the whisper of air through the branches still carried Marjorie's voice. Maybe her reflection would appear in the creek when it lay motionless. Or Julie might catch sight of her shadow disappearing into the woods perhaps on a visit to the homes of some of her Cracker friends.

She checked her watch. It was almost time to meet the tour guide. A little activity was going on in front of the house. A workman wearing shorts and a T-shirt was adding a touch of green paint to the trim. A woman in a 1930s calf-length floral dress and an apron was making her way to the front door with a bouquet of cut flowers in her hand. Another woman had bent close to the ground and was pulling weeds from the vegetable garden. Everything continued on as if Marjorie still lived there.

Eager to get started with her tour, Julie walked toward the sprawling farmhouse. This was the moment she'd been waiting for over the last week. This was more than an assignment—this was going to be a lesson in life. She knew it.

15

THE TOUR

The house looked more like a ranch-style home with a couple of added wings instead of what it actually was—a genuine historic Cracker house, dating back to the late 1800s. According to the brochure, the home originally consisted of three separate buildings. Marjorie attached them with breezeways, and she transformed the weathered pine boards by adding a coat of white paint to the main structure and dark green trim to the skirting. From what Julie had read, the Cracker people didn't paint their houses, just let them weather over time, which gave the dwellings a rustic, old-time appearance that fit in well with the setting.

As the brochure said, authentic Florida Cracker homes were built in the late 1800s and were constructed from whatever was available in the forest, usually pine boards or cypress. The foundation was raised off the ground with stanchions erected out of oyster shells and lime. The crawl space, steep metal roof, shaded porches, and wide eaves were meant to keep the house cool from the merciless sun. Lots of windows positioned on opposite walls provided cross-ventilation. With no electricity back then, fireplaces were installed in several rooms to provide heat during the brief winter.

Julie stepped closer to the entry. On the front steps stood a blonde-haired woman in a flowered housedress and apron. Julie guessed her to be in her late 30s. She'd swept her hair back in a coif like the one Marjorie favored, and she looked quite at home in front of the century-old house.

"Welcome," the woman said with a lilt in her voice. "You must be Julie. I'm Lucy." Her tone had a sing-song quality and a thick smoothness reminiscent of Southern hospitality.

There was no need for Julie to reiterate what she'd already said on the phone, how she was working on a magazine article and needed to arrange for a private tour. The woman had been expecting her.

Lucy began her spiel with a sweeping gesture toward the orange grove. She immediately shifted into character, like she'd just stepped out of the early 1900s and was about to introduce Julie to Marjorie.

"It was the spring of 1928," Lucy said. "Marjorie and Charles came to central Florida on a two-week vacation. They were so drawn to the area, they sold their house in Rochester, New York, quit their jobs, and bought this place, sight unseen, with the help of Charles' two brothers who lived in nearby Island Grove. They moved into this house a mere 18 months before the stock market crash. More difficulty lay on the horizon for them. Little did they know their orange grove was doomed to suffer from a couple of harsh winters.

"Charles got discouraged with the place and left in 1933, and here she was—a woman living alone in a mortgaged farmhouse during the Great Depression. You can imagine how hard it must have been, coming here from upstate New York where life was a lot easier. This place must have given her quite a culture shock. But it quickly became home for Marjorie Kinnan Rawlings. And, by the way, Marjorie's mother had insisted early on that their surname be pronounced KinNAN rather than KINnan."

"Anyway," Lucy went on, smiling. "Can you imagine? When Marjorie journeyed down here on the St. Johns River, she would have seen palm trees for the first time in her life. When she arrived at Cross Creek, the orange trees were in full bloom. Never before had she experienced the overpowering aroma of orange blossoms. When the oranges started to come in, and she got to cut into a bowl of that fruit—oh my! Have you ever grated orange zest into a recipe for muffins?"

Julie remembered helping Gramma in the kitchen. She nodded.

"Imagine that aroma magnified a hundred times," Lucy said. Then, she gestured toward the oak hammock, the cluster of palmettos, the flowering shrubbery arranged around the base of the porch.

"Though the state has committed to keeping the place pretty much like it was when Marjorie was here, it looks a little different from what she and Charles encountered when they first stepped foot in Cross Creek," Lucy continued. "By the time they took ownership, the orange grove and the rest of the property had been badly neglected. The house didn't look quite as pristine as it does now. They had a lot of work ahead of them. When Marjorie wrote her first impressions of the place, she didn't hesitate to share her deep disappointment over the dilapidated appearance of her Florida home—the cobwebs, the broken windows, the faded siding—not to mention the unwelcome visitors—spiders, bats, roaches, and snakes. Over the months and years, she made a lot of positive changes. She replaced the tin roof with cypress shingles, added two bathrooms, installed a generator, and hung electric light bulbs inside painted salad bowls for indirect lighting. She added indoor plumbing, and she lengthened and screened in the front porch. She planted a garden of vegetables and flowers—she loved flowers, put vases of them all over the house—and she nurtured the orange grove back to life. It was her main source of income until her books started selling. After that, her royalties supported the orange grove, instead of the other way around."

Julie took it all in and shook her head. "This is awesome," she said. "Ever since I stepped off the plane in Jacksonville, I've felt like an alien visiting a whole other country. The climate, the landscape, the entire atmosphere is so different from what I'm used to up north. Though I've traveled a little, I've never been south of the Mason-Dixon line." She took a deep breath. "And *this* place is beyond anything I could have imagined simply by reading a book. I *had* to come here."

Lucy released a youthful giggle. Here she was, a one-woman welcoming committee, and she was making the property come alive before Julie's eyes.

"You enjoy sharing this place with outsiders like myself, don't you?" Julie said.

Lucy bobbed her head and grinned. "Oh, yes. I've been volunteering here since I was 18. There's something about connecting with the past, maybe even livin' in it for a while." She lifted the side of her skirt with a flair. "I love playing dress-up, walking where Marjorie walked, touching things she touched, and helping visitors see who she really was, a person who loved nature and the people of the forest. I like to help them to view her as more than a great writer."

"I'm already there," Julie said. "For the last few days, I've been reading everything about Marjorie that I could get my hands on. My research uncovered a lot of interesting details."

She glanced around the property. "You say the state owns this land now, right?"

"That's correct. Before she died, Marjorie willed the property to the University of Florida, but they didn't have the resources to maintain it, so they passed it to the state. Now the house and property are maintained by the Florida Park Service and by a whole gamut of volunteers who love history and give their time to keep it as close to the way it looked when Marjorie lived here as they possibly can. In 2006, it was designated as a National Historic Landmark." She'd said it with such pride, it was if she owned the place herself. Perhaps all the volunteers felt that intense attachment to this slice of history.

"Impressive," Julie said.

"Nearly all the improvements on this house came from Marjorie's royalty checks," Lucy said. "The first short story she published was 'Jacob's Ladder.' She used the money to put a bathroom in the breezeway between the main building and the bedroom wing."

Julie lifted her camera and shot the house from several different angles, catching Lucy in a couple of pictures. A magazine spread often came to life with people in the photos.

As they strolled around the grounds, several questions popped into Julie's head. "I don't want to appear ignorant, but what exactly was a Cracker? " she said. "I'm not talking about the architecture. I mean the people."

Lucy dispelled Julie's remark with a wave of her hand. "No need to feel ignorant. Lots of people are confused about the term. Even those who still live around here." She nudged Julie along and led her down a path into the brush. "Before we go inside the house, let's take a walk along one of the shaded trails."

They moved from burning sunlight into the cool shadows. Lucy kicked a stone off the path and kept walking, but at a slow pace, like she was in no hurry to rush through the thicket.

"As you can imagine, arguments go on all the time about where the name originated," she drawled. "The term, Cracker, came from two possible sources—either from the sound the whip made when early settlers snapped their whips while driving their cattle through the plain. Or it could have been coined from the cracked corn moonshiners used for making their brew. A few of the locals still get into arguments over it. Some of them take offense to being called Crackers, like it's something bad. It doesn't matter to me. I'm proud to call myself a descendent of the original Crackers. That's something unique."

The deeper they moved into the forest, the thicker the brush became. The moss-cloaked oak hammock closed in on them like a huge curtain, and green leafy plants turned darker with the escape of sunlight behind the longleaf pines. Towering palm trees seemed to grow taller and spindlier. A huge blanket of pine needles covered the path ahead, and pine cones lined the trail like miniature spectators.

"All sorts of critters live in the forest," Lucy said, as though she'd temporarily escaped beyond the brush. "Deer, of course, and maybe a bear or two. Florida panthers, not to mention gators, moccasins and rattlers."

A wave of nervousness took hold of Julie, but she pushed on, determined to keep her mind on the sensory impressions and trying to ignore that a rattler might spring out of the thicket ahead. To her relief, they soon broke into the clearing and were back at the house. The experience had left Julie a little shaken, and she knew at that moment, she wouldn't be able to do as Marjorie had, settling there amidst all the vermin and the backbreaking work. It wasn't at all like Grampa's farm.

"So, Marjorie changed her entire lifestyle," Julie said. She scanned the property with fresh eyes. "She roughed it for a while, but she was able to transform the house into something more livable. How amazing."

"That's not all," Lucy said. "I think Marjorie became so enthralled with the people she met here, she tried to become one of them, at least whenever she was living here. What she encountered was nothing at all like the social climbing snobs she'd left behind. In this place, she met a whole different class of people—laid-back folks who were content to live in shacks on the edge of the creek, with no electricity, and a bathroom 10 yards away from the house. These folks shot their supper. They grew their own food, lived from hand-to-mouth, conducted business down at the steel bridge, and paid no mind to laws or law-makers."

"Do you suppose those people knew they were selling their souls when they opened up to Marjorie?" Julie said. "She told everything about them in her books. They had no secrets anymore. I have to wonder how they felt about it."

"Only one woman objected, but it didn't matter," Lucy said. "Once her work took off, those people became famous too. Marjorie's first novel, *South Moon Under*, made it onto the Book-of-the-Month Club and was named a finalist for a Pulitzer Prize. She lost to Pearl Buck's *Good Earth*. Her magazine stories 'Cracker Chidlins' and 'Jacob's Ladder,' were her first attempts at telling the world about the people who lived in the heart of Florida's forest."

Julie let her imagination run. "I've been trying to imagine

the kind of life Marjorie chose in order to gather material for those books. I spend a lot of time on the internet and in the library, a far cry from the kind of research Marjorie did. She actually *lived* her work."

Lucy shook her head and giggled. "She stayed with a family on the Ocklawaha River so she could learn first-hand how they lived. The guy was a moonshiner and a poacher. Marjorie shadowed him, even went hunting and fishing with him. As you can imagine, she didn't know a thing about outdoors living when she first got here, but she plunged right into it. In the end, she got $6,000 for *South Moon Under*. She used the money to shingle her roof. Then, another five years went by before her next big hit."

"*The Yearling*?" Julie said.

"Yep. *The Yearling*." Lucy gave a little snicker. "Funny thing, her best book almost didn't come to be. Marjorie didn't want to write a children's book, but her editor insisted she could write it *about* a child and for adult readers. He chose the title out of a list she sent him. Then, it took her a good five years of hemmin' and hawin' and scattered attempts at research, and simply living with the folks who gave her the ingredients for her characters. In the meantime, she published *Golden Apples* in 1935, then a few short stories, and finally, *The Yearling* in 1938."

Julie considered her own struggles with writing projects. Her four-year stint at the newspaper with little promise for advancement. Her failed attempt to write a novel, now stashed in a box under her bed. And more recently, stepping into magazine writing. What other forks in the road might be awaiting her? What forks did Marjorie take to get to the point of being a prize-winning author?

She looked at Lucy. The woman's face was lit up like a kid's at Christmas. She seemed to thoroughly enjoy giving this spiel for what must be the hundredth time. Yet, she obviously didn't get tired of it.

"Yep," Lucy said. "Marjorie dove into the lifestyle like she'd been cut out for it all along. She picked up the lingo of the Big Scrub people and worked those little colloquialisms into her books. Authentic. That's what I call Marjorie's writing. She brought this whole part of Florida to life and made it authentic. She took the folklore and turned it into history. She accepted who the Crackers were, both inside and outside. The old women who could kill a rattlesnake with a hoe. The unwashed little children who ran about the forest in their bare feet and could climb any tree on her property. The man who let his hogs run wild, even when they tore up Marjorie's petunia bed."

"And then she got herself an editor and published all their secrets in her books," Julie added.

"That's right," Lucy said with a nod. "Max Perkins was her fairy godfather. I don't think Marjorie could have gotten anywhere without him. A lot of ideas for her work came from Max, especially the idea for *The Yearling*."

Julie thought about the huge collection of letters she'd leafed through and how the correspondence between Max and Marjorie had gradually changed from business to personal. Julie never had that kind of relationship with Andy Jacobs, her newspaper editor. He was strictly business. Except for the day he fired her, she never caught a glimmer of compassion in those steel gray eyes. He'd softened momentarily when he let her go, and he openly expressed sadness at having to do so.

If she had any hope of having a Max-type relationship with anyone, it would have to be with Ian Fairchild. During the brief time she'd spent with him in his office, she'd connected with him on a different level. Another human being had taken more than a casual interest in her work. He didn't set any hard and fast rules, but gave her free rein to work the piece the way she saw fit. He merely fortified her with all the tools she needed and a word of encouragement. She came away from their first meeting feeling electrified.

"I can understand how an editor can make a difference," Julie said now. "Marjorie was lucky to have Max."

Lucy smiled, but sadness clouded her eyes. "After Max died, Marjorie lost much of her motivation. She lived another six years, but during that time she published only a couple more short stories and *Sojourner*, which wasn't much of a success at the time."

"So tragic," Julie said. "Can you imagine the legacy she might have left if she'd lived longer, and if she'd had Max around?"

They fell silent for a couple of minutes, as though they both had drifted off to another time. For Julie, the break offered an opportunity to mull over all they had talked about during their tour of the grounds. It wasn't only about the barn and the trail and the ambiance of the setting. She sensed a part of Marjorie still lingered there, if only in the minds and hearts of people who came to visit.

Lucy released a sigh. "Well, Julie. What do ya think? Wanna go inside the house now?"

16

INSIDE THE HOUSE

The tour of the grounds left Julie breathless. She'd entered a fascinating world and didn't want to let go of it too soon. They approached the rambling farmhouse. She paused for a brief moment of introspection. What mysteries lay beyond the screened porch? Her senses tingled with anticipation.

Lucy guided her around the side of the house where, sheltered under a carport, was a butter-colored 1940 Oldsmobile.

"This is a similar model to the one Marjorie drove," Lucy explained. She ran a hand along the side of the car and paused by the driver's door. "As the story goes, Marjorie drove like she was handling a race car, especially when she was angry. Driving fast must have been one more release for her. She lived her life that way too. She was a female version of Doctor Jekyll and Mr. Hyde. One minute she'd be calm and sweet, the next she'd literally come unglued."

Julie stopped in her tracks. Wasn't that how Mark had described *her*? Didn't he say she was a lot like Marjorie? She couldn't deny the truth. She'd lost count of the number of people she'd offended with her flashes of anger—Mark included. It astounded her that he'd stuck with her for so long.

Lucy beckoned her to the front steps. She opened a squeaky screen door and they moved into Marjorie's porch.

"This was Marjorie's favorite place to write," Lucy said. "From here she could keep an eye on the main drive onto the property, and she could admire her precious orange grove at the same time."

Julie was surprised at how cool the porch felt. The wrap-around screens let in a gentle breeze, just enough to drop the temperature a few degrees. To her right stood a round wooden table and four matching chairs with seats constructed out of deer hides. An old Remington typewriter, a glass ash-tray, and a vase of cut flowers told the story of a woman who sat there, day after day, pouring her thoughts onto sheets of white typing paper, crumpling discarded sheets to the floor, and crushing cigarette butts in the ashtray.

"I can almost picture her at work," Julie mused.

Lucy nodded. "The volunteers who maintain this place work hard to keep things pretty much like Marjorie had set it up. Charles constructed this table and chairs and a whole lot of other pieces of furniture in the house. Some items belonged to Marjorie when she lived here. Others were more recently donated because they fit the era and matched her taste in decorating."

Julie shot a few photos of Marjorie's workspace, then she turned and caught images of the other side of the porch. In contrast, it was a more relaxed atmosphere with floral-cush-ioned armchairs grouped around a tiled patio table—possibly an intimate spot where she could entertain visitors. Against the far wall was a cozy day bed where Marjorie could take a break from her work and bask in the gentle breezes wafting through the screens.

Julie followed Lucy through massive French doors into a small living room. Antique furnishings were true to the era—upholstered chairs in assorted designs and colors, a red velvet fainting couch, a tea cart equipped with all the accoutrements, as if Marjorie were expecting guests at any moment. Bookshelves and mantles held novels written by Marjorie's friends, Margaret Mitchell, Ernest Hemingway, F. Scott Fitzgerald, and many others. In keeping with her flair for entertaining, she'd converted a small closet into a liquor cabinet, and scattered about the room serving tables bearing fine china testified to Marjorie's penchant for hosting parties in this out-of-the-way hermitage.

Julie found she was enjoying this brief journey into the past. A flowered couch evoked images of Grampa and their little chats sitting side-by-side on the living room sofa. Funny how cherished moments had a way of popping up when she least expected them.

The truth was, Marjorie Kinnan Rawlings and Grampa were products of the same generation. Grampa was born at the turn of the 20th century and lived a long life. He drove around in a 1938 Hudson Terraplane with running boards and wide whitewalls. Not that Julie ever rode in Grampa's car. She'd merely seen pictures of it in Gramma's photo album.

The rest of the tour evoked more memories. The antique four-poster bed reminded her of the day the family flooded into Grampa's bedroom moments before he drew his last breath. Julie was a sophomore in high school at the time. Her heart nearly pounding out of her chest, she reached for Grampa's hand. Slowly, he laced his knobby fingers with hers. If she could have stopped the progression of his illness, she would have done whatever it took. She ached at the thought of losing this tower of strength in her life. But before the night was over, his fingers slipped away, and so did he.

Even now, fresh tears rose to her eyes. She turned her face away, unwilling to let Lucy see them. She hid behind her camera, walked about taking pictures, got interested in the different pieces of antique furniture—suitable distractions from the pain in her heart. What fascinated her most of all were the multiple photos on the walls and the book shelves and fireplaces in nearly every room of the house. There were a few pictures of Norton and a couple of Max with his fedora cocked to one side, but the majority were of Marjorie. Except for one or two in which she posed with Pat, her English Pointer, the photos depicted Marjorie alone, by herself in a variety of situations—sitting at her typewriter, relaxing on the front step, kneeling in her garden, standing on a sand dune in front of her Crescent Beach home, her dress and hair stirred by a breeze off the ocean.

A distressing thought struck Julie. In her pursuit of a career, Marjorie had spent long hours alone in this house. Is that what it takes to become an accomplished writer? Complete solitude?

Julie pondered her own life and the recent path she'd taken. Grampa would have called it a fork in the road. She shuddered at the thought of giving up her friends in favor of a career. Did she really want the kind of reclusive life Marjorie had chosen? Yet somehow Marjorie had found a way to balance everything. She soared in her career, and she not only kept her friends but added more to her growing list of acquaintances. It took a special person to accomplish all that. Julie hardly considered herself capable.

Another thought arose; a troubling one. Hadn't Marjorie also locked herself away in a prison of sorts? Or was it merely a place of escape? An escape from the tedium of everyday life in the city, an escape from people who might end up controlling her, or maybe even an escape from what she might become if left to the influences of high society?

Julie had experienced solitude in a different way. Though she'd set up certain barriers, she still experienced a flicker of guilt every time she turned off her phone, locked her door, and refused to interact with people. It turned out, what she had intended as a defense mechanism might actually destroy her in the end, if she didn't make a change.

She continued to follow Lucy through the house, listened to her describe the contents of each room. Out one door, in through another, onto a different porch in another part of the house, then outside on the lawn and into the bedroom wing through another door. The layout fascinated Julie. She had grown up in a cookie-cutter, three-bedroom, two-bath home in the suburbs. Unlike this place, going from one room to another didn't require a trip outdoors. Even Grampa's three-story farmhouse was simply built. A person couldn't get lost going from the kitchen to the bedroom or from the dining room to the front porch. But this place was like a maze, just a few afterthoughts all stuck together at the whim of a woman living alone.

There was the dining room with Marjorie's original furniture, Wedgewood china, and crystal goblets—all the fine accoutrements for entertaining the likes of Ernest Hemingway and Margaret Mitchell.

Lucy gestured toward the closest chair, which was situated with a perfect view through the window across the room. "Marjorie always insisted on sitting in this chair," Lucy said. "She didn't want her guests looking at the outhouse while eating the rich foods she'd prepared. She thought of it as an eyesore."

The kitchen fascinated Julie most of all. The open cupboard, the neat line of spices, and the iron skillet on the burner gave her the feeling someone was about to cook dinner.

Lucy placed a hand on the wood-burning stove, now lifeless and cool. "It was here, in this very kitchen, and at the Crescent Beach cottage, where Marjorie and her maid, Idella Parker, tested recipes for a cookbook. Marjorie called it *Cross Creek Cookery*. She filled it with her mother's recipes, like Ida's almond cake and her famous croquettes, plus, of course, the concoctions she'd learned in the forest, like fried cooter, gopher stew, and backwoods cornbread. The book doesn't only contain recipes. Each chapter begins with an introductory vignette by Marjorie. She said her readers were hungry for more than food. They wanted the homey gatherings she also knew how to provide."

As Julie's tour of Marjorie's farm came to an end, she joined Lucy outside on the front lawn. She turned around and swept her eyes over the entire panorama. Sunshine bathed the grass and turned it to emerald green. The garden of home-grown vegetables, planted in healthy rows, shared their enclosure with a spectrum of colors—bright orange zinnias, gold and yellow mums, purple pansies, and fiery red petunias. The barn loomed like a stark reflection of yesteryear. Once the center of activity, it now stood dormant and empty, a makeshift monument over a legacy of Marjorie's life.

Julie took in the vista with a touch of sadness. Had Marjorie's retreat died with her? Or was she still living within the orange groves and the hammocks? Was she still moving inside the house amidst the antiquated furnishings? Julie liked to imagine that people came back to visit places they loved after they were gone, though she knew better from reading the Scriptures. *Absent from the body, present with the Lord*, the Bible said. But it was okay to imagine, wasn't it? Especially when standing within a place that was steeped in so much history, a person could get completely absorbed with the one who'd immortalized it.

"Did ya get everything you needed for your article?" Lucy said.

Julie nodded. "Pretty much." She reached in her purse and pulled out $20, handed the bill to Lucy, and smiled with satisfaction. "A donation," she said. "You made this place come alive for me, Lucy. I don't know how to thank you enough."

Lucy smiled. "If ya want to know more about Marjorie, you should visit the University of Florida archives and dig a little deeper. During her career, Marjorie also wrote a number of unpublished writings. The Smathers Library has a collection you won't want to miss."

"That's a great idea," Julie said. She had planned to drive to Crescent Beach and check out the cottage Marjorie and Norton purchased there. Surely she could make time for a stop at the university. Perhaps the journey into Marjorie's life had only begun at Cross Creek. There was so much more to see.

"Where are you staying tonight?" Lucy said.

"I booked a room at a hotel in South Gainesville."

Lucy appeared shocked. "What? Wouldn't you rather spend the night right here in Cross Creek?"

The idea fascinated Julie. "What do you mean?"

"I mean the cabins. There's a half-dozen of 'em on the creek near The Yearling Restaurant. If ya want to get a taste of Marjorie's actual habitat, you'll want to take one for the night." She turned serious. "You know, it's one thing to walk through Marjorie's house and take pictures of her property and quite another to become one with nature the way she did."

"Of course," Julie said with a wave of excitement. "It's still early enough in the day for me to make the change without incurring a fee."

She stepped aside and took a few minutes on her cell phone. First, she arranged for a cabin in Cross Creek. Then she canceled the hotel room. Fortunately, they waved the late fee. The idea of camping out in the forest appealed to her, even excited her. Of course, she wouldn't actually be sleeping on the ground the way Mark did with his Boy Scout troop. A cabin would be about as close as she'd ever get to camping out.

Julie turned back to Lucy and took another look at the woman dressed in vintage clothing and looking a whole lot like she belonged in this setting. Another thought struck her.

"Is there any chance I might be able to speak to someone who *knew* Marjorie? I mean, are any of her Cracker friends still living around here?"

Lucy shrugged. "Most of those folks are gone. Norton died in 1997. He loved to talk about Marjorie to anyone who cared to listen. He described her as the sweetest person he ever knew."

Julie straightened in surprise. "You're kidding, right?"

"No, they had a special relationship. Norton really loved her."

"He must have to be able to overlook her temper." Mark immediately came to Julie's mind. She'd compared him with Norton. If he also felt that way about her, perhaps she and Mark were a better match than she'd ever imagined.

"There were others who lived long after Marjorie died and shared stories about her," Lucy went on. "There was Idella Parker, her 'perfect maid.' She could have told you a lot of juicy stories about Marjorie. She even wrote a book about the time she worked for her. Another close friend was J.T. Glisson. He also wrote a book called *The Creek*, which verifies and adds to a lot of what Marjorie wrote. As the story goes, Marjorie based one of her characters on Jake. He was born with club feet, and he loved to collect little critters. I'm afraid he's gone too."

"So, there's no one?"

Lucy cocked her head and produced a coy smile. "Well..." she said. "There's always my great-aunt Emma."

17

MARK

Mark's last class ended at 4:00. Moving like a tornado, he gathered up his papers, shoved them in his briefcase, and snuck out the back door of the college. Somehow he made it to his car and zipped out of the parking lot before Fiona showed her face.

He could grab a takeout meal, hunker down in his apartment, and complete work on his PowerPoint presentation. He'd be leaving in three days for Chicago. It was crunch time. But first, some physical exercise. A quick workout at the gym would get his endorphins going.

He made it to the gym in 10 minutes, grabbed his duffle bag from the trunk, and hurried inside. He was on high speed now and wasn't about to slow down.

He changed in the men's locker room, jammed his clothes in a locker, and headed straight for a treadmill. He placed his gym bag on the floor beside it. After 30 minutes of hard running he still hadn't cleared his mind. Even in her absence Fiona was bothering him. He didn't want to take her on the trip with him, but he was stuck. He worked up a good sweat and moved to the weight room. He pulled his gloves out of his gym bag. First thing, he tackled the free weights, went through his usual routine, but more intensely now. His breathing was labored, not his usual controlled puffing. The whole time, he thought about the trip to Chicago. It was supposed to be a happy time, the epitome of his career to date. But it promised nothing but trouble.

He kept an eye on the far corner where a couple of jocks had gathered around the heavy bag. They took turns pummeling the thing, laughing, and egging each other on. The second they cleared away, Mark switched to his boxing gloves and made a dash for the bag.

The events of the last week had drained him. His meeting with Melanie had gone nowhere. She couldn't help. Neither could human resources. Now he was fighting mad. He lit into the bag with all his might—jabbing, punching, pounding until he thought the thing might split apart.

"Whoa there." The voice came from behind him. He steadied the bag and turned to face his best friend.

Greg was laughing and shaking his head. "Who on earth are you mad at?"

Embarrassed, Mark took a deep breath. "Was I that obvious?"

"You bet you were. I'd hate to think whose face you're attacking, but I can guess." He snickered. "Maybe it's a good thing you're taking it out on an inanimate object. Tear the thing up. Nobody's gonna get hurt. And nobody's gonna care, except maybe the people who run this place."

They shared a laugh. Mark gazed into the twinkling gray eyes of his best buddy. How he admired the guy. Nothing ruffled Greg. Even though his parents rejected his wife, Greg had maintained a positive attitude, even kept in touch with his folks. Could Mark have behaved the same way if his father rejected Julie? He wasn't sure. As it turned out, Al Bensen and Julie Peters got along just fine. They'd bonded like a magnet and a piece of steel. He even invited her down to Florida for a visit. Too bad she was about six hours away from where his father lived. She might have been able to make a side trip.

Greg was staring at him with mirth in his eyes. He ran a hand through his flock of blond hair and slowly lost his smile.

"What's going on, Mark?"

He shrugged and made a disgusted face. "Let's get a smoothie at the snack bar. I'll fill you in."

"Okay, buddy." Greg patted him on the arm.

He pulled off his gloves, grabbed his gym bag, and started for the front of the gym with Greg trailing close behind.

The snack bar ran the length of the lobby. The menu board listed practically every type of smoothie a person could want plus wraps, salads, homemade soups, and other heart-healthy options.

Mark ordered a banana/peanut butter smoothie. Greg chose a strawberry/lemongrass drink. They grabbed a cafe table by the window, out of earshot of the snack bar crew.

Mark spent the next 15 minutes moaning about Melanie's new assistant. "She won't leave me alone. I walk around the college on eggshells, thinking any moment I'll run into Fiona. I'm sick of all the phone calls and now that note. And guess what? She's going to Chicago with me. Melanie can't do a thing about it. It seems the little princess' father runs the college."

Greg cocked his head, and his eyebrows came whimsically together. "Wait a minute, buddy. Are you telling me you're upset because a beautiful girl is infatuated with you? Most guys would give their eye teeth to have such a problem." He shook his head and laughed.

"You don't understand, Greg. It's not a simple problem. This girl is stalking me, and I can't do a thing about it. I'm afraid she's gonna cause trouble between Julie and me."

"I see." Greg nodded and turned serious. "Melanie can't help because the big boss is calling the shots, right?"

"Right."

"So, go to the big boss."

"Huh?"

"Tell the girl's father what she's been up to. Maybe *he'll* do something to stop her."

He sipped his smoothie, bought some time to think. "I don't know. Melanie said he put his daughter in this job because he's trying to straighten her out. Apparently she's been trouble for a while. I doubt he'll want to change anything based on what I tell him. Anyway, it's her word against mine. Don't forget, this is his little girl. He's gonna believe *her*."

"You could get a restraining order."

"Yeah, right. They'll laugh at me. She hasn't done anything yet. No threats. No accusations. What? They're gonna arrest her for *liking* me too much? C'mon, Greg."

His friend gave a little chuckle. "It must be awful to be irresistibly cute."

Mark sneered at him. "Look, I'm stuck. I'm leaving Sunday afternoon for Chicago, and Fiona is gonna tag along. My presentation will take place Monday morning. Then it's back home again. We'll only be gone for one night, but it'll be long enough for her to start pushing again. I'm tellin' ya, Greg, if she acts up, I'll talk to her father when we get back."

"Good."

Mark slumped forward. "Not good." He stared at his shoes. "Not good at all. I'm gonna feel like a little kid tattling on a bully. Only this time the bully happens to be a *female*."

Greg leaned close and rested a comforting hand on his shoulder. "Listen, it's gonna be all right, man. This too shall pass. That's what my dad always said whenever I came to him with a problem. And you know what? A couple of weeks later, I'd look back, and I'd see he was right."

Mark scrunched up his lips. "I'll keep it in mind." He finished his smoothie and leaned back, crossing his arms. "Speaking of your dad, what about you and Lakisha and all the in-law drama? Any success getting them to change their tune?"

Greg let his hand slip from Mark's shoulder. He dropped back in his chair and grunted. "I'm afraid not. Lakisha's parents are coming around, but they're Boston people. Mixed marriages are common on their turf. When they first met me, they warned us that not everyone would accept our union. But, Lakisha's sisters got after them, and they finally accepted our marriage. Now, they're getting excited about having this grandbaby."

"Maybe *your* folks will come around too, eventually. After all, they came to the wedding, didn't they?"

"Yeah, but they didn't stay long. My parents live on a farm. In the boonies. They've been so cut off from everything, they live in their own little world."

"They're Christians, right?"

"Sure, but they have these antiquated standards, and they won't bend, not one little bit. They're stuck in the Old Testament where God forbade Israel to intermarry with alien cultures, or at least that's what they called this marriage."

"That's absurd. It had less to do with racial differences and more about keeping His people from idolatry. It was a whole different scenario. Lakisha's not some idol-worshiping heathen. She's a Christian."

"Right. I tried to tell them that."

"And?"

Greg's eyebrows came together in a sarcastic frown. "You haven't seen them bringing baby gifts to my house, have you?"

He shook his head. "I'm here for you, buddy. If there's anything I can do..."

Greg managed a smile. "I'll let you know. For now, pray for us. Pray Lakisha won't get stressed out over my folks. I want her to have a healthy baby. And pray for everyone to get along one of these days. I don't think I can deal with having my kid play sports or do a piano recital or graduate from high school without her grandparents being present. Kids need their grandparents. So, keep praying, Mark."

"You've got it, man."

"Now," Greg said, draining the rest of his drink. "What do ya say we take turns and mutilate that heavy bag? I think the two of us can get in a couple of good punches and destroy the thing."

Mark couldn't help but smile. Having an ally made his problem seem less formidable. Greg had his own troubles, yet he was there for Mark. Wasn't that what best friends did?

Just knowing they had each other's backs was enough for Mark. His manic workout hadn't helped nearly as much as Greg's gentle touch. He could leave the gym with a clear mind. Spending time with Greg created a cathartic effect. He could tackle his project, maybe even complete it tonight.

On his way home, he picked up a pepperoni pizza. At the apartment, he worked on his speech while eating, unconcerned over the dollop of tomato he spilled on his notes. Once he developed his talk, he could toss them in the trash and give the presentation without them. He possessed a photographic memory, grew up reciting Bible verses and memorizing whatever dates and events he needed to learn for his classroom studies. In his work at the college, he often gave extemporaneous speeches whenever called upon to do so. This was pretty much the same thing.

He worked until midnight. The slides came together nicely. Flutes and lyres played softly in the background and set the mood. He practiced his narration a few times. The visit at Moody would be a trial run. He could watch the students' reactions, evaluate the slide progression, and make changes later. Then he could insert a narration directly into the presentation, perhaps hire a professional with a magnetic voice. He could make the finished product available to colleges across the nation. Students could visit Bible lands without ever having to leave the classroom.

Once the finance director set a price, the bulk of the proceeds needed to go to the college with a small stipend for himself. He'd roll the money over into another project. Most of all, he wanted to be recognized among his peers. He'd been wallowing in the shadows far too long. This could make a huge difference in his career.

But if things didn't go well in Chicago on Monday, he'd either have to make improvements or give up the project altogether. Melanie would give him a patronizing pat on the back and find some other job to keep him busy. The question was, how understanding would she be if he hadn't resembled the brother she'd lost a few years ago? Would she have taken him under her wing like she did? Or would he merely have blended in with the other instructors, just another face in the crowd?

Whatever the case, he wasn't about to give up now that he was so close to realizing his dream. Julie would expect nothing less from him. She would needle him and push him and get in his face. She wouldn't let him quit. Mark couldn't help but smile. He needed Julie more than ever. If only he could get her to admit that she needed him too.

18

THE CABIN

After stopping for dinner at an Italian restaurant in Micanopy, Julie drove to the cabin. She had to admit, Lucy's suggestion added another element of backwoods living to Julie's growing collection of mind-blowing experiences. The tiny block structure, painted a deep blue, resembled a doll house beneath the canopy of oaks on the banks of the creek. The ground—mostly sand and scattered patches of grass— sloped down to the water's edge. The creek rested between two banks and trailed off to the right beneath a wooden bridge and beyond. Like a tinted mirror, the water reflected the bordering palmettos and scrub grass, and on the other side people's houses stood precariously close to the water's edge. Julie gazed at the bridge and wondered if it might be the same bridge where Marjorie's forest friends used to settle their differences.

Overhead, the beginning of a crimson sunset flickered amongst the tops of the trees and cast spears of light onto the creek, creating a scene reminiscent of one of the famed Highwaymen paintings.

Julie reluctantly tore her eyes away and unlocked the door of her cabin. Inside the one-room structure, another sensation of yesteryear enveloped her like a warm quilt. The small space accommodated a sleeping area, a living room, and a kitchenette, plus a tiny bathroom with a shower.

The decor was reminiscent of the 1930s and '40s, the era Marjorie made famous in her books. The furniture was simple—a full-size bed with a flowered bedspread, a maple armoire, and a Formica table with two hardwood chairs. A small reading light stood on the table, and a plain, free-standing lamp cast its light on a corner of the small room. Except for the flat-screen TV, the microwave, and the Mr. Coffee machine, Julie could imagine she'd gone back to another time.

She chuckled softly. Mark would love this place. He'd been a Boy Scout leader for many years. He'd spent a lot of time outdoors, starting fires with a couple of sticks, putting up a tent, and fishing for his breakfast. He'd talked about taking her on a camping trip someday. Now she looked around the cabin with all of it's comforts and figured this was about as close as she'd ever get to sleeping outdoors.

After a refreshing shower, Julie slid into her pajamas, brewed herself a cup of herbal tea in the microwave, and settled down at the little table to go through her notes. She spent a couple of hours rearranging their sequence, then, using her tablet, she wrote a couple of sample paragraphs to get her story started.

The first few lines came easy.

Not all Florida roads lead to beaches and theme parks. Some lead to the very heart of the peninsula. They meander through an unfettered blend of forests and marshland, a magical escape from the impersonal world of paved highways and strip malls, gated subdivisions and country clubs.

The next two lines flowed easily from there, but it was time to stop. The activities of the day had exhausted her. A morning plane ride, the drive from Jacksonville, the tour of Cross Creek, switching to a cabin costing double the price of the hotel room, and spending two hours beside a table lamp typing out her notes. She looked at her watch. It was coming up on midnight. She wanted to get started early tomorrow, but her mind drifted to Mark. She wondered what he might be doing. Probably hard at work on his PowerPoint presentation. She smiled. How many men kept busy with their own interests while their fiancées ran off to another state to do her own work project? She could think of only two. Norton Baskin and Mark Bensen.

Though busy with his hotels and restaurants, Norton managed to fit in with Marjorie's routine. Mark hadn't yet adjusted to Julie's new schedule. What was it he'd said to her before she left for Florida? *"Most women won't even go to the bathroom by themselves."* She'd laughed with him, but a subtle sarcasm lay beneath his comment.

She picked up her cell phone and punched in his number. He answered immediately.

"Hey there."

"Hi, Mark. I thought I'd give you a call before I went to bed."

"So, you're still at Cross Creek?"

"I am. But, I'm not at the hotel where I told you I'd be staying. I booked a cabin at a campground by the river. You'd love this place. It's quite rustic. And the creek is right outside my door."

He laughed softly. "You've already immersed yourself in the culture, haven't you?"

"Yep. I'm soaking it all up. Hopefully I'll come away with a better understanding of what drew Marjorie here. The natural setting is awesome, probably a lot like it was when she moved to this place. The roads are paved now, and much of the forest has been cleared, but the area has stayed pretty much like it was nearly a hundred years ago. You can drive for miles and never see a house."

Briefly she described her tour of the farm. The misty freshness of the Florida climate, the steady rasp of locusts in the orange grove, the tree-lined property, the old barn, and the rambling farmhouse.

"My guide was fabulous," she said. "Her name is Lucy, and she knew a lot about Marjorie's private life. Tomorrow, I'll be meeting Lucy's great-aunt Emma. She's one of the locals who knew Marjorie. This is what I need, Mark, to talk to someone who can fill in the missing pieces."

"It sounds like you're making good use of your reporter skills. All that research and now a special interview. I'll bet you can't wait to meet the woman."

"It's no different from what we did when we traveled to Patmos. The plane ride across the Atlantic. The ferry across the Aegean Sea. The trek up the rocky hillside. Meeting Yanno, eating lunch at his favorite cafés, sitting in his living room and drinking his herbal tea."

"Yes, and you got a free ride on his Vespa, didn't you?"

She laughed. "That was quite an experience."

"So, just like in Patmos, you're soaking everything up, and now you've settled into a cabin by the creek. Sounds fascinating."

"I'm experiencing a slice of Marjorie's life. Today I walked where she walked, and tonight I'm sleeping very close to where she slept. Tomorrow I might even eat what she ate."

"What do you mean?"

"There's a restaurant here by the cabins called The Yearling. I'm guessing the menu will include a lot of authentic Florida dishes. Anyway, from the outside it appears to have a rustic, down home atmosphere."

"Wish I could be there to enjoy it with you," Mark said.

She ignored the hint of sadness in his tone and tried to keep the conversation light. "You've got your own project, Mark. By the way, how's it going?"

"I finished the PowerPoint today. I only need to go over it a couple more times and rehearse my speech."

"I'm so proud of you."

"Well, I'm proud of you, too. When you start a project, you see it through to the end. It's one of the things I love about you, Julie."

She didn't respond. An awkward silence fell over the airwaves.

"You still there?" Mark said. There was a tremor in his voice.

"Yes." She breathed a heavy sigh. "How are things going with that woman? What's her name? Frances?"

"Fiona."

"Whatever."

"The way things stand right now, she's set to go on that trip with me. Believe me, I tried to prevent it. I talked to Melanie, but her hands are tied. It seems Fiona's father controls everything that happens at the college."

A flood of heat rushed to her face. "So, that's it?"

"You don't have to worry about her, Julie. Or let's put it this way, you don't have to worry about me. You can trust me."

More silence. She didn't know what else to say. She didn't want to sound like a jealous shrew. Yet a flicker of anxiety nagged at the back of her mind. What if Mark got tired of waiting for her? A sadness engulfed her. Their wedding plans were hanging like a broken strand of Christmas lights, but she didn't know what to do about it or what to say to convince Mark she wasn't backing out. She simply needed more time.

"When I get home, you'll be getting ready to leave for Chicago," she said.

"Yeah. I leave Sunday afternoon. Listen, how about we take a drive Saturday, maybe visit my favorite hillside retreat?"

Julie remembered the magical place. They'd stood on the edge of the rise and looked out over moss-covered hills, a cascade of wild flowers, and off in the distance, a scattering of lakes that resembled pieces of broken glass. It was there that Mark got down on one knee and proposed to her. Now he wanted to go back. A ray of hope entered her heart, and the flush on her cheeks dissipated.

"Sounds good to me," she said.

"Do you think you might have absorbed enough of Mother Nature by then?"

"Not a chance. This trip has kind of pricked my interest in the good ol' outdoors."

He laughed, and the tension eased a little more.

"Well, I need to get some sleep," she said. "I have to get up early tomorrow."

"Okay," he said, but there was a quiver in his voice.

"Is there something wrong, Mark?"

He made a kissing sound. "Be safe, Julie. I'll see you Saturday morning."

And the line went dead.

19

AUNT EMMA

Julie slept with the window open that night. Her cabin was equipped with air conditioning, but she wanted to experience the kind of evening Marjorie experienced sleeping in a house with no electricity. A soft breeze fluttered the tops of the palm trees and made a soothing rustling sound. Gradually, an entire orchestra of wildlife tuned up outside the screened window. High in the treetops locusts screeched like a chorus of violins. Cicadas clicked out rhythms like accompanying timpani. Within the scrub, crickets chirped their high-pitched tones, and from the edge of the creek, frogs croaked in response, much like one of those two-part inventions she had to practice on the piano when she was a child. Just as those Bach pieces kept a musical dialogue going back and forth on the keyboard, the wildlife in the scrub performed their own melodic discourse.

Growing up in the suburbs, the only night sounds Julie could recall were the high-pitched squeal of an emergency vehicle and the honking of car horns in heavy traffic. Now she was falling asleep to nature's symphony.

She snuggled beneath a light blanket and gazed out the window at a star-dappled sky. At some point the wildlife concert ceased, and an unearthly stillness settled on the creek. Only the hoot of an owl from somewhere high in the branches interrupted the quiet.

She awakened before dawn to the tapping of a woodpecker on a nearby tree. The world outside her window was bathed in a gray fog. The mist oozed through the screen and tickled her nose. Gradually, the sky grew lighter, the fog lifted, and the sun scattered its gold through the branches of the hammock.

She lay still for a while and soaked up the atmosphere. The trees outside her window stretched their branches like black fingers, etched against the wakening sky. She inhaled deeply of the fresh morning air. She was experiencing a small taste of what Marjorie's life must have been like waking up every morning in Cross Creek. The natural setting was great for a couple of days, but Julie didn't think she could live here permanently. Marjorie had spent a good 20 years in this place. Though such a lifestyle carried the promise of peace and relaxation, it also guaranteed days and even months of solitude, maybe more than Marjorie had planned on having. Perhaps that was the reason she ran off at times to Crescent Beach or New York or Washington. Maybe she missed her socially elite friends. Maybe she needed to hang onto the culture she grew up with before she lost it completely. Or maybe it was just to be close to Norton again, if only for a few days.

As the world outside Julie's window brightened, a fresh group of musical artists took the stage. Within minutes the trees were filled with chirps and trills, warbles and metallic strains of the feathered friends Marjorie had written about— the redbirds, whippoorwills, mockingbirds, and whooping cranes. Julie could only imagine which of them might be serenading her at that moment.

Groaning, she pushed herself out of bed and headed for the bathroom to freshen up. As she washed her face, excitement kicked in. Today she was going to meet Lucy's Aunt Emma, a first-hand witness to the life of Marjorie Kinnan Rawlings. If she was alive back then, she had to be close to 100. Would she be able to reach back in her memory nearly 80 years?

Julie stared at her image in the mirror. Yesterday's bright sunshine had tinged her cheeks to pink. She didn't need a single dab of makeup today. She ran a brush through her hair, pulled it back in a ponytail, and quickly dressed in white slacks and a pale green cotton blouse. She traded in her walking shoes for a pair of white sandals. No trekking through the brush today. She was going to visit a woman who was about to bring Marjorie back to life.

Before she left the cabin, she shut the window. Then she grabbed a fresh notebook and her purse and stepped outside, making sure the door was locked before she went to her car. Somehow, locking a door in this setting didn't make sense. From the way Marjorie described Cross Creek, people came and went at will. Screen doors banged constantly in the Big Scrub. If things got a little tense, the men—and most of the women— simply loaded their shotguns and kept them ready to fire at whoever encroached on their land. Most of the time, *visitors* didn't touch what didn't belong to them. These folk took more pleasure in giving than in receiving.

Julie had begun the transformation from newspaper reporter into Cross Creek explorer and magazine writer. By the time she left this place, she expected to be a different person altogether. The thought both thrilled and terrified her.

She pulled out her cell phone and was about to do a search of breakfast places, when the ringer went off in her hand. She hit the answer button. It was Lucy.

"How was your time in the cabin?" Lucy said. "Did you sleep well?"

"Better than I have in weeks," Julie admitted to both Lucy and to herself.

"Have you had breakfast yet?"

"Not yet, I was about to search for a place."

"Well, stop searching. My Aunt Emma has invited us to have breakfast at her house. I'm on my way to the cabin. I'll pick you up, and we'll go straight to Aunt Emma's. She makes the best hotcakes. And guess what, Julie. You'll be having breakfast in a real Cracker house, this morning."

Julie marveled at how everything was falling into place. She'd been on a journey, and except for the necessary but mundane arrangements of a flight, a rental car, and lodging, she'd simply been going along for the ride for the last 24 hours. Surprising gifts were dropping in her lap. With Lucy as her guide, a door had opened for a visit with a real Cracker woman in her authentic Cracker house. It already was obvious—someone greater and wiser than Julie was in charge of this project. It was like Grampa said, she only needed to choose the right fork and then see what happens.

While she waited for Lucy, Julie paced the sandy path that ran between the parking area and the creek. Two men drifted noiselessly by on a small fishing craft, barely making a ripple. The Yearling Restaurant also stood dormant, but all around it nature was coming to life. In the parking lot was a lone palm tree, like a sentry watching over its domain. Lucy pulled up next to it and beckoned to Julie.

She hopped in and they drove onto the main road and over the wooden bridge.

"Is this the same bridge Marjorie wrote about?" Julie said. "The one where people settled arguments and conducted business?"

Lucy nodded. "It is."

"Wasn't it supposed to have steel bars?"

"Good observation," Lucy said, smiling. "Back in 1939, a log hauling truck ran off the road and slammed into one of the steel trusses, sending a good part of the bridge into the creek. Three months later they started to rebuild the bridge, and this time they did it with reinforced concrete. You can read all about it in J.T. Glisson's book. He knew as much about The Creek and maybe a bit more than Marjorie did. He'd lived there all his life."

They continued on the pavement for several miles then turned onto a pitted dirt road and headed deeper into the forest. On both sides, hammock grew thicker until they were enveloped in shadows. Lucy turned on the car's low beams. They drove on into near darkness. An occasional break in the tree line allowed a quick shaft of light onto the road ahead, then the world fell back into utter darkness.

Julie's throat tightened. She wasn't used to giving complete control to another human being. She preferred to be in charge most of the time. Now she felt helpless. She was heading into unfamiliar territory, and she wasn't doing the driving. Someone else was. She was about to say something about being on the wrong road, when they broke through the brush into a large clearing bathed in full sunlight. At the far end stood a traditional Cracker house looking much like it must have when it was built more than a hundred years ago. Julie forgot all about her angst and just stared at the intriguing homestead.

The front lawn was anything but lawn. It consisted of large swaths of sandy soil with an occasional clump of scrub grass. Ducks and chickens roamed freely about, pecking the ground where someone had tossed kernels of corn. A chicken-wire fenced garden looked like it could use a little tender loving care. Inside were a few straggly stalks drooping with ears of corn, a couple of tomato plants ripe for the plucking, and two rows of cabbages and lettuce wilting in the heat of the day. To one side of the property, a small grove of orange and tangerine trees boasted a crop not yet ready for harvest.

Julie turned her attention to the house. Its weather-beaten pine siding was a dull, bluish gray. The tin roof sloped downward over a wide front porch, and broad eaves ran around the perimeter. A short walkway attached the tiny main house to an even smaller structure, which, as Julie had learned, generally housed the bedrooms. Both buildings were raised off the ground on tiny pillars constructed of rocks and shells. Their haphazard construction left the foundation listing slightly to one side.

As Julie got out of the car, two mongrels of no recognizable breed burst from beneath the house, snarling and barking. Lucy stepped in front of Julie and blocked their path.

She raised her hand. "Baby Socks! Sugar! Settle down."

At her command, both dogs slowed their pace and pranced closer, their tales wagging, and their tongues hanging out the sides of their mouths. Julie edged out from behind Lucy and bent over to greet the dogs. The miniature welcoming committee jostled against each other to get close to their new visitor. She petted their bobbing heads, reveled in the feel of soft fur, the lap of wet tongues against her fingers.

Julie had regretted growing up without a dog. Many of her childhood friends owned a dog or a cat—little non-critical buddies that followed them around, loved, and worshipped them, no matter how they looked or smelled or messed up. With a sharp command, Lucy sent the dogs fleeing for the cool shelter of the crawl space. And it was no wonder. It was mid-morning, approaching the hottest time of the day.

The screech of a screen door drew Julie's attention to the front porch. The smallest woman she'd ever seen emerged. Hunched over a four-legged cane, she took baby steps to the middle of the porch. Her bony frame disappeared inside her oversized house dress. She wore an apron and had wrapped the ties around her tiny waist several times. A pure white fluff of curls crowned her head, and her skin had that leathery, suntanned look old people get when they spend a lot of time outdoors in the sun. Everything about her—the smile that sent deep creases into her cheeks, her sparkling blue eyes, the tilt of her head to one side—seemed to be saying, *"I'm so happy you came to visit me."*

Julie pulled out her camera and captured the little woman and her classic home in a couple of shots. Then she followed Lucy up the front steps, taking care to keep her balance on the uneven boards. Lucy made the introductions, and Aunt Emma beckoned them inside the house. Immediately the aroma of pan-fried bacon tickled Julie's nostrils. Though she rarely ate pork, saliva rushed to her mouth. Mark once described how roughing it in the wild could activate people's taste buds, sometimes for things they usually turned up their nose at. Suddenly, eating outdoors over a campfire made sense. A menu of fresh-caught fish, wild game, or in this case, bacon sizzling in an iron skillet, would do just fine. She certainly wasn't about to insult Aunt Emma by refusing to eat whatever the woman placed before her.

She was surprised to find the kitchen cool and comfortable. Though Aunt Emma obviously had kept her little Cracker house intact, she hadn't shied away from a few modern conveniences. A window-size air conditioner sent a cool breeze into the kitchen.

Julie surveyed the room. On the counter stood a microwave and a toaster oven, and in the corner a small refrigerator hummed. Other than those modern inventions, the rest of the kitchen was steeped in traditional Cracker—a wood-burning stove, an old-fashioned pie cupboard, and on the top of the stove, a set of cast iron cookware and an antique metal coffee pot.

Aunt Emma shuffled back and forth from the table to the stove and assembled plates of hotcakes, bacon, and stewed apples for each of them. Lucy helped her place the food and a pot of coffee on the table, then she grabbed the chair beside Julie. Aunt Emma crowded in on the other side of the tiny tea table. There was barely room for a crock of butter, a carafe of honey, and condiments for the coffee. Julie smiled at the simplicity of it all. She couldn't be more impressed if she were eating prime rib at an expensive restaurant.

Aunt Emma reached out and wrapped knobby fingers around Julie's hand. Lucy took Julie's other hand. As Aunt Emma launched into a lengthy giving of thanks, memories surfaced. Julie bowed her head. First, she was back at Grampa's farm, and the family was gathered for Thanksgiving dinner. There were her two uncles and their wives, plus her eight cousins, her parents, Rita, and best of all Gramma and Grampa. She went from there to Patmos. Now she was seated in Yanno's living room, and he was blessing their mid-morning tea and cookies. Those were happy memories.

She was ashamed to have neglected making the ritual a regular part of her life. If two old men and an aged woman could acknowledge the source of all good things, why couldn't she? Mark did. Whenever they ate together, he made sure he blessed the food. But that had always been a part of Mark's life. Julie, on the other hand, had stopped thanking the Lord when she walked away from everything else. That would change, of course, once she and Mark married. Perhaps by then, she'll have started a ritual of her own.

Over breakfast talk centered around Aunt Emma's failing garden, her need for someone to come and reap the remaining produce, and her desire to put up more preserves on the shelf in her pantry. Lucy promised to come out with her two sons and take care of her needs. The two boys could work the garden, and Lucy could help her aunt with the canning. Aunt Emma smiled with satisfaction.

Julie couldn't believe how her appetite had awakened. A slather of butter and a generous coating of honey got her digging into the hotcakes like she hadn't eaten in a week. She caught Lucy staring at her with a smile on her lips. Aunt Emma also stared with pleasure from across the table.

"It must be the fresh air at The Creek," she said, apologetically.

Lucy and Emma shared a giggle and continued eating.

Julie downed three slices of bacon. For the first time in ages she savored the crisp, hickory-smoked flavor. A bowl of stewed apples had a strong cinnamon taste, a satisfying end to the morning meal.

The coffee, however, left a lot to be desired. Julie took one sip of the thick, black liquid, shuddered, and added a healthy serving of cream and two teaspoons of sugar. She laughed to herself. That was how Mark drank his coffee, tons of cream and several bags of sugar. He doctored up the brew until it no longer could be called coffee. As for Julie's cup, no matter how much sugar she added, it still resembled what people jokingly referred to as "paint thinner." She took another sip, then left the rest in the cup. Lucy leaned close and whispered in her ear. "You just got a taste of chicory, makes the coffee darker and stronger."

"And more bitter," Julie said, keeping her voice low.

"It's the old way," Lucy said. "Aunt Emma grew up with chicory coffee. It doesn't affect her in a bad way, though. In fact, maybe it's what's keeping her going."

They laughed together. Julie looked across the table at the old woman. She apparently hadn't heard a word they'd said and was now draining her own coffee cup.

When they finished eating, the three of them cleaned up the kitchen then moved to the living room. With Aunt Emma's approval, Julie kept her camera handy and shot random photos of the inside of the house, also catching the little woman whenever she could. It all amounted to visual note-taking. Once she sat down to write her story, those photos might come in handy.

Aunt Emma's living room was a literal museum of antique furniture and collectible lamps, glassware, and ceramic statues depicting animals, birds, and cherubs. The furniture was eclectic—a red velvet sofa, a brown wing-backed chair, two padded armchairs, and a recliner with a multi-colored granny quilt draped over its arm, most likely Aunt Emma's favorite place to sit. End tables in nearly every type of wood and in a variety of shapes and sizes stood in various places about the room. Each one held either a lamp or a statue or both. On the sideboard stood a 14-inch TV set and a vintage radio carved from dark maple with a huge dial in the front.

Julie settled for one of the armchairs, startled when the cushion sank a few inches under her weight. She kept a notebook and pen handy, but she'd already made up her mind. If she really wanted to connect with Marjorie, she'd have to just sit and listen to whatever the old woman had to say.

Aunt Emma shuffled into the living room and paused in front of an antique-framed mirror on the wall. She removed her apron, straightened her shirt collar, and tweaked a few of her snow-white curls. Then she smiled. It was as if she'd said, "I'm ready for my close-up, Mr. DeMille."

20

INTO THE PAST

As Julie expected, Aunt Emma toddled over to her recliner. Lucy rushed to the old woman's side, grabbed her arm, and lowered her into the seat. Julie eyed Emma with interest. From what Lucy had said during their drive, her aunt lived in the same house in the forest all of her life. She'd never left, not even to shop in the big city. Other people, like Lucy, did her shopping for her, what little bit she needed. Other than a few groceries, she lived off the land or what neighbors provided from their daily catch of fish or their hunting trips into the brush.

Julie glanced about the room. The old furnishings, the dust-laden antiques, and the kerosene lamps took her back more than 80 years. She had to admit, the dilapidated Cracker house was the perfect setting for a journey back in time.

Aunt Emma cleared her throat. Before Julie could ask a single question, the old woman launched into an account of what life was like in the 1930's and '40s in Cross Creek. Her voice trembled as she talked about the overgrown clump of forest where she first caught sight of "the lady from up north."

"I was borned and raised in The Creek, the third of seven children," she said in her slow, Southern way of talking. "My grandparents built this place in the late 1800's. We was poor. Lived off the land. Back then, we raised a couple o' goats, a lazy ol' cow that gave milk whenever she felt like it, the usual chickens and ducks, and of course dogs. We always had to have dogs."

Julie laughed softly and nodded. Hadn't two of the friend-liest guard dogs she'd ever seen greeted her on Aunt Emma's front lawn less than an hour ago?

"I was two years old when Mis' Rawlins' moved here in 1928," the old woman mused. "I later learned her and Charles come here for a two-week vacation and ended up buyin' the propity for upwards of $14,000. It was a lot of money in those days. She put $7,000 down and took out a mortgage. My folks said they couldn't imagine what kind of uppity folk bought that old house and then went through all the trouble o' fixin' it up. But even when it was fallin' apart, it were a lot nicer than our place."

Emma coughed a couple of times. She pulled a lace-trimmed handkerchief from her dress pocket and spit into it.

"Sorry," she said, folding the handkerchief in a little ball.

Julie gave her a friendly smile.

"By the time I was 10," Emma went on, "I'd gotten used to seein' Mis' Marjorie come an' go. I'd made it a practice to keep an eye out for that fancy car of hers. Sure enough, I'd hear it clackin' over the bridge, and I'd run after it to get a better look. Couldn't catch it though, not even if I took the shortcut. That woman tore down the dirt road like she was in a race, kickin' up sand and stones, and cuttin' down whatever plants got too close to the edge. Me an' my brother Seth walked a mile to get over to The Creek. If her car was parked there under the awning she'd built on the side of the house, we knowed she was at home."

She coughed again and turned her attention to Lucy who was curled up on the sofa with her legs folded underneath her.

"Dear, will you get me a glass o' water? My throat's a tad dry."

"Sure, Aunt Emma. Be right back."

Lucy unfolded her legs, nearly leaped off the sofa, and hurried into the kitchen. She obviously didn't want to miss whatever Aunt Emma might have to say next. Emma fell into polite silence and waited for her niece to return. Lucy was back in mere seconds. She handed her aunt a frosty glass of water. Emma sipped long and hard, then she set the glass on a ceramic coaster on the table by her side. She took a deep breath and continued.

"One day, when we got to the propity, Mis' Rawlins was jest gittin' outta her car, and oh my. Me an' Seth was amazed at the size of that woman. She looked about as tall as my daddy. She was a little bulky for a genteel lady, small shoulders, but bosomy on top and heavy from the waist down. She had small hands though and dainty little fingers. And her feet looked like they belonged to a child."

Julie soaked up the description of Marjorie. None of the photographs she'd seen revealed such details. And after seeing the film, *Cross Creek,* she'd imagined Marjorie as slim and feminine as the actress who played her part. Not so, apparently.

"She warn't what you might call beautiful," Aunt Emma said. "She was more handsome, and she had the prettiest gray-blue eyes I ever seen." Emma's face took on a youthful glow, like she was remembering something pleasant. "She was somethin'." Emma went on, her voice soft. "She'd fashioned her hair in one of those swept-back styles with a buncha pins, like the high society ladies do. Her clothes reminded me of a magazine ad I once seen. They was a little too fancy for backwoods living. And she wore nice shoes. Not somethin' you'd want-ta' wear trekkin' through the woods."

"Did you speak to her?" Julie said.

"No, we was too scared. She caught us staring at her from inside the shadows. For only a second, she flashed those gray-blue eyes at us. I was certain I seen her wink. Then she turned away and unloaded the trunk of her car. She lifted out two huge grocery sacks, and she carried those bags like they was nothin' up the steps of the house, and she disappeared inside."

Emma drank more water, and though her hands were shaking, she managed to return the glass to the table.

Last night, in the privacy of her cabin, Julie had jotted a list of questions in her notebook. Now, seated amongst the age-old furnishings and a woman who looked as if she'd walked right out of the past, she preferred to let Emma dredge up whatever she could recall. She gave the old woman a nod to go on.

Aunt Emma didn't hesitate. She tilted her head to one side and smiled like she'd made another trip into the past. "Ever so often, when our chores was done, me an' Seth trekked over to Cross Creek and tried to catch sight of Mis' Marjorie fixin' the place up or plantin' the garden. Else she'd be typin' away at that tom-fool machine o' hers. When she wasn't workin' or writin' she'd be spendin' her time with the local folks. She even hired a couple of blacks to work the house and propity, but I think she had them there because she needed someone to talk to." The lines on Emma's face gathered into a frown. "Back then, the whites didn't accept the blacks like they do today. Some even used the "n" word. Even the blacks sometimes poked fun at each other that way, but they didn't want no one else to do it. One of my best friends was a little colored girl who lived deeper in the forest in a little shack with her Mama and Papa and baby brother. Me and her used to play down by the river and—sorry, I'm gettin' off track."

Aunt Emma's little rabbit trail brought a painful twinge to Julie's heart. Maybe times hadn't changed as much as Emma thought. Julie's own best friend was facing bigotry on a different level. It wasn't bad enough Lakisha and Greg endured occasional sideways glances from strangers who didn't approve of bi-racial unions. What hurt Lakisha more was not being able to win the acceptance of her in-laws.

Then there were folks like Aunt Emma. The old woman apparently never cared what color someone was. Like Julie, she'd latched onto a best friend who was another color, and they got along great. When it came to friendships, who saw color, anyway? Julie couldn't imagine life without Lakisha. She'd been a rock in a storm to her, knew everything about her and loved her anyway.

Aunt Emma shifted into a more comfortable position and moved back to the subject of Marjorie. "Most of us began to think Mis' Marjorie didn't move to Cross Creek just to get away from the big city. She was purposed, though we didn't know until later what her purpose was. Unbeknownst to us, that woman was about to write stories about all of us and then show 'em to the world. She started minglin' with the Cracker folks over in the Big Scrub on the other side of the Ocklawaha. She wanted to learn what they knew, fish where they fished, and eat what they ate. She plunged in with such a passion it was up to the people to decide whether they resented her intrusion or welcomed it."

Emma shook her head and giggled like a little girl. "In 'most no time at all, Mis' Marjorie's appearance begun to change. She swapped out those fancy, store-bought frocks and started walkin' around the propity in frumpy house-dresses, socks that didn't match, and men's shoes. She let her hair go ever which-way, drank like a fish, and smoked like a chimney, even in public when it was unheard of for women to do so. Some said the alcohol was what changed her. I think it was frustration over her writing and her feelings of loneliness—first, when her and Charles split up, and later, whenever Norton weren't around."

Lucy was curled up again on the sofa. She leaned slightly toward Emma. "Tell Julie about some of the things she did for the people, especially during the holidays."

"Oh my," Aunt Emma said, as if a light bulb had gone off in her head. "When she wasn't holed up in the house writin' on that clickety-clack typewriter o' hers, she was out gettin' to know a few of her neighbors, sharin' stuff she'd made in her kitchen, or askin' for down-home recipes. And there was no question about it, Mis' Marjorie had a heart o' gold. She didn't only take from the people. She gave. When Christmas rolled around, she showed up on our doorstep with a box o' clothes for us kids." Emma smiled sweetly. "Besides sweaters fer everbody, the box held a black, velvet dress with a big red bow for me, pants and shirts for my brothers, and store-bought shoes fer all of us. There was a fruitcake and a bottle of whiskey for my parents, candy for us kids, a doll for me, and cars and trucks for the boys. Before she left, she set out a smoked ham and a couple o' bags of oranges and tangerines, fresh-picked off her fruit trees. We all knew Marjorie's grove was supposed to be for business, but after her husband cut out, she shared a lot of her gatherins' with her neighbors." Emma glanced up at Julie. "Would you care for a tangerine, dear? There's a bowl of 'em in the refrigerator."

Amused, Julie shook her head and grinned. "No, thanks. The wonderful breakfast you made was quite enough."

Emma nodded, and her face glowed with a rare youthfulness. "It turned out, Mis' Marjorie did the same for lots of poor folks, both whites and blacks. She shared what she had. There was a story that one of her maids once stole some things from her and took off, but Mis' Marjorie didn't call the police. Didn't even take it out on the girl by whippin' her when she came home with her tail between her legs. She welcomed her back in her employ and let the whole thing pass."

Emma frowned then. "Now, don't get me wrong, Mis' Julie. That woman was easy-goin' most o' the time, but there was plenty of times when she lost it. Sometimes, there was so much shoutin' and cursin' goin' on over there, we could hear her back at my house more'n a mile away. Well, maybe we didn't always *hear* it, but we sure heard *about* it.

"It warn't long after Mr. Charles left that Mis' Marjorie started throwin' parties. Whenever there was a full moon and a party goin' on, me an' Seth snuck out and traipsed on over there. We knew it was party time 'cause all day long we could hear the rumble of automobiles goin' over the bridge makin' a familiar clunk-clunk sound on all them loose boards. One night, when the moon was full, the two of us plotted to go over there and spy on one of her highfalutin' get-togethers. Folks mentioned names that didn't mean anything to us at the time, but now I know how important they was. F. Scott Fitzgerald, Ernest Hemingway, and my personal favorite, Margaret Mitchell. Mayor M.C. Izlar drove up from Ocala. And there was that editor friend of Mis' Marjorie's, Max somethin'-or-other."

"Perkins," Julie said. "Max Perkins."

"Don't matter. They was all drinkin' and smokin' and carryin' on like they'd just been elected to office."

Julie never went to high-society galas, never knew what it was like to rub elbows with the rich and famous. But she *had* attended more than her share of church functions and weddings. Except for Lakisha's wedding, she could have passed on all of them. Even at those functions, people put on airs, so you never got to know who they really were. It took a personal tragedy for Julie to find out.

Unknowingly, Aunt Emma had opened another door of amazing truths for Julie to contemplate. Not only was there a definite divide between the colored and the whites back then, but also between the rich and the poor. Apparently, in the heart of the forest, people were either black or white, rich or poor. No in-between. Yet, Marjorie somehow bridged every gap, maybe for the purpose of writing her books, maybe because she had a heart for the underdog. In any case, she found a way to break through the barriers and get to really know people.

Julie supposed her own family would be considered wealthy by the old-time Cracker standards. Her father was a CEO in a big company. Though they lived in the same house since Julie was born and lived frugally, the family never wanted for anything. Julie's church often took up collections for the poor, and she recently had gotten involved in a ministry to the homeless.

It wasn't until she went to Patmos that she got a glimpse of what truly destitute people looked like. During her visit with Yanno, when the time came for him to greet his visitors, he sent her and Mark into the dining room where they could observe from the shadows. She'll never forget the humble, world-weary folks who came plodding through the old man's door. Each visitor came in with a different need.

And each one brought some sort of payment, though it was rarely money. Sometimes they handed him a loaf of home-made bread or a sack of vegetables. He received their gifts graciously and later passed them into the hands of someone who needed them.

Aunt Emma finished off her glass of water and breathed a sigh. On cue, Lucy rose from the comfort of the sofa and hurried into the kitchen to refill the old woman's glass. Julie stared at Emma and mentally willed her to stay awake. What if the old girl nodded off in the middle of their visit? All the talking and remembering surely had taken its toll on her already.

Emma gazed back at Julie and her blue eyes sparkled like those of a teenager. Somehow, inside this woman a young girl was still trying to get out.

Julie could hardly wait for Lucy to get back with Emma's glass of water. She felt like a little girl herself, and this was a story-telling festival, and the key speaker was a fascinating old woman who'd been there and still remembered how it was.

21

MORE MEMORIES

J ulie didn't take her eyes off of Emma. The woman was an enigma from head to toe. Though she looked like one of those elderly folks who sit drooling in a wheelchair in a nursing home, this dear lady exuded a girlish personality far beneath her years. Inside she hadn't aged at all. Her memory was as sharp as an axe blade.

Lucy returned from the kitchen and handed Emma the glass of water. The old woman fumbled with the glass and took a little sip. Then she tilted her head in that whimsical way older people do when they're about to say something important.

"You seen my two dogs out there in the yard?" Aunt Emma said, a smile crinkling her face.

"Uh, huh," Julie said, nodding. "They gave me a nice, wet welcome."

"They's my pride and joy," Emma said with nod and a wink. "Mis' Marjorie loved dogs too. She owned this black-and-white huntin' dog named Pat. You could see him a mile away if he stood still long enough."

Julie chuckled. "There's a nice picture of Marjorie and Pat on the wall at the house."

Aunt Emma nodded. "Thanks to Lucy, I seen it too. My lovely niece gave me a tour of the house a few years back. Just walkin' through it brought back a ton o' memories. Mis'

Marjorie took that dog everwhere with her. Sometimes he even rode in the back seat o' that car o' hers. One day, he got a little too frisky out in the front yard. He leaped over the cattle guard and ran straight into the street about the same time a car came around the bend. I was standin' at the side of the road. It all happened so fast, I couldn't do nothin'. Poor thing died right there in the street. Mis' Marjorie probly drank herself to sleep that night."

Emma froze for a moment, like she might be trying to regain her composure.

"Tell her about Norton Baskin," Lucy said, quickly changing the subject.

Aunt Emma nodded. "Oh, yes. A few years after Mis' Marjorie's divorce from Charles, Mr. Baskin started hangin' around the propity. People said he was there to help out, but my mama knew better. 'That man's got his eye on Mis' Marjorie,' Mama said at supper one night. Sure enough, they got to be a couple after a while. 'Course, he warn't there all the time. He ran a hotel in Ocala, so he sometimes disappeared to take care of business, I guess." She chuckled like she was about to reveal a secret. "The maids said when he spent the night in Cross Creek, Mis' Marjorie made him sleep in the spare bedroom. She kept their relationship real decent. Even after they got married, they spent an ungodly amount of time apart. Not me. No sir. I never spent a day away from *my* husband. Denny an' me, we always was together, day and night, night and day, week after week, month after month, until he died. That was 15 years ago, and I still feel like I hear him comin' out of the bedroom. We was married 60 years and never uttered a harsh word betwixt us."

Emma slowly shook her head, and a sadness crept into her

eyes. "Can't say that about Mis' Marjorie. She could make a loggin' man cringe with that sharp tongue o' hers. Most o' the time, I suppose she was in the right. Don't know for sure. But Norton, he was a mild-mannered fella. Laughed a lot, and liked to tell jokes, or so I heard. Me an' Seth seen him come and go. He dressed like a real businessman, nice suits, starched shirts, and pretty ties. He was handsome, too. His hair looked like a pile o' gold threads. They set off a glitter whenever he stepped out in the sunlight. Norton was a military man, served in the war driving an ambulance on the front lines. He wouldn't have left his duty, 'cept he got deathly ill with a stomach problem and ended up flying home for treatment."

Emma paused to drink more water. Julie eyed her with concern. How long was the old woman going to last before she needed to take a bathroom break? The casual visit over breakfast took up most of the morning. Then there were those water breaks. Julie hoped they could keep going without another interruption. It was already well past noon, and she wasn't ready to leave yet. Then the old woman set down the glass and kept right on talking.

"Now, I need ta make somethin' clear about Mis' Marjorie's parties. Sure, she liked to entertain. She enjoyed wearing long, black gowns and dressin' up like she was about to get an award. The thing was, she was at home whether she was wearin' an evening gown and high heels or if she was in riding pants and men's boots. She could tip a glass o' champagne or guzzle whiskey from a flask in a paper sack. It didn't matter to her, one way or t'other.

"The sad thing was, she spent more time alone than with other people. 'Cept for the servants who worked her farm and took care of her house, Mis' Marjorie lived like one of them hermits who hole up in their cabin and lock everyone else out. I suppose it were the only way she could write all them books."

Emma shook her head and grunted. "There was times I'd venture near the propity, and all I could hear other than the sounds of nature was the clicking of that fool typewriter o' hers. She'd sit in the screened porch for hours rippin' up yellow note paper, tearin' sheets out of the typewriter, cursin' a blue streak, and startin' all over again. A couple o' times I crept up closer to the house and got a look at her work table. Next to the typing machine was an ash tray loaded with burned out cigarette butts and a paper sack. Some said the little bag contained a flask o' whiskey."

Emma tilted her head and smiled at Julie. "Heard enough?"

"No, I could listen to you all day," Julie said. "But I don't want to tire you."

"Tire me?" Emma let out a giggle. It sounded oddly youthful for a woman her age. "I'm just getin' started, girl." She gave her arms and legs a little stretch, released a contented groan, and settled back in her chair. She squeezed her eyes shut, like she was searching her brain for a forgotten memory.

"Now, let's see," she said, opening her eyes. They sparkled with moisture. Emma cleared her throat and let out a little cough. "Here's somethin' you need to know about Mis' Marjorie. She mighta been a no-nonsense person, didn't put up with no arguments, and stood her ground no matter what. But she showed compassion for the little folks and even stepped in when she thought somebody was bein' unfair. One time, a couple of her neighbor men were goin' at it at the bridge, arguin' about who owed t'other one money. It started out like a simple misunderstandin', but their words was buildin' into somethin' bigger. 'Bout the time they were gonna start punchin' each other, Mis' Marjorie come along, whipped out her wallet, and settled the whole matter in five minutes. The two men walked away friends agin'."

Aunt Emma chuckled and stared off at nothing in particular. "Oh, yes. A lot o' disputes were settled on the old bridge. Us kids used ta' go over there and swing on the steel bars like a bunch o' monkeys. Those was fun times. Other than Mis' Marjorie an' her friends, we didn't have ta' worry about any cars comin' along disruptin' our play, 'ceptin' once a day when the mailman come over the bridge."

Still chuckling, she shook her head. "There was other times when Mis' Marjorie stepped up and settled a problem between the locals. They never thanked her for it, not with words. But sometime over the next few weeks, she'd find a couple o' killed rabbits on her front porch, or somebody maybe snuck up in the middle of the night and mended the break in her fence or left a fresh-made cornpone on her back step. Crackers are a proud folk, but they like to be fair."

Julie tilted her head quizzically. "You keep using the word 'Cracker.' Isn't that a derogatory term?"

Aunt Emma gave a little shrug. "Some say it is. But it's who we are, and we should be proud of it. The word sets us apart from the other forest people. It's our identity."

"These days, it's even become an architectural term," Julie said. "Lots of people build their homes in the old Cracker-style—but furnished with modern conveniences, of course." She paused, then got back to the main topic. "What else can you remember about Marjorie?"

"Well, there's not much more to say about her," Emma said.

Her voice was starting to sound a little scratchy, like maybe she'd been talking too long. "As you already know, she loved animals. It warn't long after Pat was killed but Mis' Marjorie got herself another huntin' dog. She named him Moe. And she kept a couple o' cats too. Smokey was always hangin' around."

"Did you ever go inside the house?" Julie said.

Emma shook her head and a sadness clouded her eyes. "Nope. Most o' the time, I watched from a distance. Believe me, a person can see and hear an awful lot from the bushes. I was curious, of course, couldn't stay away for long. But if I wanted to know more, I depended on reports from the servants and other folks who gabbed about Mis' Marjorie."

"Did she ever speak to you?"

Another shake of Emma's head, but this time she smiled. "Only when she delivered toys and clothes and food to us poor folk at Christmas time. Then she said a whole lot about taking care of ourselves and not giving up. After that, she'd drive off in that car o' hers. I'm not kiddin' when I say that woman drove fast. She talked fast, walked fast, and drove fast. I think she was on high speed for most of her life."

"Did she change at all after she won the Pulitzer?"

Emma narrowed her eyes like she was trying to choose between two different stories, then raised her chin like she'd made up her mind.

"Some folks thought she got a tad more uppity, like she thought she was better than everbody else." She shook her head with emphasis. "Not me. And not my brothers or my folks. She'd been real kind to us at holiday times. The funny thing was, with no phone and the telegram service sometimes gettin' messed up, she didn't find out she'd won that prize until it was too late for her to go to the big New York party they'd planned for her. She celebrated by herself in that big ol' house o' hers."

The wrinkles on Emma's forehead deepened and moisture filled her eyes. "I guess you already know, Mis' Marjorie went to an early grave."

Julie nodded. "She was 57."

Out of nowhere, a terrible sadness filled the room. Emma brought out the lace-trimmed handkerchief again. She dabbed at the tears oozing from her eyes. "Mis' Marjorie took sick a lot, made bunches o' trips to the hospital over in Flagler. But she always bounced back and started right in with her stompin' and cursin' agin', jest like before. Wouldn't go to the doctor until she couldn't bear it no more. She was a tough one."

Julie shifted in her chair to get more comfortable. She stared at Emma. The old woman sat twisting her handkerchief in her hands, like she was about to fall apart.

"How long was it before you found out she'd passed?" Julie said.

Emma shook her head with sadness. "It warn't long. Bad news travels fast in the forest." She frowned then. "Did you know Mis' Marjorie's buried a few gravestones away from Zelma Cason? She didn't want to spend eternity anywhere near that miserable traitor." She paused and blotted away more tears. "There's never gonna be another Marjorie Rawlins' Not in a million years."

The old woman fell into heart-wrenching sobs. Julie and Lucy rose at once and rushed over to her. They knelt on either side of her, stroked her back, and held her hand.

Julie looked at Lucy. "Perhaps this is getting too taxing," she said. "I certainly don't want to cause her any pain."

Lucy nodded. "We should go," she whispered.

They stood to their feet. Emma leaned back in her chair and mopped her face with the already damp handkerchief.

"So sorry," Emma said. "I've read pretty much everthing Mis' Marjorie wrote. Saw the two films, too. They didn't tell half the story. For me, it was like losing an old friend, though I never did get close enough to call her that."

Lucy stroked her aunt's fluff of white hair. "You may very well be one of the last living human beings who got to see her in the flesh," she said. "Marjorie Kinnan Rawlings put Cross Creek on the map. She left a legacy, Aunt Emma. Now Julie's going to print a lot of what she learned here today. So, thanks to you and your fabulous memory, the legacy will go on."

Julie leaned close and gave Aunt Emma a hug. "Don't get up," she said. "Lucy will show me out." She straightened and took one last look at the frail little woman. "Thank you for welcoming me into your home. And for your stories about Marjorie and The Creek."

Emma smiled and gave a little wave of the handkerchief. "You come back sometime and see me."

Julie gathered her things and made her way to the door. A lump had settled in her throat. She tried to swallow it, but it remained. Tears flooded into her eyes. There was no telling if she'd get to visit Cross Creek again. Yet those few hours she'd spent with Aunt Emma would stay with her for a long time to come.

Julie and Lucy stepped out onto the front porch. The afternoon sun was beating down with a vengeance. Julie put on her sunglasses. She was at a loss for words. She'd entered another world, and she wasn't ready to leave it. She gazed into the hammock at the palmetto spears, the palm trees, and the moss-draped live oaks. Somewhere, deep inside that thicket, wildlife moved unseen. Maybe a herd of deer, a raccoon family, and even a mama bear with her cubs. Julie had begun to imagine all sorts of magical images. It seemed forest living affected humans in a way city life never could.

"I'll take you back to the cabins," Lucy said. "Then I'll come back and help Aunt Emma into bed for a little nap."

"Thank you for arranging this visit. I love your Aunt Emma."

"So does everyone who meets her," Lucy said with a smile.

They headed for Lucy's car. Emma's two dogs didn't bother to come out in the heat of the day.

"So, what's your plan now?" Lucy said.

Julie checked her watch. "I still have plenty of daylight. I'll take a drive up to Crescent Beach and check out the cottage. I understand someone else owns it now, so I won't be able to go inside. There's supposed to be a research library in St. Augustine. I guess I should stop there too."

"And tomorrow?"

"My flight doesn't leave until the afternoon. I'll make arrangements to visit the university and check out the archives, like you suggested."

"And, before you leave Cross Creek, be sure and visit Marjorie's gravesite," Lucy said. "Antioch Cemetery is just a short drive from the cabins. You'll want to say good-bye to Marjorie."

After leaving Aunt Emma's, Julie cued in the University of Florida archives on her cell phone, pulled up the Smathers Libraries, and was able to arrange with the archivist to visit in the morning. Then she took a run up the coast along

Route A1A. Following the car's GPS, she made a couple of turns and located the Crescent Beach cottage Marjorie and Norton once owned. Old photos had depicted it as an isolated cottage with few neighbors. Now the area was jam-packed with home after home. The tiny house was dwarfed by larger mansions and a string of hotels.

As she gazed at the simple cottage, one word came to Julie's mind. *Charming.* Whoever owned the house now must have wanted to keep it looking much like it did decades ago. Julie's imagination soared. To think Marjorie played host to famous writers and actors in this house. She drove away, wishing she could have gone inside.

With time to spare, she made a stop at the St. Augustine Historical Society Research Library. A young man greeted her warmly and pulled out some files. The records showed that Marjorie purchased the home in 1939 for several thousand dollars from her Pulitzer Prize award for *The Yearling*. After MGM bought the film rights for $30,000, Marjorie used some of those funds to add a wing for an office. Many famous figures walked through the front door over the years. Apparently, Marjorie and Norton shared some of their best times in that little cottage.

After Marjorie died, Norton remained at the Crescent Beach property until the 1960s, then he moved to St. Augustine Beach.

The society's records showed that, over the years, the Crescent Beach cottage passed through a couple of different owners and at one time was listed for more than $3 million. Perplexed, Julie shook her head. Why hadn't the state officials taken as much interest in the Crescent Beach property as they had in Cross Creek? Finances, perhaps. Or maybe there was a huge difference between high-end properties compared to a hovel in the woods.

As she drove away from St. Augustine and returned to the cabin on the creek, Julie pondered the staggering amount of information she'd gathered. How was she going to make all her notes fit a 3,000-word magazine article? In truth, she'd gathered enough information to write an entire book. And what about the photos? Somehow, she'd have to send Ian a dozen out of more than 100 shots. The project was already too big.

22

MARK

Once again, at quitting time, Mark cut out of his office and left the building without seeing a sign of Fiona. Melanie had done as much as she could over the past couple of days. She'd kept her assistant so busy she didn't have time to venture over to his side of the campus. Still, he had a creepy feeling someone was watching him, maybe following his car, standing outside his apartment building, tailing him wherever he went.

It was probably his imagination, yet he spent an inordinate amount of time looking over his shoulder. He drove out of the parking lot, peered in the rear-view mirror, and breathed a sigh of relief. Nobody there.

He immediately phoned Greg. "You done working yet?"

"Yeah, I've been home for two hours."

"Wanna spend a little time together, maybe take in a movie?"

"Don't tell me you've finished the PowerPoint," Greg said, a mix of surprise and praise in his voice.

"Yep, I'm done. I can't do anything more with it until I try it out in Chicago. Julie's still in Florida, and I'm free for the evening."

"A movie sounds good. Lakisha already told me she wants to get to bed early tonight. She spent the entire day cleaning our house, and she's exhausted. Doesn't even feel like cooking. Got a particular film in mind?"

"As a matter of fact, I do. The Vintage Cinema happens to be showing *Cross Creek*. I'd like to get a look at the place where Julie's stompin' around right now, maybe glean enough from the film to be able to talk intelligently about her project and show her I'm interested in her work."

"Sounds like a plan. I saw the movie ages ago, but I could stand to sit through it again."

"You're a true friend, Greg. Listen, I'm heading for the apartment. I'll take a shower and meet you at the theater at 6:45. The movie starts at seven."

"You've got it, pal. Later."

Mark couldn't help but smile. He'd come out of college with a ton of friends, but none of them had stuck by him like Greg had. The guy went beyond the call numerous times. Like two years ago when Mark tore the meniscus in his right knee during a 5-K event. Greg gave up the race halfway to the finish line in order to help Mark get to his car. Afterward, he chauffeured him to his doctor's visit, to the surgery clinic, and anywhere else he needed to go. He spent many days at his apartment, keeping him company until he could get back to work.

Then, when Julie broke off their relationship, who showed up to give him comfort? Greg. While Mark insisted on sitting home and moping, Greg ushered him out the door to one of their favorite hangouts, got him laughing again, and made sure he didn't starve. The Bible said something about a friend who is closer than a brother. Greg was such a friend. As far as Mark was concerned, he couldn't get any closer to him if they shared the same blood.

On his way home, Mark swung into the drive-up lane at a fast food restaurant and ordered a hamburger and fries. He ate the burger before he reached his apartment. He finished off the fries and a milkshake in front of the TV during the 5 o'clock news. Julie was right. The *Springfield Daily Press* was on its way down, and Jason Redding, the WPIX news anchor, had jumped on the story and even seemed to enjoy commenting on it.

With a sigh of disgust, he turned off the TV and headed for the shower. Now he could look forward to spending a relaxing evening with his best friend. He changed shirts a couple of times, settled on a T-shirt with a *Star Wars* silk-screen, a birthday gift from Greg a couple of years ago, and a pair of distressed jeans. He wasn't trying to impress anyone, merely wanted to kick back tonight. Anyway, they'd be sitting in the dark for most of the evening.

He left home at 6:30 and made it to the Vintage Cinema parking lot in plenty of time. There was Greg, pacing the sidewalk in front of the marquee, a border of peanut bulbs illuminating the name of the film—*Cross Creek*.

For Greg to agree to a retro movie was also a big deal. He usually gravitated to futuristic films *action flicks*, yet here he was, standing on the corner of Sixth and Elm, and in his hand, two tickets to see a 1983 film based on a 1942 book.

Mark strolled up to his friend. "Thanks, man, what do I owe you?"

"Nothing. My treat."

"Okay, then I'll get the popcorn and Cokes."

They found the theater about half-full. Thursday evenings didn't draw a big crowd. The building itself looked like it was built in the 1920s and never went through any renovations. Red velour drapes hung on the two side walls between dark panels displaying gold-framed artwork from another era. Except for six dimly lit wall sconces and strips of floor lighting, the theater lay in near darkness.

Greg selected a couple of seats in the middle of a row about two-thirds up the sloping aisle. Mark's seat sagged beneath his weight, and the seat in front of him was mere inches away. He settled in and flipped one leg over the other knee, scrunching his long limbs inside the close space. Greg did the same, settled down, and dug into his popcorn.

"This is the life," Greg said, keeping his voice soft. "No worries. No pesky clients. Just a couple of hours to escape and forget about the outside world."

Mark nodded and took a long drink of his Coke. "I appreciate your taking time away from Lakisha. You sure she's gonna be okay?"

Greg nodded and let out a snort. "She was like a workhorse today. Don't know what got into her, but she needed to get the house in order, like she was expecting company. Then she collapsed in bed with a book and told me to go have fun."

The previews came up on the screen. More vintage films, most of them black-and-white. Then, in the tradition of the old-time film houses, they ran a dated newsreel followed by a Bugs Bunny cartoon.

"Those were the good ol' days, weren't they?" Mark said. "My dad used to take me to old movies when I was a kid. He figured it might help me get more well-rounded."

"Smart man," Greg said.

Mark and his dad shared a unique bond. After his mother died, the two of them grew so close, they were more than father and son. They were best friends.

Greg didn't have that kind of relationship with his father. To Howard Davis, it was all about the farm and having his son take over when he couldn't handle it anymore. But Greg took off after graduation. He put himself through college and ignored the rift between them.

"Do you ever regret not going back home to work the farm?" Mark said.

"Sometimes." Greg surprised him with the admission. "But only to make my parents happy and to hear my dad say he was proud of me. Otherwise, I believe I made the right decision."

The thing was, Greg liked his job, and he was married to Lakisha, one of the nicest women Mark had ever met. The two were a perfect match. They balanced each other well, with Lakisha, the well-to-do daughter of a Boston lawyer, and Greg, the product of a humble rural couple blending together like the salty popcorn and sweet Cokes the two of them were consuming at that very moment. If opposites did attract, Greg and Lakisha were prime examples.

For her to be cleaning up a storm at their house didn't make sense. Lakisha never put things away after using them. She let the dinner dishes sit in the sink until the next morning. And she spent far too much time looking for things she'd misplaced, a real problem for Greg who was one of those guys who preferred to have a place for everything and everything in its place. While Lakisha lived a relaxed lifestyle and took her time getting ready to go out, Greg didn't like being late. But he rarely complained about her, except in fun.

"Is Lakisha going through some sort of transformation with the baby coming?" Mark said.

"What do you mean?"

"The cleaning bit."

Greg shrugged. "Who knows? If that's what's happening, great. Maybe now she'll put stuff away when she's done using it."

The wall sconces dimmed, and the giant screen flickered to life. Mark and Greg immediately settled down, munched on their popcorn and sipped their sodas. They were like two kids playing hooky from school. Greg had spent the last couple of weeks complaining about having to do the laundry and wash the dishes. For Lakisha to shoo him out of the house was like being released from prison—at least that's how Greg put it. As for Mark, he could lose himself in a good movie. No classroom full of students. No papers to grade. No PowerPoint pressures. And most of all, no Fiona.

The movie ended. The popcorn tubs were empty, the Cokes were drained dry. Mark and Greg unfolded their legs, and with a chorus of grunts pushed out of their tightly-spaced seats. They left the theater with a few stragglers and stepped out in the glow of streetlamps.

"Great film," Mark said. "First time I ever saw it."

Greg nodded. "Yeah, it brought back some memories about the farm. Of course, my life wasn't quite that difficult. We had a tractor and lots of other tools to keep things running."

Mark chuckled. "I can picture you bouncing around on a tractor and hauling crates of corn to the barn."

Greg made a face of disgust. "Let's not go there. I'm very happy sitting behind a desk. Now, whaddaya say we get something to eat? My treat."

"Isn't it my turn?"

"Nah, I've got it tonight. You can take our next date out."

Mark smiled at his friend. "In that case, let's skip the fast food joints."

"I already know what I have a taste for," Greg said. "How about some hot wings? There's a place right around the corner."

Ten minutes later they were seated in a booth looking over a menu that boasted the hottest wings in town. Fortunately for Mark, they also offered soups and salads, plus an assortment of sandwiches.

"You get the wings," Mark said. "I'll have this toasted ham-and-cheese special."

"What? You can't handle a little heat?"

"Not tonight. My stomach has been in an uproar for the last couple of days."

"I won't say her name," Greg said, though he didn't have to. Mark didn't want to talk about his trip to Chicago or anything else to do with work. Thank goodness, his friend understood.

They placed their order and settled back with two cups of coffee.

"The movie made me a little more familiar with Julie's project," Mark said. "I'm glad we went to see it."

"They sure picked an attractive actress to play Marjorie, didn't they?" Greg said.

"Steenburgen? Yeah, they tend to do that. I doubt the real Marjorie looked like her. And what about the cinematography? Do you think that part of Florida still looks like a jungle? I'll tell ya, Greg, those scenes got me worrying about Julie. You know, snakes and bears and gators. That's really not her bag."

"You should know what Florida's like. Haven't you been down there several times to visit your father?"

"Yes, but he lives on the coast. You know, sandy beaches, towering high-rises, lots of activities for seniors. Cross Creek is in a whole different part of the state."

"I guess you'll have to ask Julie what it's like, but I'm guessing they've cleaned the forest up quite a lot since the 1930s."

"You're probably right, Greg. I hope it won't be a huge disappointment to her. She got it in her mind to get a feel for the kind of life Marjorie Rawlings experienced. If it's all highways and condominiums now, she's not gonna be happy. No matter what she's writing about, Julie likes to immerse herself in the culture. She wants the real thing, but without the dangerous critters."

"Has she said much about it?"

"We talked on the phone last night. She sounded excited, said she toured the old house, and it looked pretty much the way it used to be. I guess the state's been maintaining everything pretty well. They even rebuilt the old barn to look like it did back in the day. From what Julie said, a good bunch of volunteers come in there and keep things going."

"Then don't worry about critters. Julie can take care of herself. She'll get the story if she has to tear the place down."

Mark snickered. "That's what I'm afraid of."

Suddenly, Greg's phone rang. He checked the screen. "Unknown caller," he said.

"Maybe you'd better answer it, make sure nothing's going on with Lakisha."

Greg cued in the call. He looked at Mark. "It's my neighbor."

As he listened to the voice on the other end, his face turned ashen.

Mark straightened in his seat. "What's wrong, Greg?"

"They've rushed Lakisha to the hospital. I've gotta go."

Mark grabbed the check. "I'll take care of this. You get going. I'll be right behind you."

23

JULIE

Julie needed to relax. The lights were on at the Yearling Restaurant, a few steps from her cabin. She walked inside and was led to a small table in a dimly lit room with a subtle orange glow and an aura of tranquility, precisely what she needed after a long day.

She looked over the menu, amused by the number of marshland critters listed there. In addition to venison, catfish, and frog legs, the restaurant offered alligator cooked in a number of different ways. After all, she was no longer in Springfield. She was in the heart of the forest, and all of those creatures were easy pickin's here. The question was whether or not to try one of those rare delicacies.

A burst of boldness overcame her. She ended up ordering a side salad and the "Yearling Sampler," which, besides tomatoes, fried onions, and mushrooms, included frog legs, gator tail, and conch fritters. "Why not?" she said with a shrug, and she handed the menu back to the server.

While she waited for her food, she allowed herself a mental escape back into the forest, drawn there by the strains of Willie "Big Toe" Green's blues played simultaneously on a guitar and a harmonica. Between songs, the big black entertainer lowered his instruments and interacted with the patrons. His deep South accent, casual demeanor, and backwoods humor helped maintain the atmosphere of the Florida eatery.

She enjoyed her meal more than she expected, though she could curse the person who'd said gator and frog legs tasted like chicken. No matter how much breading or batter the chef applied, they still tasted gamey. The gator tail seemed more like veal with a fresh, pink texture beneath the breading. The frog legs were larger than she thought they'd be. She ended up liking the assortment well enough to clean her plate. Tasting the foods Marjorie relished gave her one more way to stay connected with her favorite author.

Julie already had smelled the fresh scent of the longleaf pines. She'd run her hand over the faded boards on the side of Marjorie's barn, had stroked the bark of a palm tree, had let a soft clump of Spanish moss slip through her fingers. She'd walked where Marjorie had walked—within the orange grove, into the brush, along a dirt path, up the stairs to the house, through each room. She'd watched the long-necked cranes strut along the edge of the property, had listened for the cries of the whippoorwill and the red bird, and had fallen asleep to the music of cicadas and locusts. Now she'd used one more of her five senses in her quest to sample every aspect of Marjorie's life in the forest.

The restaurant was laid out like a mini museum. When she finished eating and paid the bill, she strolled down a long hallway past more eating areas where people dined in the presence of a stuffed bear, an angry bobcat, a ten-foot alligator with his mouth open wide, a broken-down canoe, and a mix of woodsy settings, all images from *The Yearling*—both the movie and the book.

Before leaving the restaurant, she paused at a hallway where tons of used books were on display. Curious, she scanned the spines. Many of them focused on local history, fishing, hunting, and nature, including most of Marjorie's books, and all of them for sale. She picked up a copy of *Cross Creek Cookery*, Marjorie's cookbook, and flipped through the pages. It contained a mix of Ida's recipes and down-home concoctions Marjorie had tested with Idella Parker, her "perfect maid" for many years. At the beginning of each chapter, Marjorie had added little vignettes that would prove entertaining. Without hesitation, she pulled out her wallet and bought the cookbook—one more treasure to add to her Rawlings collection.

She left for the cabin, expecting to get a good night's sleep. She needed to leave early in the morning if she wanted to stop in Gainesville before catching her flight. Also, first thing before leaving The Creek for good, she'd have to visit Marjorie's grave in Antioch Cemetery. Afterward, she'd head straight for the George A. Smathers Libraries at the University of Florida. An internet search had showed that the library held a large collection of Marjorie's unpublished writings, including letters from troops she'd written to during World War II, some correspondence from Norton, plus other notes and memorabilia. If Julie wanted to get into the heart and soul of the woman, she couldn't bypass this unique opportunity.

She had almost reached the cabin, when the scent of burning firewood tickled her nose. Curious, she followed the scent to the banks of the creek. Several people sat in plastic outdoor chairs around a fire pit. A dancing blaze shot sparks into the sky and lit up the circle of rocks around the pit. The fire's glow illuminated the side of a nearby oak that had a large gash in its trunk, looking an awful lot like it had been struck by lightning. Nevertheless, it continued to stand, tall and strong, as if nothing in the world could topple it.

Julie paused at the edge of the clearing. One of the shadows near the fire pit waved her closer. "C'mon. We're roasting marshmallows."

Someone else held up a bottle. "Beer?"

"No thanks, but I'd love a marshmallow." She sauntered over and accepted an empty chair.

In the cozy half circle were two men and three women, all in casual dress—shorts, jeans, tank tops, and T-shirts. Introductions went around the small group. One young woman spoke with a British accent. She told Julie she was a college student on break. The others said they were on vacation from different jobs. When Julie told them who she was and what she was doing there, they lit up with interest.

"My *awnt* is a writer," the British girl said.

Julie's interest was pricked. "Is that right? What does she write?"

"Mostly research papers and a little poetry."

"Is she published?"

"Blimey, yes. She's quite famous in London."

Julie eyed the others with interest. "Have you people been to The Rawlings Farm?" she said.

Two of the women nodded and said they enjoyed the time they spent there. One of them, a middle-aged redhead, spoke about the "step back in time" she'd experienced.

A guy named Hal grunted. "We're goin' there tomorrow. Can't say I'm lookin' forward to it. Sounds boring as hell. I can think of a whole bunch of other things I'd like to do."

His remark sent angry prickles to Julie's cheeks.

"Boring?" she snapped. "Why do you expect it to be boring? Have you no interest in history? Don't you know Marjorie Kinnan Rawlings put this place on the map? What are you doing here if you didn't come to see her farm?"

Hal leaned back and raised a hand like he was fending off an attack. "Uh, sorry. It's not my thing. My wife wants to go, so I'll tag along—you know, make her happy."

Julie leaned into his space. "Look, Hal. You should try to be a little more open. You never know what you might learn about the past. One of Florida's most famous writers, if not *the* most famous, lived on the property almost a hundred years ago. Haven't you ever read *The Yearling,* or at least seen the movie?"

Hal cocked his head to one side, like he'd gotten a flash of memory. "Oh, yeaaah. I did see that flick when I was a kid. So, that's where we're going?" He turned toward the woman on his other side.

She jabbed his arm playfully. "Be nice, honey. Maybe you should think about taking up reading. You might learn something."

He looked back at Julie. The fire bathed his face with color and caught a flicker of remorse in his eyes. "Sorry, lady. I didn't know we were gonna step on hallowed ground tomorrow." He sounded sincere, but Julie detected a hint of sarcasm.

She was about to lash out again when she caught herself. She'd been trying to curb those outbursts and here came another challenge. She had to calm down. Mentally, she started counting. One...two...three.... She didn't finish the count. "It's okay," she said.

As a peace offering, Hal held out a stick with a nicely browned marshmallow on the tip. "Friends?" he said, with a hopeful grin.

Julie slid the marshmallow off the stick. "Friends." She bit into the crisp outside and savored the gooey inner part. Momentarily she was a teenager again, sitting around a campfire at the beach with her friends. *Sure. Friends.* Not one of them stuck by her after the rape. Maybe their parents kept them away. Maybe they chose to avoid her. She never knew.

Suddenly the British girl lurched out of her chair and pointed at the creek. "Look! There they are. That guy at the gas station was right."

Julie stared beyond the girl's outstretched arm at the still, lifeless water. There along the creek's edge on the opposite side, between cypress knees and tufts of river grass, was a row of red dots, like tiny lights illuminating the marsh.

Julie stood to her feet. "What are those things?"

Hal burst out laughing and stood up. "You mean the red lights along the shore? You don't want to go anywhere near 'em," he said. He took a swig of beer, laughed again, and cast a smug look at Julie. "Ya mean I know something you don't know?"

Julie scowled at him at the same time his wife stepped up and gave him a poke in the arm.

Hal lost his smirk and raised his beer bottle in the direction of the creek. "Here's to the collection of gators lookin' back at us from the other side. And I can pretty much guarantee, there's a whole slew of em on this side, just beyond the bank, lookin' back at 'em."

Julie took a step back. The riverbank couldn't be more than three or four yards away. Alligators were supposed to be quick. They could outrun a man, right? What did people say? Run serpentine instead of in a straight line. They can't turn fast.

She checked her watch. It was 9:45. She needed to get to bed so she could start out at the break of dawn. She said her goodbyes, even shook Hal's hand, and went to her cabin. The first thing she did was turn off her phone. Not even Mark would be able to reach her tonight.

Mark tried calling Julie several times from the hospital. All of his calls went to voicemail. While Greg was in the intensive care unit with Lakisha, Mark stayed in the emergency waiting room on one of those uncomfortable chairs. He scowled at the row of plastic seating. Sick people shouldn't have to sit in discomfort while waiting to be seen. Heck, *well* people shouldn't have to sit there either.

He was the only one in the waiting room. At this hour, people were finishing dinner or getting ready for bed. Thursday night was quiet in Springfield. Less traffic than on weekend nights, thus fewer accidents. Nor was this a holiday when all kinds of illnesses and injuries kept hospital emergency rooms busy.

He checked his phone to see if Julie might have responded to his messages. Nothing. So far, all he knew was Lakisha suffered a serious cramping episode and was rushed to the hospital. He left such a message on Julie's phone and added an agitated, "Please call me," at the end.

A flood of guilt washed over him. He shouldn't have dragged Greg to the movies. The guy needed to be home with his wife. If they hadn't turned off their phones in the theater, maybe Greg would have gotten the call a lot sooner. Now, all Mark could do was wait. And pray.

He leaned forward and folded his hands. But, what to say? He had no idea what was going on behind those double doors. He had to rely on the usual spiel, ask God to guide the doctors' hands, to give them wisdom, and to help Greg through the ordeal. *And please save Lakisha and the baby.* He'd said similar prayers for people he barely knew. This time it was personal. Greg was his best friend. Lakisha was Julie's best friend. They were like family, maybe even closer than family, if that were possible.

Funny how his daily monologues suddenly changed into heartfelt pleas for help. He felt like those students who had little time for God until a school shooting happened under their noses. Then they gathered around a flagpole, linked arms and prayed to the God they'd been ignoring for most of their young lives. Or how about those busy individuals who rarely saw the inside of a church, but dropped to their knees at a candlelight vigil when heartbreak hit close to home?

Mark couldn't fault them, because he himself had become lax in his prayer life. Why did it take a horrible tragedy for him and most other people to recognize a need for God's intervention? He couldn't recall the last time he prayed with intense passion, except for...

Suddenly he was 12 years old again, and his mother was in the hospital, fighting for her life. Back then, he had no trouble talking to God from the depths of his heart. He'd poured out his anguish on the floor of the waiting room. He'd sent up a child's heartfelt plea for God to spare his mother. He didn't get the answer he was hoping for. His mother died that very night.

Several weeks had passed before he read the note his mother left him. In it, she'd said she was ready to go, that she'd be waiting for him and his father to join her one day in heaven.

You need to let go, too, my son, she'd written. *God has great plans for you. Stay true to your faith and choose a righteous path to follow. I'll be watching.*

Even then, he'd felt lost, like God hadn't heard his prayer, or maybe hadn't cared. Tears stung his eyes. His mother's note had kept him believing, and with his father's guidance, he pursued a career in Christian service. Yet, in the back of his mind, an inkling of doubt remained. Why didn't God let his mother live? It was a bitter lesson that God might not answer his prayers to his liking. There were times when the Almighty's plan differed from his. Numerous times. He could only hope for a favorable answer tonight.

Grateful to be alone in the lobby, he located a box of tissues on a side table, mopped the flood from his cheeks, and resumed his prayer, when Greg came through the double doors. The poor guy didn't have to say a word. The dire expression on his face said it all.

24

JULIE

Once again, Julie left the window open. She drifted off with wood-ash residue from the campfire seeping through the screen. It was the closest she'd probably ever get to sleeping outdoors. She'd never gone camping as a youth, so she welcomed the rugged ambiance of being a small part of nature. Perhaps Marjorie enjoyed a similar outdoor wilderness experience when she spent her first night in the dilapidated house with its broken windows and missing boards.

Like Julie's first night in the cabin, the chirping of crickets and the rasp of tree frogs continued their persistent melody, punctuated now and then by the hoot of an owl perched somewhere high in the branches of a nearby oak.

She didn't know when she'd passed from awareness of the natural setting to slumbering peace. When she awakened, the morning light was turning the darkness to the gray of dawn. She sprawled on top of her bed, stretched her arms and legs, and took a couple of deep breaths. Her flight home was scheduled for 3:15, which meant she'd have to get to the airport before 2:00. She could grab a quick breakfast, visit Marjorie's gravesite, and head to the University of Florida in Gainesville to complete her research. She could spend a couple of hours there and still have time for lunch at the airport before boarding her flight.

Satisfied with her plan, she headed for the shower. There

was plenty of time. She stood under the spray and let the hot water ripple down her back. She thought about Marjorie having to shower under rainwater running off the metal roof and stumbling along a muddy path to the outhouse in the middle of the night.

The woman often left Norton's cozy hotel suite and a comfortable home in the north in order to... what? Live in near poverty amongst a people who shunned her in the beginning and later came to be some of her best friends?

But what if Marjorie didn't leave the comforts of home to embark on such an adventure? What if she hadn't chosen to live in the wild for more than 20 years? What if Max Perkins hadn't encouraged her to put those impressions in a book? Where would her legacy be?

Conviction swept over Julie along with the cascade from the showerhead. When she went to Patmos to find Yanno, didn't she hobnob with the locals, try to win their trust, and even pretend she wasn't a reporter? And wasn't her motive strictly for the story?

Her morning shower began to pelt her with guilt. She turned off the tap, toweled off, and hurried into the main room to throw on some clothes. She grabbed a skirt and top, suitable for the plane ride, and put on her walking shoes.

She left a tip for the maid on the kitchen counter. Since she'd paid for the cabin in advance with a credit card, she only needed to toss her luggage in the car and take off.

She turned the key in the ignition and glanced at the clock on the dash. It was 9:30. She'd wasted so much time in the shower, she'd cut her time nearly in half. She still needed to visit Marjorie's gravesite before heading to Gainesville. Afterward, she'd have to make a two-hour drive to the airport, ditch the rental car, and check in at the gate. She'd badly miscalculated her schedule. Is this what life in the forest did to people? Did such an environment mess with the concept of time?

Breakfast was out. Thankfully, she'd packed a couple of power bars in her bag along with some bottled water, enough to keep her going until she could grab something at the airport. She threw the car into drive and took off toward the Antioch Cemetery.

The GPS route took her across Highway 301 to a long, paved road that seemed to go nowhere, then to a dirt lane peppered with loose sand and gravel. The car's wheels kicked up a dust storm behind her. The vegetation on either side of the road—mostly scrub pines and palmetto bushes—grew denser as she continued. Fingers of sunlight squeezed through the branches and dropped silver pellets on the road ahead. Julie frowned. Had she entered the wrong location? Nothing looked right. Why would an icon of literature be buried out here in the boondocks, away from civilization?

She was about to give up and turn the car around, when up ahead she spotted a small white sign on the side of the road. As she drew closer, the words came into view, *Antioch Cemetery*, and an arrow pointing to the right. Another half-mile and the semblance of a cemetery came up on the left behind a chain-link fence with a solitary gate.

Julie parked on the grassy soft shoulder, looked up and down the road, and swallowed. She was alone in a backwoods wasteland, and she was about to enter a deserted cemetery. She left the car and crossed the street. Taking in a deep breath, she lifted the chain to release the gate and stepped inside. Her internet search had provided basic directions to the actual gravesite. She checked her notes—*Go to the small utility building.* Okay, easy enough. The structure stood out like a sore thumb amidst the nondescript tombstones. *Turn left, go 45 paces west.* Did they mean men's paces or women's paces? She sighed her frustration.

She walked slowly between the rows of graves, ignored the upright monuments, and concentrated her attention on the flat slabs of concrete. Then she spotted them. Norton and Marjorie, side-by-side in eternal peace.

She glanced around the graveyard at the scrub trees in their own last stages of life, some of them consumed by shrouds of Spanish moss. The graveyard, with its meager spread of unkempt lawn interspersed with patches of sand, made a bleak setting for the grave of one of America's most revered authors. All around headstones, markers, and a few monuments had turned black with mold. Tufts of dying grass rimmed their edges, and there was no sign of cut flowers anywhere, neither living or plastic. The air was thick, only the sound of crickets penetrated the stillness. A distressing sense of loss swept over her.

Sighing, she turned her attention to the two slabs. One, the grave of Marjorie's *Beloved Husband, Norton Sanford Baskin, 1901-1997,* and the other, the final resting place of a woman who'd lived like a vagabond, moving from one location to another and ultimately finding her resting place in the Florida wilderness.

She drew closer to Marjorie's grave, easily identified by the mementos someone had placed on the top. There was a tiny plastic deer, two small stones, a few pens and pencils, and to Julie's chagrin, a miniature bottle of Jim Beam. Marjorie's fans had honored the woman with remnants of her life's loves. Julie snickered softly, yet a certain sadness consumed her. She stared at the words etched into the slab, *Marjorie Kinnan Rawlings, 1896-1953, wife of Norton Baskin,* and, farther down, *Through her writing she endeared herself to the people of the world.*

A life cut short. How much more of a treasure would Marjorie have left the world if she'd lived a few more decades? Few writers could describe God's creation as prolifically as Marjorie had. Using her five senses, she'd gathered the riches of Florida's natural environment and swept a world of nature onto the page. With her typewriter, she'd groomed those images into stories that lived on long after she died. Marjorie left her readers more than a taste of central Florida's wealth. She left them a banquet.

A sob rose to Julie's throat. Tears flooded into her eyes. Here, in an obscure graveyard, a few miles from Marjorie's beloved Cross Creek, hidden away in a remote part of the forest, slept a woman who should have been entombed in a magnificent sepulcher on the grounds of the property where she'd lived for 25 years. Didn't Marjorie deserve more than this? Or was it her final wish to be tucked away out of the public eye, a glaring reflection of the hermitic way she lived her life?

Though she was pressed for time, in the stillness of the burial ground, as bright sunlight bathed the slab over Marjorie's grave, Julie allowed herself several minutes of heartfelt weeping. When she started this project she never suspected how profoundly she'd be affected by someone whose books she'd read. The truth was, Rawlings had become more to Julie than a writer to be admired.

Over the past two days she'd come to know the real

Marjorie, the woman who chose to stray from her comfortable, elite lifestyle to mingle with a people who existed on what they could scrape up from the dregs of the forest. Ultimately, Marjorie learned everything she could from them, and then she wrote about this rare and fascinating culture existing a short distance from her readers' mundane world.

Julie pulled herself away from the gravesite, wiped the tears from her face, and left through the gate. She slid inside her car and sat still for a few seconds. Then, she took one last look at the rundown cemetery, turned the key in the ignition, and drove away.

During the drive to Gainesville, Julie continued to ponder the events of the last couple of days and her unexpected emotional upheaval. When she'd first started out on this journey, she'd approached the assignment like she always did while working for the newspaper. Get the facts, seek out some interesting interviews, sort through the materials, and *Bam!* Write a story to impress her editor and hopefully anyone else who reads it.

But this was different. From the moment she stepped foot on the Cross Creek property, Julie had entered another world. What she knew from her career no longer existed. She'd been caught up not only in Marjorie's work but in her life. And wasn't that the goal? Didn't magazine writing differ from newspaper reporting? For these travel pieces, wasn't she supposed to tell all she could about people along with describing where they lived?

Somehow this work had disrupted her life. All along, Marjorie had been speaking to her, not only through her writings but through Lucy, through Aunt Emma, through nature itself. Overnight, Julie's concept of her own past had started to change and a little bit of Marjorie's fortitude had seeped into her spirit. Until this trip, she'd been allowing the attack in the past to stifle her future. Now she felt ready to fight back.

She still needed to make one more stop before catching her flight out of Jacksonville—The University of Florida. The drive went faster than she had expected. She located the school's libraries behind a block-long brick wall with George A. Smathers' name emblazoned there. After parking her car, she walked across the street to the library entrance and punched in the phone number to the literary archivist, a Mr. Fred Thomas.

Minutes later, a tall, thin man looking surprisingly like Gregory Peck approached her. He could have walked onto the film set of *The Yearling,* and no one would have questioned his presence there. Fred's welcoming smile put her at ease. Vertical lines creased his cheeks, and his sky-blue eyes sparkled like diamonds. He obviously enjoyed ushering visitors into the coffers.

Together they walked into the library, and Fred, as he asked her to call him, immediately fell into an animated spiel about Marjorie's collection. Julie listened intently and filed some of the details in the back of her mind. There was no telling what gems might come from this learned man. He'd told her he'd been in charge of the archives for 12 years. Surely, he had acquired a wealth of information.

"In addition to Marjorie's published writings and biographies about her, the archives also hold a massive collection of her unpublished works and a great deal of her correspondence," Fred told her.

"I can't wait to take a look," Julie said. Then, she filled him in on the research she'd been doing for the past two weeks. "I've read through Marjorie's letters to Norton Baskin and the correspondence with her editor, Max Perkins," she said. "But, apparently many more documents exist."

"Oh, yes, many more," Fred said with a flair. "For example, we also have letters Norton wrote to her. You'll want to take a look at them. And of course, there's fan mail from her readers—housewives, servicemen, college students, even ministers. She didn't throw anything away. Kept every letter and postcard. Marjorie loved her fans, and they loved her."

The department was on the second floor of the building, behind a set of glass doors with a security lock. Fred pushed the buzzer, and a female college student released the lock from behind her desk in the center of a massive room, its four walls lined with a colorful array of books in all sizes, plus glassed-in shelves guarding literary artifacts of noteworthy value.

A couple of side tables held large computer screens available for research projects, and several mahogany tables ran the length of the room down the center. Fred directed Julie to one of those tables. He paused there and recited the rules.

"No water bottle, no food, no purse, no briefcase," he said, his tone serious. "And no pens."

"No pens? How can I take notes?"

Fred walked to the counter and drew a yellow No. 2 pencil from dozens in a ceramic jar. He held it in front of Julie. "With this," he said. "Pens leak."

Of course, this was a fragile collection. Until now, she'd assumed she could handle her research like every other story she'd worked on for the newspaper. As a reporter she was able to delve into police reports and public records with few restrictions. Obviously, something far more delicate was stored here.

Fred walked to a rolling stand with several items arranged in a row on the top shelf.

"After we talked on the phone, I pulled these out for you, so they'd be ready when you arrived," he said, and his smile came back. "I suggest you start with this." He rested his hand on a large box. "You said you wanted to see letters. Well, here they are. We only require that you keep the folders in the order in which you find them and the letters exactly the way they've been placed inside each folder."

She nodded in agreement. Hopefully, she could get through enough of this collection before she had to leave for the airport. Obediently, she placed her belongings in a locker and pocketed the key. She was grateful to be able to keep a notebook with her. Other than that, it was only the yellow No. 2 pencil. Nothing more.

Fred showed her each of the binders on the metal shelf and insisted she take only one binder at a time to the table. Other than the box of letters, a folder containing Marjorie's biographical writings and early drafts caught Julie's attention.

With just two hours remaining, Julie needed to get right to work. She thanked Fred, and he left the room.

Julie dove into the large box of letters first. Such a treasure trove might open more doors of understanding. What did Marjorie's readers think about her work? They were complete strangers, yet she'd let them into her life through her writing. Yet there was much more to her than most people could ever imagine. A wave of smugness took over. Julie already had learned volumes more about this complex and somewhat evasive author who locked herself away in the solitude of a Florida wilderness, a recluse who came out only when she wanted to and never under pressure from anyone else.

As Julie flipped through the letters inside the different files, more enlightenment surfaced. Marjorie's audience spanned all ages and genders and personalities, all levels of intellectual prowess, from young children to college professors, from the descendants of backwoods people to wealthy entrepreneurs in the big cities. *The Yearling* was translated into 29 different languages. By now, nearly everyone in the world had heard of Marjorie Kinnan Rawlings.

Julie carefully turned each fragile piece of correspondence. A 16-year-old girl who was suffering with tuberculosis wrote to Marjorie from a private rest home. A merchant mariner told her he spent most of his off-duty time reading her works and had finished *The Yearling* in three days. An Army corporal based in San Francisco complimented her "word painted pictures of wilds." A young officer candidate in a training squadron wrote that he read *Cross Creek* while traveling to school in Miami Beach. *"It helped a boy from the Northwest to really appreciate Florida,"* he wrote. A zoologist praised her accuracy of nature and called *The Yearling "a literary treasure."* And a clergyman confessed he'd based an entire Sunday sermon on a quote from *Cross Creek:* "Sift each of us through *the great sieve of circumstance and you have a residue, great or small as the case may be, that is the man or the woman."*

Julie sifted through the slips of paper, careful not to crease or tear any of the delicate treasures. At length, she raised her head from the collection and checked her watch. She'd spent a full 90 minutes on the one box and had hardly made a dent. With only another half-hour remaining before she needed to leave, she reluctantly put away the box of correspondence and turned her attention to the binder containing Marjorie's personal notations.

The bound volume offered a wealth of unpublished gems typed on fading paper—Marjorie's inner musings scrawled in pencil on long yellow sheets and afterthoughts scribbled on tiny scraps of parchment, plus early drafts of some of her famous works, all of them encased in sheer protective sleeves. While Marjorie's books revealed the curiosity and the fascination and the drive of this famed writer, here, in this collection, Julie had found her soul.

"I find I have been in acute need of solitude," Marjorie wrote, and in a later document, *"Among the small things of tree and grass, life is not always idyllic."*

Nevertheless, Marjorie's solitude and idyllic lifestyle was interrupted briefly when one of her best friends, Zelma Cason, sued her for $100,000 for what she claimed were unflattering descriptions of her in *Cross Creek*. Word later came out that Zelma had tried to get other people Marjorie had mentioned in her book to submit their own lawsuits. Instead, they all sided with Marjorie at the trial.

Greatly troubled by the lawsuit, Marjorie mentioned it many times. Julie read the notations with sadness. It seemed people who gain fame and fortune are often at the mercy of the jealous and the greedy. She couldn't help but think something stronger than hurt feelings drove Zelma Cason to attack her friend. Julie had seen similar battles during her job as a newspaper reporter. She'd written plenty of stories about heirs grappling for their father's fortune and cut-throat litigation between former business partners. Sometimes, a hidden evil surfaces in the midst of those conflicts and people show their true sides under the guise of demanding fairness. Underneath it all, as Julie quickly had learned, lay greed and jealousy and self-aggrandizement. Never having met Zelma

Cason, she couldn't say one way or the other what drove the woman to sue one of her dearest friends. But she must have felt less than vindicated when she received only one dollar from the suit.

Julie shook it off and continued to dig through Marjorie's unpublished files. At times, Marjorie spilled her thoughts randomly on the pages. She acknowledged her quick temper, even apologized for it. She also admitted to the frustrations of trying to get published. Several of her short stories, one after the other, were rejected, and though she earned some success working for newspapers and magazines, it wasn't until she met Max Perkins that her work began to soar.

Julie continued through the binder and discovered truths of a different nature. Though Marjorie was busy writing stories and articles, she still made time to support the nation's war effort. She sold war bonds and volunteered as an airplane spotter while at her Crescent Beach home on the Atlantic.

Though she plunged into those unpaid positions with fervor, she still made time to write multiple letters to military personnel, obviously one of her favorite pastimes from the amount of mail she received. In a yellowed fragment of notepaper, she humbly stated, *"My only contribution of any value was a voluminous correspondence with men in the Service."*

In another place she boasted, *"Lonely soldiers and sailors wrote me from all over the world, literally from Greenland's icy mountains to Africa's tropic shore."*

Though Marjorie's personal life revealed a mix of flare-ups, mistakes, excessive drinking, and a self-centered obsession with her work, another side of her also came through in this pile of letters, not only in her own writings but in the writings of other people who appreciated her work and developed a deep love and respect for her. Julie shook her head in wonderment. To be adored by so many people throughout the world had to be mind-boggling. Yet despite Marjorie's mounting popularity, she often admitted her need to disappear within the shadows of the forest.

While living with Norton at his hotel in St. Augustine, she wrote, *"Most of the time I escaped to Cross Creek from the too public life."*

Too public life? Didn't Julie do the same? When circumstances got overwhelming, didn't she flee from people, even those who cared about her? Didn't she block their phone calls? Didn't she barricade herself in her apartment, crawl into a self-made refuge that was more of a prison than a place of comfort? Marjorie got to run off to The Creek, but where could Julie go to escape? And truthfully, why should she? No one was threatening her anymore.

She checked her watch again. It was time to go.

She had the receptionist contact Fred and tell him she needed to leave. Carefully, she put everything back the way she'd found it. She retrieved her belongings from the locker and was ready when Fred appeared.

"Did you find what you needed?"

Julie shrugged. "I could have spent more time here, but I believe I have enough for my project."

He ushered her out of the building. Julie hurried to the parking lot. Depending on traffic, she expected to be at the airport an hour before takeoff.

During the drive, she thought again about Mark and Lakisha and how she cut them off whenever she got busy or distracted, or worse yet, when she was dealing with personal issues. At those times, she should have been letting her friends in, not blocking them out.

She suddenly realized her phone hadn't rung for two days. Like always when she got busy with a story, she'd turned it off.

At the next traffic light, she pulled her phone from her bag and turned it on. There were multiple calls and texts from Mark. A cold chill went through her. Something had happened. Mark rarely persisted after a couple of calls. Frowning, she cued in his last text.

"Lakisha was rushed to the hospital. It doesn't look good. Call me."

25

MARK

Mark had given up trying to reach Julie. He was fuming. What kind of marriage were they going to have if she kept cutting him out of her life? They needed to find common ground before they walked down the aisle. Julie's best friend was in the hospital, and he couldn't tell her about it. Is this what he could expect months and even years down the road?

For now he was concerned about Greg and Lakisha. The news wasn't good last night. The doctor told Greg there was a chance Lakisha might lose the baby. They put her on full bed rest. She couldn't even get up to use the bathroom unassisted. Poor Greg looked like he'd been run over by a train. He barely got the doctor's report out of his mouth when he broke down in sobs. Mark did all he could to comfort him, but what should a person say at a time like this? From his own experience with his mother, he knew mere words were not enough. Stay close, let the hurting one feel your presence, and for the love of all that is holy, don't spout off any overused platitudes.

Against his better judgment, he'd left the hospital around midnight, went home and tried to sleep. This morning, he phoned Greg and learned there'd been no change, so he went to work. He should have called in sick. Melanie certainly would understand. Instead he'd gone to the lecture hall, conducted two sessions with one more to go before he could leave for the hospital. He needed to get out of there before one of his students corralled him for extra guidance.

Please God, don't let Fiona start her stuff. He was going to have to move fast if he wanted to avoid her. Greg needed him. The memory of his friend standing in the emergency waiting room, his face drawn, his eyes red from crying, sent Mark scrambling out the back door and sprinting to his car.

When he got to the hospital, Greg was sitting in the waiting area.

"I need another change of clothes," he said, holding out his house keys. His voice cracked with every word.

"Of course." Mark took the keys and started for the door, then hesitated. "How is she?"

Tears rose to Greg's already redlined eyes. "Still no change," he said. "They want to keep her on bed rest with her feet elevated, and they've put a monitor on her. She spotted a little through the night, but she hasn't dilated yet. The baby hasn't budged." He shook his head despondently. "This is all new to me, Mark. I have no siblings, never even been around a pregnant woman. I don't know how to help my wife."

Mark placed a hand on his friend's shoulder and drew him close. "I'm in the same boat, Greg. We both led the life of an only child. Now we're having to step beyond that place." He stroked Greg's back. "I haven't stopped praying. Even while I was lecturing my students, I inserted little thought prayers. I had to stand at that miserable podium when I wanted to be here, with you."

Greg bowed his head. "Thanks, buddy."

Mark held him tight. "I'm yours for the rest of the day. Whatever you need."

Greg nodded and backed away. "I'm not gonna leave her

side. Lakisha and our baby mean everything to me. My life is nothing without them."

"I know." Mark backed away. He left his friend standing there looking like a lost sheep and hurried to Greg's house to get him a change of clothes. He filled a duffel bag and made the trip back to the hospital in less than an hour.

As he was walking into the lobby, his cell phone went off. He grabbed it. Finally. It was Julie.

Her voice was frantic. "Mark, oh Mark, how's Lakisha? Is she okay? What happened?"

He told her the little bit he already knew. A little amniotic fluid had leaked from the protective sac around the baby. For a while, Lakisha suffered cramps, but they had subsided, and she was now resting in a private room. For the time being, only immediate family members were allowed to visit.

"I've been spending every free hour in the waiting room. Where are you, Julie? Lakisha needs you."

"I'm almost at the Jacksonville airport. I'm so sorry I missed your calls. I turned off my cell phone, and I was so busy I forgot to turn it back on again. I read your text message a few minutes ago. I pulled off the road to call you, but I'll have to get moving if I want to make my flight. I need to turn in this rental car and get to the gate." Her voice shook like she was about to panic. "I'm sorry I've been so self-absorbed, so insensitive that I've cut you out of my life. I'm going to try and do better. Please, don't give up on me."

"Give up on you? Never. I love you, Julie. There's nothing you can do to change the way I feel about you."

"I love you too, Mark."

"Be safe."

They hung up. Mark stared at his dead phone for a minute.

It was obvious Julie was struggling with emotions he might never understand. How could he help her? Like Greg couldn't face life without Lakisha, he couldn't imagine going another day without Julie. She meant everything to him.

As he headed for the waiting area in the maternity section, his personal issues faded into oblivion, and his concern for Greg and Lakisha took over again. He hadn't been allowed inside the room yet. His friend had come out every hour to give updates. Greg had stayed there for a while, just sat and talked with Mark, like he needed to tap into his best friend for strength to keep going.

He'd even said as much. "I don't know what I'd do if I didn't have a friend like you, Mark."

But what if Lakisha lost the baby? And worse, what if she were to die? What kind of help could he be to Greg then? The loss of his mother had left some kind of a curse on him. Afterward, he'd avoided situations when people were dying. Even when his uncle passed away, he made an excuse why he couldn't go to the funeral. The same thing happened when his aunt died six months later. How could he be strong for Greg when he himself was crumbling?

He texted Greg, saying he'd returned with his duffel bag. Moments later, Greg came into the waiting room. Mark set the bag on the floor, and the two of them sat together.

"I'm trying to get the nurse to let you come in and visit Lakisha," he said.

The thought of seeing someone on the brink of death sent cold shivers down his spine. "It's okay, Greg. I'm good just sitting here. When you're ready, I'll run out and get you some dinner."

Greg chuckled. "Great, Mark. If not for you, I'd forget to feed myself."

"It's the least I can do. So, tell me, how's she doing?"

Greg gave him another update. "Lakisha smiled at me for the first time since they brought her in. That's a good sign, isn't it?"

"Sounds like it."

"I have to believe they're gonna make it. I have to—" Greg stopped short, his eyes on the open doorway.

Mark followed his gaze and turned around, shocked to see Greg's parents standing there. The two of them seemed to have aged a little since the wedding. It was the last time he'd seen them. Both of them had lost a few pounds. Their frail bodies bent slightly forward, the veins on their hands appeared more prominent, their shoulders were hunched making them look shorter and less intimidating. Howard Davis' bald spot had eased back a little on the top of his head, and Mildred's yellow curls had strands of gray woven through them.

Greg slowly rose and faced them. An uncomfortable silence fell on the room as each of them waited for the other to speak. With awkward shuffling, the old couple moved closer to Greg. His father placed both hands on his shoulders. His mother started to weep.

Greg appeared dumbfounded. "I–I didn't think you'd come."

His father stuck out his jaw and gazed into his eyes. "You called us, Son. You needed us. Did you think we'd turn away from you in your time of need?"

Mildred mopped her face with a handkerchief. She blew her nose and continued to cry.

Howard shook his head. "I'm sorry, Son. How is Lakisha? And the baby?"

Mark stood up to acknowledge their presence. He kept

his eyes on Greg. Tears were running down his friend's face.

"She's doing a little better, but she's not out of the woods yet." Greg said, then fell into his father's arms. "Oh, Pop. I don't know what I'll do if I lose her."

The older man stroked his son's back. "Now, Gregory, don't you give up. Your mama and I have been praying. She checked with the midwife who lives down the road from us, and she said this kind of thing happens all the time. It's merely a little bump in the road."

Mildred spoke up then. "What your father said is true, Gregory. The midwife knows everything about pregnancy and childbirth. I believe your wife and baby are going to be just fine."

Greg reached out and took his mother's hand. "I sure hope you're right, Mom."

"Can we see her?" Mildred asked, her voice so soft it was almost inaudible.

Greg looked his mother in the eye. "You want to see Lakisha?"

Mildred nodded and let out another gusher of tears. "We have so much to say to her. I need to apologize for being such a terrible mother-in-law. And now, with the baby—"

"Wait a minute." Greg backed away from them. "Are you telling me you're ready to accept my marriage?"

Howard nodded. "You can thank the midwife for that too. She must have lectured us for an hour about what's important—family and supporting each other through good times and bad times. I'm afraid we failed you, Son. We got so caught up in our own ideas of what's moral and right, we forgot we needed to take care of each other. It's like the midwife said—our family is what really matters."

Greg succumbed to another onset of sobbing so intense he crumbled into a chair. There, with his father and mother comforting him, he released three long years of pain.

Mark rose and quietly slipped from the room. Greg needed to be alone with his parents. They were satisfying a need even Mark couldn't fill. He burst through the outside door and inhaled deeply of the fresh air, now sweetened by a midday rain. He walked around the side of the hospital and picked up a paved trail circling the grounds. His thoughts moved from Greg's problem to his own. Julie was coming home, and they obviously had a lot to talk about.

26

JULIE

After making it through security, Julie stopped at a cafe in the concourse and bought a sandwich. She took it to the gate to eat it there. The overhead board indicated her flight was running an hour late. Though she was anxious to get home and see Lakisha, she was stuck in the Jacksonville airport. There was nothing she could do about it.

She chose a quite spot away from the other passengers, took a couple bites out of the sandwich and stuffed the rest back in the bag. She'd lost her appetite.

She needed to talk to someone. But who? Someone who could tell her what was happening with her best friend. Julie knew little about pregnancy and childbirth. She'd never been pregnant, and she generally shied away from women who were, except for Lakisha of course. She thought about Rita. Her sister often talked about having her own family one day. Now she was in nursing college. Julie checked her watch—2:55 on a Friday. Rita might be on her way home from school by now.

She punched the button for Rita's number. Her sister picked up on the second ring.

"Julie! So great to hear from you. What's up, girl?"

Bypassing all the amenities, Julie plunged right into her concerns about Lakisha. "Help me understand what's happening, Rita. Surely, some of your studies have addressed child bearing."

"Wow, this is intense. Hold on a minute. I'll call up some of my notes on my computer."

"You're home?"

"Yeah, I had a half-day schedule today. Friday, you know."

Except for Rita's steady breathing, the airwaves were silent. Julie could picture her sister bent over her monitor, her hands flying over the keyboard, her dark eyes scanning the information, her fingers clicking to another image, and then another.

"Okay," Rita said, at last. "Here's what I gathered from last year's classes. My notes say cramping early in pregnancy is normal because everything is changing. How far along is Lakisha?"

"Six months."

"Hmmm. She's still in her second trimester. Cramping usually doesn't happen at this stage, unless she's having twins."

"No one has mentioned twins. She lost a little amniotic fluid."

"Oooh, not good."

Julie's pulse began to race. "Please, Rita."

"Sorry. Listen, if Lakisha happened to be in her third trimester, I'd say it was Braxton Hicks. But the sixth month is too early for them."

"Braxton Hicks?" The term sounded dreadful. "What on earth are they?"

Rita let out a little giggle. "Just false labor. Nothing to be concerned about."

"I see. So, what about Lakisha? What's happening to her?"

"Well, I don't know enough. Are they just cramps or actual contractions?"

"I don't know."

"Is she nauseous or vomiting?"

"I don't know. I'm not there, Rita. I'm in an airport trying to get home." Her voice had gone up an octave. She was losing control.

"You're gonna have to settle down, Julie. You can't do anything where you are now, but once you get home, take a cab to the hospital. Don't drive. You're not in any condition to drive. You might end up being a patient yourself."

"I can handle it," Julie said, though she wasn't sure.

"Why don't you relax, go and see your friend, and call me when you know more."

Julie breathed a long sigh. "Alright, Rita. Thanks for what you told me so far."

"Julie."

"What?"

"Is there something else going on?"

"What makes you ask?"

"I can hear it in your voice. Sister's intuition, I guess."

Why not tell her everything? Rita was always there for her, through all the trauma and for months after. She was the only one who believed Julie's story. She also was the one who informed Julie when her attacker was caught assaulting another teenage girl, and she'd sent her the newspaper clippings of the trial. A pillar of the church, people had called him. He almost got away with a terrible crime. Thank God, he'd been caught. The guy could rot in prison, for all she cared.

"Mark and I have postponed the wedding," she said, matter-of-fact like.

"Aw, I'm so sorry. Why on earth did you postpone it?"

"Mark sensed I was on overload."

"And you?"

"I'm not sure I can handle what it takes to be a wife and mother."

"Are you still having nightmares?"

"Sometimes." She began to feel like she was in Doctor Balser's office spilling out her psychological problems.

"I did a little research," Rita said, sounding an awful lot like their mother. "I know what's going on with you, Julie. Do you want me to tell you what I found?"

She straightened her shoulders, prepared for whatever might come. "Yes, tell me. So far, I've been able to forgive the people who turned their backs on me. Other than that, I still feel lost and alone."

"Okay. Let me ask you a few questions, first."

"The airplane's not even here yet. I have all the time in the world."

"Aside from nightmares, are there times when you re-experience the trauma of the attack, like you're reliving it?"

"I try not to, but sometimes it happens unexpectedly. Something I see or a comment someone makes reminds me, and it's like a huge wave of negative memories crashes over me. I can't function afterward, not until I put it away and get my mind on something else."

"Okay, question number two. Are you an emotional ping-pong ball? Up one minute, down the next? Easily provoked, maybe even cruel at times?"

Julie couldn't deny the truth. She sometimes lashed out at innocent people who meant her no harm. Like Hal, the guy at the campfire last night. Fortunately, she'd caught herself before their little back-and-forth turned into a major blowout.

"I think you know the answer without me saying anything," Julie said. "Sometimes I can't control my mouth. I get angry and anything can come out."

"True," Rita said. "But after the incident, another side of

you showed up. A lonely side. You disappeared in your bed-room and refused to speak to anyone. Not even me. You hid yourself away to suffer alone, and you didn't let any of us in. Think about it, Julie. Do you still do that?"

"Do what?" Heat rushed to her cheeks. She pinched her lips shut.

"You know what I'm talking about." Rita's voice became firm. "Do you still hide yourself away whenever you're over-whelmed? Do you shut out people who love you? Do you turn off your phone, lock your door, and crawl into yourself?"

Tears oozed from Julie's eyes. She brushed them away. "I do," she said, meekly. "But I don't know how to stop."

"One more question," Rita said. "Get ready for this one."

Julie breathed a long sigh. "Go ahead. Hit me with it. I can't feel much worse than I already do."

"Sorry, Julie, but I'm trying to help."

"I know. So, what's your last question?"

"Have you become emotionally numb toward members of the opposite sex? Are you afraid of marriage and intimacy?"

She blushed. How foolish. This was her sister she was talking to. She could say anything to Rita. "Well, I have to admit, I cringe at the thought of being intimate with anyone. Including Mark."

She brushed another tear from her cheek. "So, what's your diagnosis?" She truly did want to know what her sister was driving at.

"It's simple, and I'd be surprised if your therapist hasn't picked up on it."

"What? Do you think I'm mentally ill or something?"

"Not exactly. I believe you're suffering from PTSD."

"What?"

"Post Traumatic Stress Disorder."

"I know what PTSD stands for. Why do you think I have it? Isn't it something combat soldiers experience?"

"Sure it is, but PTSD also can affect people who go through other traumatic events. The loss of a child. A bad traffic accident. Even divorce. And, yes, women who've been molested. My classes only dealt with the basics, but your therapist should be able to verify if you have it. He also should be able to help you overcome it."

Julie slumped back in her chair. "Heal?" she said. "How? I've been trying to heal for six years now."

"Oh, Julie. What you experienced no teenager should ever have to go through. All I know is, certain medications help with different aspects of PTSD, like insomnia and mood swings."

She lurched upright. "No way am I going to muddle up my brain with drugs. I need a clear mind to do my work."

"Hold on, Julie. I can almost see your face turning red."

Julie took a couple of deep breaths. "Okay, I'm settling down, but don't suggest drugs again. I will *not* use them. Anyway, my therapist is a family counselor. I don't think he's licensed to prescribe medication."

"He'll certainly have other methods, Julie, but you're the one who has to get better, and you're the only one who will know what's working and what isn't. Promise me you'll make an appointment the minute you get back home."

"I already have an appointment, but my first priority is to go and see Lakisha. I need to make sure she's okay and isn't about to lose her baby."

A flight announcement came over the public address system. "I've gotta go, Rita. They're calling my flight."

"Take care, Julie. I love you."

231

There it was again. Someone near and dear had declared love for her. First Mark. Then Rita. And she knew without a doubt Lakisha would say the same words the instant Julie walked into her hospital room. Even more importantly at this moment, she realized she also loved *them*. They meant the world to her, and somehow, she needed to find a way to let them know.

27

THE HOSPITAL

J ulie went straight to the hospital from the airport, but she didn't take Rita's advice and hail a cab. She drove her own car—carefully and methodically weaving through traffic at a reasonable speed, nearly holding her breath until she arrived at the hospital.

She found Mark in the maternity ward waiting room. They embraced briefly, then she backed away and stared into his eyes. The brilliant blue had faded slightly, as if a cloud had passed over them. Worry lines creased his brow. It was obvious Mark's heart was breaking for his best friend.

"I'm here now, Mark. I'm not leaving."

"I know."

"How's Lakisha?"

"The last I heard, she's stabilized, but they're concerned about the loss of amniotic fluid."

"It's too early for her to deliver. The baby won't make it."

"They said something about possible surgery to prevent dilation. If she can hold off for another few weeks, she'll be in the third trimester. Then the child will have a chance."

"Yeah, a *slim* chance." She shook her head. "Greg must be a bundle of nerves."

Mark gave a sad shrug. "He's holding up."

"Can we go in?"

Mark nodded. "They lifted the restriction. Lakisha's out

of danger for the time being. Greg said she's smiling and chattering away now. I haven't gone in yet, not sure I can handle it."

"We'll go in together, Mark."

He took Julie down a long corridor, almost to the end, and turned into room 134. Julie went through the door first and stopped dead in her tracks. She didn't try to hide her shock. Hovering at Lakisha's bedside were Greg's parents.

Her first impulse was to rush toward them and tear them away from her friend before they caused more trauma for the poor girl. She hesitated. Greg's father and mother were holding Lakisha's hands. Their heads were bowed. Indistinct whispers rose from their tiny huddle.

Greg sat in a corner chair, his head down, his hands folded on top of his knees. Was he praying, or was he simply exhausted? Probably a little of both. The good thing was, his parents had come, and they were praying with Lakisha.

Julie thought she'd shed all the tears inside her before coming to the hospital. She'd cried in the airport gate area. She'd wept silently during the flight, trusting her sunglasses to hide her red-rimmed eyes. And she'd cried off and on while driving to the hospital. Yet another flood of tears spilled from her eyes at the sight of Greg's parents making peace with their daughter-in-law.

These were good people. Though they'd taken a bitter stand against Greg's marriage, they had reconsidered their rejection. Why did it take a near tragedy to get some people to put aside their petty differences? The good thing was, they'd left the farm, probably in the middle of a workday, and had come to support their son and his wife.

She reached for Mark's hand and turned to look at his face.

His eyes were on Greg's parents. Tears were puddling in his eyes. A tenderness struck Julie's heart. Here was a man who wasn't afraid to cry in front of people, yet he had the strength of a warrior. He stuck by his convictions, never wavered, and he exuded a confidence she'd rarely seen in anyone else. Mark was a wonderful mix of strength and tenderness. And he was in love with her. How lucky could a woman get? And how dumb to have not appreciated him more.

Marjorie's letters to Norton showed her what it could be like to really connect with a man. Though Julie had read only one side of their correspondence, Marjorie not only exposed her own heart, she'd written enough praises about her husband to reveal his heart, too.

Now caught in an emotional upheaval, she vowed to do what Rita had suggested. She was going to stick with the weekly sessions with Doctor Balser. It was time to tear open the wound from her past and allow it to heal from the inside out. Her relationship with Mark depended on it.

Just then Howard Davis turned around. "Sorry," he said a little sheepishly. "We didn't know anyone had come in."

The Davises backed away from Lakisha and let her hands slip from theirs. "I guess you want to spend some time with our daughter-in-law," Howard said. Julie detected a surprising hint of pride in his voice. "Mildred and I will go out to the waiting room," he went on. "Take all the time you need."

The man's humility squashed any ill feelings Julie may have harbored against him. No longer did she view him as a stubborn old coot who'd made her best friend's life a living hell. He'd finally come around and had made peace with his daughter-in-law, Julie could no longer fault him for his past behavior.

Greg's mother smiled sweetly at Julie as she passed close to her on her way out the door. Julie nodded and smiled back, relieved to see the wall of bigotry had come down.

With the Davises out of the room, Mark went over to Greg and rested a hand on his shoulder. Julie rushed to Lakisha's bedside, grasped her hand, and leaned close to plant a kiss on her cheek.

"You gave us quite a scare, girl," she said, then studied her friend's face. Lakisha's coffee-and-cream complexion glowed with fresh confidence. Her dark eyes sparkled, and there was a hint of a smile on her lips.

Lakisha gave a little shrug. "Sorry to create such a fuss."

"No, I'm the one who should be sorry," Julie said. "I should have been here for you."

Her friend's smile broadened. "You're here now."

"Yes, a day late. What kind of a friend am I anyway?"

"Look. I'm glad you got to go on your trip. You couldn't help it if you were a thousand miles away when this happened. But what did you do the minute you got home? You came to see me. Now, *that's* friendship."

Julie stared with anxiety at her friend. Bright-eyed, exuberant, independently strong Lakisha lay weak and helpless on a hospital bed. Lakisha, who never caught anything worse than a cold, and here she was, flat on her back, like a bird with a broken wing, dependent on frail humans to figure out a way to save her baby.

"Tell me what I can do for you. Anything. Just name it."

Lakisha shook her head. "Just keep going as you were. Write your story. Fulfill your obligation to your editor. Show me what you can do with this new job of yours. I'm not going anywhere. I'm fine. The baby's fine."

"Don't be ridiculous, Lakisha. Nothing else matters to me at this moment except for you and your baby. If I have to, I'll call my editor and ask for more time."

Lakisha laughed softly. "Nice thought, Julie, but it looks like I'm gonna be stuck here for a while. I can't even use the bathroom without having to call the nurse's station. They even make my bed with me in it. Can you imagine? No privacy at all."

Her comments brought a giggle to Julie's throat.

Greg rose from his chair in the corner and approached the other side of the bed. Mark followed and stood beside Julie. Greg hovered close to his wife. Poor guy. He appeared to be in worse shape than Lakisha. His hair looked as if it hadn't seen a comb in two days, like he'd merely run his fingers through the tangles. A five o'clock shadow had taken over his jaw, and his clothes had a wrinkled, slept-in look. Despite his disheveled appearance, he managed a smile.

Julie eyed him with concern. "Are you taking care of yourself, Greg?"

He gave a half-hearted shrug. "I haven't left my angel's side for more than 10 minutes, and I don't intend to. See that chair over there?" He nodded toward the corner. "It opens up into a single bed. The cafeteria is down the hall. And, thanks to Mark, I have a clean change of clothes. I can stay here indefinitely."

"What about your job?" Julie said. "We're here. Your parents are here. Surely we can relieve you for a while."

"My boss has given me a leave of absence. If I had to go in, I'd be a mess. But you do as Lakisha says, Julie. You complete your work and stop by whenever you can. And you know, there's always the phone."

Here in a hospital room, with Lakisha confined to a bed and Greg shedding all other responsibilities to be with her, brought another stark reality to Julie. These two were more than a couple who chose to live together. Like it said in the Bible, when two people marry, they become one.

She glanced at Mark. He was staring at her, his blue eyes misting over. She loved a man who could let down his defenses and cry without shame. If she could give herself completely to him, they also could become one, like Greg and Lakisha were.

Lakisha didn't need her to give up everything else to sit constantly at her side. She had Greg. The guy looked like he was about to crumble, but in truth, he was a pillar of strength.

She acquiesced. "Okay, you two. I can do as you said. But I'll be ready to come to the rescue if needed. You have to call me about any changes."

"We will," Greg said. "I promise. But we want you two to keep going with your lives. Mark already has given up too much of his free time." He gazed at Mark with appreciation. "Listen, Buddy, you've gotta take care of your PowerPoint and do the best job ever. Go to Chicago, and don't cloud your mind with worries about us. Our doctor has everything under control. The nurses have been great. They don't leave Lakisha alone for very long. And her folks are coming down tonight from Boston. Only God knows how many of her sisters and brothers they'll drag in here with them. So, you see, we have a great support system."

"Okay, Greg. I'll try to keep things as normal as possible," Mark said. "And I'll make sure this woman stays on her assignment."

He placed a hand on Julie's shoulder. His touch gave her

a sense of security. The problem was, she wasn't at all like Lakisha, dependent on a relationship with a good man. She was more like Marjorie. Obsessively strong. Independent. Keeping the man who loved her at a safe distance.

But Julie wasn't always so aloof. Before the assault, she dreamed of being totally immersed in another person. After watching her grandparents' live and work together, she wanted to become someone's wife, someone's mother, and eventually someone's grandmother. One incident, one brutal attack, one moment in time, had changed her forever. Now she wanted to change back, but she didn't know how. It was more important than ever to get with Doctor Balser.

She leaned closer to Mark, pleading with him without words to be her strength. As though reading her mind, he slid his arm around her. What a relief to have someone protect her—but from what?

Reality struck. From herself.

They left quietly, so Greg and Lakisha could grab a few moments alone.

In the hallway, Mark stopped walking and faced Julie. "I think it's best if we skip our picnic tomorrow. You can get to work on your story, and I'll give my PowerPoint one last look. We can grab some lunch and come back here in the afternoon."

"Sounds like a good plan," she said. "I'm eager to start writing while everything is fresh."

"And, don't worry about Lakisha," he said. " I have a feeling everything's gonna be all right." She thought she heard a tremor in his voice. She dismissed it.

28

SATURDAY

Julie spent Saturday morning working on her magazine piece. For the travel portion, she gave a full-page description of her impressions of Cross Creek. Later, she planned to add other prime locations—the scenic drive past Marjorie's Crescent Beach home, and, of course, the gravesite. She began to weave in various particulars about Marjorie. Challenges came. There was so much people didn't know about the famed writer, she could have written an entire book about her. Or several books.

She sifted through her notes and selected what she thought to be the most interesting details. By lunchtime, she was ready for a break. She tapped in Mark's number. He was already on his way to her place. She quickly freshened up in the bathroom, then she grabbed her purse and hurried outside as he was pulling up to the curb.

He suggested fast food, and she didn't quibble about it. The sooner they could get to the hospital the better.

"Okay if we eat in the car?" she said.

Mark grinned at her. "I do it all the time. I just order something I can hold in one hand while I drive with the other."

His remark brought a laugh to her throat. "Sounds safe enough."

He pulled up to the drive-up window at McDonalds. Their order took longer than normal. Or did it? Was her anxiety getting the best of her?

They finally got back on the road. With Julie picking at her salad with a plastic fork and Mark taking huge bites out of a cheeseburger, they made it to the hospital in less than a half hour.

They found Greg sitting on his chair/bed next to a fold-up chair and with a chessboard on the table in between them. He looked up and beckoned Mark to the other seat. "Time for a quick game?" he said. He'd already set up the pieces on both sides of the board.

Mark didn't hesitate. He grabbed the other chair and hunched over the chessboard.

At that moment, Julie blended into the wall. She should have been used to disappearing whenever Mark and Greg got a chess game going, or during any other of their innumerable guys-only activities.

Lakisha sometimes griped about their disappearances. Julie didn't. To her, it was like taking a breath of fresh air. She even hoped he'd leave once in a while so she could get some alone time. It wasn't that she didn't like to be around Mark. But all the time? In that respect they were different from Greg and Lakisha. Those two walked around like their shirts were sewn together.

For now, she could spend a little girl-time with Lakisha. She started toward the bed and stopped short. Her friend was sound asleep.

"She's been resting a lot," Greg whispered and went back to his game.

Julie tiptoed up behind Mark and placed her hands on his shoulders. He turned his head and gave her a welcoming smile.

"They're hoping to send her home on Monday," Greg said. "She'll have to remain on bed rest, maybe for the duration of the pregnancy, or at least until she reaches the eight-month mark. If the baby comes then, she'll be viable."

Julie balked. "That's so far off. Lakisha will never want to be bedridden that long."

"She'll have to," Greg said, frowning. "Somehow, we'll have to keep her down."

His comment both pleased and troubled Julie. Pleased her, because Greg was including her in everything, like he expected her to help out. And troubled her, because it wasn't going to be an easy task. Lakisha would be wanting to get back to work. A baby was coming, and they could use the extra cash. Somehow, Julie was going to have to convince her best friend to take it easy—for the baby's sake.

Julie remained by the two men. They moved their pieces methodically but smoothly, like they knew what they were doing. Except for Mark giving her a crash course in what the pieces were called, she never caught on to how they were supposed to move. Chess was nothing like the checker games she used to play with Grampa. Now *that* was a challenge. What Mark and Greg were doing made no sense at all.

Mark moved his knight. "Check," he said.

Greg stared at the board and shifted his jaw back and forth, like he was concentrating.

Julie didn't dare say another word. Up until now, they'd each made lightning moves on the board, like they'd planned their strategy well in advance. Now the play had gone into slow motion. Greg eased his king to another square. Mark pursued. Then they stared at the board again. They reminded Julie of those cartoon characters who get caught in a hot chase and then leap into the air and freeze.

It was Greg's turn. After what seemed like an hour but was

only a couple of minutes, he shoved his king to another square.

Mark pressed his finger against his lips and stared at the board. Julie shifted from one foot to the other. The checker game with Grampa would have been over by now.

She was about to egg him on, when he advanced his bishop. "Check again," he said.

Greg blew out a long sigh. "I can see your next move, buddy. You've got me." He laid his king down and slumped back in his chair. "I'm done."

Mark rose and offered Julie his seat. She settled into it and turned her attention to Greg. Mark was merciless. Mr. Perfect had to win. He could have thrown the game—anything to help Greg feel better. After all, hadn't the guy been through enough? She cast a disappointed eye at Mark, then turned back to Greg.

"Are you holding up okay?" she said softly.

Greg snickered. "It's been tough. This is all new to me. I don't know what to expect, and to be honest, I'm terrified."

"I was glad to see your parents were here. Did they stay in town?"

"Yeah, they'll be here until Sunday. Then, my dad has to get back to the farm."

"He has a work crew, doesn't he?" Mark said.

"Yes, he does, but he wants to be there to supervise."

Julie eyed Greg with concern. He needed family at a time like this. "Did Lakisha's parents come down last night from Boston, as they had planned?" she said.

Greg bobbed his head. "They did, then they checked into a hotel. They plan to stay the weekend, but her father has clients scheduled for Monday, and her mom still teaches at the university up there. I doubt either one will cancel their commitments. Anyway, you can expect to see a steady flow of Lakisha's siblings coming and going over the next few days. If we don't set some rules, it's gonna look like a regular block party in here, only without the loud music."

Julie remembered the huge crowd of relatives at Lakisha's wedding. "She has thee sisters and two brothers, doesn't she?"

"Yeah, plus a slew of nieces and nephews, aunts and uncles, and an extremely active set of grandparents. There's no telling who will pop their heads in here, but we've got to be ready. I don't want Lakisha to get over-excited."

Julie's concerns took another path. "Is there anyone who can stay behind and help out when Lakisha goes home?"

Greg shook his head with an air of despondency. "They all have jobs—except for her grandparents, and they're in their 70s."

"I'll do what I can," she said. "I can go grocery shopping, do your laundry, maybe clean the house. Of course I'll spend most of the time sitting with Lakisha."

Greg stared at her with disbelief in his moist eyes. "Are you kidding? With all you've taken on right now? I refuse to take any time away from you, Julie. Neither will Lakisha stand for it."

"You're gonna have to go back to work next week," Julie said. Though she didn't know how she was going to juggle her job while taking care of her friend, it was something she desperately needed to do. It was a first step in caring for someone else instead of herself.

"I can come to your house during the day, while you're at work," she told Greg. I can set up my computer and finish my article, while Lakisha takes a nap or watches one of her soap operas."

It was the least she could do for a friend who'd stuck by her when she also was down. They'd made a pact several years ago and had faithfully kept it, year after year.

"No, Julie." Greg's tone sounded firm. "I can't let you jeopardize your new job by playing nursemaid to my wife. "I'll figure someth—"

"I'll do it." The high-pitched voice came from the doorway.

The three of them turned toward the opening. The light in the lobby backlit what appeared to be a tiny angel in a soft blue dress and a white sweater that seemed to have sprouted wings. The figure floated into the room and shuffled up beside Greg.

"Are you serious, Mom?" he said. "You want to help?"

She leaned back and gazed at him with tear-filled eyes. "Of course, Son. Your father will be busy at the farm, and I've got all the time in the world. I can take care of Lakisha. I'll keep house for you, and cook your meals, like I used to do. It'll make me feel needed again."

"I–I don't know what to say." Greg choked out his gratitude.

"Just say we can do this for you," a deep voice insisted. His father stepped into the room. "Everything's gonna be okay, Son. But you gotta let us help after all the heartache we gave you young 'uns."

"Then it's settled," Greg said, more to Julie than to anyone else. "You can do your work and come over whenever you need a break. You can relieve my mother, so she can take time to do something for herself. And I can go back to work and not worry."

"I'm all for it," Julie said, smiling.

His father drew close to Greg. "I'll take your mama home tomorrow so she can pack her bag. Let us know when you need her, and I'll bring her back."

Greg frowned, like another thought had struck him. "You need to know, this means you two won't get to see each other for weeks, not until Lakisha's out of the woods."

"Oh, yes, we will," Howard said. "I'll come out on the weekends. After 40 years of marriage we can stand a few days apart. Don't you agree, honeybunch?"

Mildred gazed into her husband's eyes, her own eyes sparkling like those of a young bride. Unknowingly, they were showing Julie another side to marriage, far removed from the type of relationship she might have imagined. It amazed her how two people continued to look at each other with love in their eyes after nearly 40 years together. These two obviously had reached that place. So had her Grampa and Gramma before they died. Probably Marjorie and Norton had it too. Perhaps the simplicity of farm life and dependence on a natural environment had created a special kind of bond. Whatever it was, she envied them.

She hoped to experience such a connection 40 or 50 years down the road and to be able to look into Mark's eyes and experience the same thrill she felt right now. She'd heard it said that love is a choice a person makes every day. Something bigger and better must lie beyond the words, "I do." Something that could turn a shallow commitment into an unshakeable vow and stand the test of time. A flicker of hope made its way into Julie's heart. In this hospital room she'd witnessed love and commitment expressed by two distinct generations. Despite her self-sufficient independence, Julie could imagine herself in such a relationship, and for the first time in six years, she was willing to fight for it.

29

SUNDAY

Mark woke up Sunday morning with a nervous knot in his stomach. His anxiety stemmed from two concerns. One—was he going to pull off the presentation Monday morning at the college? And, Two—did Fiona Askren still want to go there with him?

He hadn't seen or heard from the woman in several days, but then he'd done everything he could to avoid contact with her. When he wasn't teaching a class, he locked himself in his office. And when his day ended, he skipped out before anyone knew he'd left the building. She hadn't phoned him, hadn't knocked on his apartment door, hadn't even shown up *by chance* wherever he went. Perhaps she'd given up the pursuit.

He slid out of bed and headed for the bathroom, went through his usual routine, took a hot shower, and massaged some gel in his hair. *Or maybe the little panther was lying low for the big lunge.* It was no wonder he felt vulnerable. If she went on the trip with him, once they left Springfield he'd be at her mercy. He needed to come up with a defensive plan, some way to keep their contact to a minimum.

If only he and Julie were already married. He could have brought her along on the trip. But she wouldn't have been able to spare the time. She needed to get to work on her own project, and she'd never let him drag her away from Lakisha for two days.

He went to his closet and selected a pair of khaki pants, a brown-and-blue speckled shirt, and a blue blazer—a suitable combination for church, the flight, and his presentation. He'd packed his bag last night after coming home from the hospital. He checked the contents, made sure he didn't forget anything, then opened his briefcase and went over the PowerPoint materials and handouts.

The thought of standing before an unfamiliar audience, perhaps 200 students plus staff, got his nerves jangling again. What if Fiona grabbed a seat in the front row and ogled him with those sultry black eyes of hers? How was he going to concentrate?

He clenched his jaw. He didn't need this kind of pressure. Not while his best friend's wife was in the hospital fighting for her baby's life. And not while he was trying to make things work with Julie. There was no doubt, Fiona was a knockout. Most men would have crumbled by now. But he'd set his goals. He'd established a solid career. He'd chosen the woman he wanted to spend the rest of his life with. He wasn't about to throw it all away, not for an overnight fling and certainly not for a woman who, once she'd made the conquest would probably move on to the next poor slob.

He'd made arrangements with Julie to have breakfast out and afterward go to church together. This had been their pattern since they returned home from Patmos. If things worked out for them, they'd keep the same routine for years to come. His mother had started him in the habit of attending church and, after she died, his father carried on the ritual as if by doing so he was able to maintain some sort of stability in Mark's life. Mark didn't resist. There existed a certain comfort in keeping the old habits going, a familiarity that offered a sense of tranquility and wholeness he hoped to pass on to his own children one day.

Mark left the apartment and drove to Julie's condo. She was probably going to ask him about the trip. He was going to have to set her mind at ease. His mouth went dry, and his heart began to pound. He clenched his teeth. Somehow, he was going to have to convince Julie that he wasn't interested in Fiona and never would be.

When Julie opened her door to let him in, he nearly melted. She stood there in an emerald green dress that set off the color of her eyes. Her fiery red hair hung in gentle folds to her shoulders. She looked more beautiful than ever. The Florida sun had added a hint of color to her cheeks. When she smiled, she literally glowed.

They left immediately for the Pancake Cafe. Julie talked animatedly during breakfast. She shared more details about her trip, described the places she'd gone and the people she'd met. She gave colorful details, made Florida's backwoods come to life for him. His own trips to Florida had always ended up at the beach for visits with his father. It was an entirely different part of the state. High-rise condominiums and hotels lined a sandy shoreline, and paved roadways led to side streets with pristine homes, palm trees, and lush gardens. What Julie described was a more secluded part of the state, enveloped in forests, far from the heavily trafficked roads that took tourists to theme parks and ports of entry for cruise ships. He wondered if it was anything like how the movie had depicted that part of Florida.

He waited until after they finished eating their pancakes to talk about his trip. With time to spare before church, this was probably the best opportunity for him to address the issue. As he explained about Fiona's father and how Melanie couldn't stop the woman from invading his space, he kept his eyes on Julie and tried to read her mind. On the outside, she was beaming, obviously refreshed from a good night's rest and reassured by a positive phone call from Lakisha that morning.

He plunged ahead, covered everything from the time Fiona insisted on going on his trip to Chicago. He made sure Julie understood his reluctance to have the girl accompany him. He couldn't report the situation to human resources. The woman had been a pain in the neck. Julie already knew about the phone calls and Fiona's spontaneous visit to Mark's office. Plus, he'd read the note to everyone at the table the night before Julie left on her trip. He had nothing to hide. At the same time, his hands were tied. Fiona was going on the trip, and he couldn't stop her.

When he finished, he sat back and waited for the explosion. It didn't come. He eyed Julie with curiosity. He'd expected her to fly into a rage. That was one thing about Julie. She didn't hesitate to let him know what was on her mind, whether he wanted to hear it or not.

But she didn't say a word. She merely stared at him with those green eyes of hers.

"She hasn't tried to contact me since she sent the note," Mark persisted. "Maybe she's given up and moved on to someone else; Jimmy Nolan maybe."

Julie smirked. "It doesn't sound like there's much you can do about it."

"You can trust me, Julie," he said.

"I know." Her voice sounded unnaturally calm and accepting.

"You *did* hear what I said, didn't you—that Fiona's going on the trip?"

"Yes."

Mark frowned in puzzlement. "And you're not upset?" He caught himself. "What I mean is, most women wouldn't stand for their guy traveling with another female."

She giggled. "Mark, I trust you. To be honest, I've experienced an epiphany of sorts. Over the past week, while I was researching Marjorie, I began to understood some things about myself—things I'm not proud of. Then I observed Greg's commitment to Lakisha and how his parents demonstrate their love for each other. They have something I want for you and me."

"Really?" Mark was not only amazed, he was impressed.

She reached across the table and grabbed his hand. "Our next appointment with Doctor Balser is Wednesday. I'm gonna address a problem my sister thinks I have."

He raised his eyebrows with interest.

"Rita believes I might be suffering from PTSD," Julie said. "If that's true, it's time I allowed my therapist to dig into my past and help me recover from it."

He stared in bewilderment at her. "What a breakthrough, Julie. You know, Rita's diagnosis makes sense."

She giggled and her eyes sparkled, like she'd just opened a much wanted birthday present. "Don't worry, Mark," she said, still laughing. "You'll be there to hear everything Doctor Balser and I discuss. I think you'll like what you hear." She gently squeezed his hand. "For now, I want you to relax, go on your trip, and do a fantastic job with your presentation tomorrow morning. Do what you can to avoid Fiona, but know that I trust you."

Dumbfounded, he stared at her as if seeing her for the first time.

"We'd better get to church," she said.

He paid the check and walked out to the car with her. Though he wanted to press her for more information, he backed off. Julie was calling the shots right now, and he kind of liked it.

The pastor's message gave Mark a boost of confidence. Not only in himself but concerning his relationship with Julie. Pastor Joe's sermon was titled, *"Fruitful Loving."* He used as his text the Fruit of the Spirit passage in Galatians 5:22-23. Mark considered those attributes on a personal level. *Love,* of course, served as a springboard for all the rest of the fruit, and it was the easiest to acknowledge in how he felt about Julie. Then Pastor Joe described what he considered the products of love—*joy, peace, patience, gentleness, goodness, faith, meekness,* and *self-control.*

By the time the sermon ended, Mark was convicted that those virtues weren't meant only for a male-female relationship. They were supposed to spill into every area of his life. With people like Greg and Lakisha, of course, and so many others who crossed his path. Melanie, his co-workers, even Jimmy Nolan who got on his nerves at times. And yes, even people like Fiona. If nothing else, he needed to exercise patience and gentleness.

He left the church with a huge lump in his throat. They drove to Julie's condo without uttering a word. He glanced at her. There were no worry lines on her forehead. In fact, she had a hint of a smile on her lips.

They said goodbye at her door. Mark didn't ask to come in, nor did Julie suggest it. His luggage was already in the backseat of his car. He needed to get to the airport. He drew her close, and she pressed her cheek against his chest. He rested his chin on her forehead. His throat tightened, and he couldn't speak. They'd reached a place in their relationship when a wink or a smile or a slight caress was enough.

He leaned away, planted a kiss on her lips, another on her cheek, another on her forehead. She blushed in his arms.

"Hurry home," was all she said, but it was enough for him to take with him for two days.

He could handle anything now—even Fiona.

When he arrived in the airport gate area, there she was, dressed in a formfitting outfit far too seductive for air travel. She was made up like a showgirl, and she strutted around like she was about to go onstage. Didn't she know how disgusting she looked?

Immediately, he tucked his pastor's sermon in the recesses of his mind. The hairs on the back of his neck rose and he forgot all about practicing patience and gentleness or any of the other fruit he was supposed to have.

While most of the men in the gate area appeared to enjoy Fiona's prancing about, Mark chewed his bottom lip in shame for her. After spending time with Julie, he could see no comparison. Julie's wardrobe consisted of tasteful dresses and slacks. Even when she wore shorts or a swim suit, they were modestly made. Wherever they went, she didn't try to draw attention to herself. In fact, the opposite was true. Julie shriveled up at times, like she preferred to remain in the shadows.

Now he was going to be traveling with a village streetwalker. When she stepped up beside him, several men gazed after her, and though the envy in their eyes bolstered his ego for a moment, his heart was somewhere else.

"So, you got your way, didn't you?" He didn't try to hide his annoyance.

She tilted her head and slipped her hand in the crook of his arm. "I did," she said with an air of boldness. "You're all mine for the next two days."

He pulled away from her and found a seat in the waiting area. She dropped into the seat beside him and slipped one leg over the other, exposing her thigh. He looked away, tried to focus on the woman with the baby at the end of the row, the man pacing the floor and looking at his watch, the teenager with his thumbs flying over his iPhone.

"Wait here," he said, rising. He left his baggage with Fiona, which meant she'd have to stay put in order to keep her eye on it.

He approached the agent behind the desk. "What do I need to do to change my boarding pass to an aisle seat in a different row?"

She smiled and checked her computer screen. "I have two aisle seats available, plus a first class option for an extra charge."

"I'll take one of the coach seats, please, either one. And make sure the other seats in my row are already occupied."

Her eyebrows came together quizzically. She flashed a glance at Fiona, returned to the screen and punched in the change. Seconds later, she handed him a new boarding pass. It was that easy.

He returned to the waiting area and settled into the seat beside Fiona. Fortunately, their time together would be brief.

She eyed him with skepticism. "What was that all about?"

"Nothing."

"Come on. You're up to something."

"It's nothing, Fiona. Relax."

He reached in his briefcase and pulled out a copy of *Great Destinations* magazine he'd purposely brought along as a distraction.

"My fiancée works for this magazine," he said, hoping she'd catch the underlying message.

"I know."

He frowned and gave her a sideways look.

"Don't be surprised, Mark. I made it my business to learn everything about you."

He crumpled the magazine. "Oh, really? You shouldn't have bothered, Fiona. I'm attached. I love my fiancée, and I have no interest in looking elsewhere."

A young man in the next row turned around and stared at him, his eyes wide, his brows raised in surprise. Mark glared at him and sent him back to his own business.

Fiona rambled on about her job, and how, working in the main office, she could look up anyone's file. Mentally he blocked out her monologue, scanned a few travel stories, and mumbled a prayer under his breath. He nearly collapsed with relief when their flight was called.

As he followed Fiona down the jetway, a smug smile tugged at the corners of his mouth. She was in for a big surprise when he walked past their row and settled in his newly assigned aisle seat.

Sure enough, she raised a scene, called his name twice, then plunked down by the window with a noisy huff.

Mark pulled a similar stunt later at the Palmer House Hotel. After checking in and getting Fiona settled in her room, he went back to the desk and asked for another room on a different floor.

"And please don't give out my room number to the woman

who checked in with me," he said as firmly as he could. The clerk nodded with understanding.

Early Monday morning, before the sun was up, Mark slipped on his jogging clothes, laced up his running shoes, and headed out to the street. The Illinois climate was a tad chillier than back home. The blast of cool air invigorated him. He was good for about 10 miles this morning.

He did some mild stretches then hit the pavement. His breath came out in frosty puffs. He checked the street sign, got his bearings, and headed for the Riverwalk. The wind pressed against his back, urging him on. He needed the push, reveled in it.

A wedge of orange at the horizon cast golden streaks across a patch of cirrus clouds overhead. It was a beautiful morning in Chicago, maybe a good omen for the rest of the day. Somehow he needed to get through his presentation without a hitch. How would he explain things to the board if the program didn't go well? He didn't want to fail, not now.

He picked up speed and moved along effortlessly, like he'd been saving his energy for such a moment as this. He reached the shoreline and turned north. There was something exhilarating about running in unfamiliar territory, like he'd entered another world, maybe another life for the moment.

Julie would be getting out of bed about now, eager to get started on her own project. A cup of tea and a piece of toast and she'd go right to work. Her research was done. She'd finished it up in Florida last week. Now it was just her and her computer, and a pile of notes at her side.

He checked the time. He'd been running for 20 minutes.

Endorphins were surging. Sweat gathered on his brow. With the rising of the sun, the temperature went up 15 degrees. He kept going at the same speed, farther and farther from the hotel.

Then, suitably hyped, he reversed his direction. Another half-hour passed. It was the beginning of a warm summer day. He was amazed at how the air could change from a penetrating chill to instant warmth. If not for the wind, Chicago's atmosphere might match what he enjoyed in Springfield.

He was a block from his hotel. He slowed to a jog, checked his pulse, tapered off to a gentle lope, and, finally, a stroll into the lobby. He bypassed the elevator and took the stairwell, two and three steps at a time, to his floor.

Feeling invigorated, he headed straight for the shower, finished his grooming routine, dressed quickly, and luggage in hand, he hurried out the door. Back on high speed, he checked out of the hotel, grabbed a blueberry muffin and a cup of coffee from the continental breakfast bar on his way out, and hailed a cab on the street.

He started eating the muffin during the drive to Moody Bible Institute. It was still early, but he wanted to get there before the students started flowing into the auditorium. Plus, he needed to avoid Fiona. Let her fend for herself. In fact, she could pack up and go home, for all he cared.

From out of nowhere, the pastor's sermon revived in Mark's brain, and a stab of guilt struck his heart. It was easy to practice those godly attributes with Julie. After all, he was in love with her. It was easy to be joyful and patient with Greg and Lakisha. And his dad? Not a problem.

But the truth was, he hadn't been kind or helpful or patient with Fiona. Her father had given her the position at the school for good reason. She'd been trouble. Was it Mark's job to straighten her out? Probably not, but he was in a good place to help someone else. This woman needed guidance. She'd sort of admitted it to him that day in his office. Hadn't she said something about needing brotherly advice? Whether he wanted to admit it or not, the job had fallen to him.

He finished off the muffin as the cab swung onto Wells Street. The driver pulled into the drop-off parking lot and let him out. From there, he made a short walk to the entrance of Dryer Hall where he'd been told he'd be speaking. The rest of the morning went by like a dream. At one point, he faced an audience full of young, excited faces, with a few older folks—probably staff members—thrown in.

He concluded his presentation to an unexpected rise of applause, whistles, and cheers. His confidence restored, he could hardly wait to get back home to make a few minor changes and start setting up more engagements. Melanie would be pleased. So would the board.

Now, only one more task pressed on his mind. He needed to make things right with Fiona. First, he'd have to apologize for being so harsh with her. Then he'd have to get through to her how her behavior was offensive, not only to him but to other people she might encounter in life. This time, he didn't ask the gate agent for a different seat. During their two-hour flight home, Fiona was going to be a captive audience, whether she liked it or not.

30

JULIE

On Monday morning, Julie started reviewing her story from the time the sun came up. Like every other article and book a person wrote, it had to start with an attention-getting hook. The main thing was to grab the readers' attention right from the start. She felt she'd accomplished that already with the lines she'd jotted down while she was in the cabin in Cross Creek. She reread them now.

Not all Florida roads lead to beaches and theme parks. Some lead to the very heart of the peninsula. They meander through an unfettered blend of forests and marshland, a magical escape from the impersonal world of paved highways and strip malls, gated subdivisions and country clubs.

She also considered the title she'd settled on when she first read Marjorie's biography about how she started writing stories at the age of 11. *Felicity,* she'd called herself then. The name had stuck in Julie's head. Felicity. "Intense happiness." She scrolled to the top of the page and entered her working title: *In Search of Felicity, In the Footsteps of Marjorie Kinnan Rawlings.*

So, she had a title and the travel portion. The next step posed a number of challenges. She needed to weave in as much information about Marjorie as possible. For a story like this, the human element was crucial. It could bring the article to life. The rest of the text and the sidebar had to flow from the beginning paragraph, and somehow she had to squeeze in as much information as she could from her pile of notes. She worked on the piece all morning.

At lunchtime Doctor Balser called and confirmed her appointment for Wednesday at 4 p.m. Mark's last class would be over at 2:00. She wanted him there with her, if for no other reason than for moral support.

She pulled a pre-made salad from the fridge and brewed a cup of tea. When she finished eating, she freshened up and headed out the door to go to the hospital. She arrived in Lakisha's room to find her best friend sitting on the edge of the bed holding a vase of cut flowers.

"From Greg's parents," she said with a teary-eyed grin.

Julie leaned in to admire the spray of carnations and irises. "They're lovely."

"Howard's bringing Mildred here this afternoon. When they learned I was being released from the hospital, she insisted on taking care of me after I get home."

"I remember her saying that," Julie said. "How sweet of her."

Lakisha began to sob. She brushed tears from her cheeks. Her sparkling, dark eyes touched Julie's heart. "Sometimes God works a bad situation into something good, right?" Lakisha murmured.

"He sure does," Julie said. She drew close for a hug. "I can attest to that." She backed away and gazed at her friend. "Look at *my* life. Where would I be right now if I hadn't met Yanno? Not to mention the great support system I have with you and Greg, and of course, Mark."

Lakisha smiled. She knew everything about Julie's experiences—the good and the bad.

Julie looked about the room. "So, where's Greg?"

"He went down to get the car. I'm waiting for an aide to whisk me out of here."

She no sooner said those words than a young woman in a candy-cane striped smock came in pushing a wheelchair.

Julie expected to spend an hour visiting with Lakisha in the hospital room before getting back to work. The interruption could take more of her time than she'd planned on. First, they needed to drive Lakisha home and get her settled. Greg couldn't hang around. He had to leave for work. Julie would follow in her own car and then be stuck there waiting for his parents to show up, maybe not until late afternoon. Her best friend sat there beaming, like she was about to be released from prison. Julie couldn't simply make her comfortable and say, "So long." She'd have to put off writing her article until tomorrow. She breathed a sigh. Her friend was worth the sacrifice.

Such was one of the many changes Julie had faced during the past few days. She wasn't going to shut out her best friend anymore, and she wanted to treat other people better—Mark, of course, and Greg, and her sister, and her parents. People who cared about her. People she'd conveniently compartmentalized. Now she was facing the first of several challenges. She was having to put aside her own plans and set her full attention on Lakisha.

"I'll stay with you until Greg's folks show up," she said. "Just let me know what you need."

Lakisha shut her eyes and squeezed out a tear. The woman had just came through a life-threatening trauma. And she wasn't completely out of the woods yet.

A softening came to Julie's heart. "It's okay, Lakisha. I'm here. I'm not gonna leave you alone."

Lakisha opened her eyes and took hold of Julie's hand. "I've never felt so helpless," she said, her voice thick with emotion.

"Time to go," the aide said with a cheery giggle.

Julie grabbed Lakisha's bag off the bed, and followed them out the door.

Greg was waiting by the curb with the car door open. Julie handed him Lakisha's bag, which he tossed in the back seat. He gave her an appreciative nod.

"I'll see you at the house," Julie said, and she took off for the parking lot.

A part of her hoped Greg's parents might already be there. But, the reality was, Howard and Mildred lived a good four hours away. He was one of those slowpoke drivers who tie up the passing lane. A far cry from an Indy 500 driver. More like a lumbering snow plow. The truth was, a normal four hours could turn into five or six with him trawling along.

She went inside the house and found Lakisha already seated in her recliner in the living room with a multi-colored quilt on her lap. Greg was darting from room to room, grabbing things she might need—a box of tissues, a glass of water, the book she'd been reading, the TV control, her cell phone. He crowded everything together on the little end table at her side.

Julie stood back and took in the scene. The man could run himself into an early grave if he didn't slow down. She had to smile though. This was true love in action. Not many women were lucky enough to find a husband like Greg. But Julie knew without a doubt, Mark had the same qualities. He'd already demonstrated his unwavering loyalty, in spite of all her senseless mood swings.

He'd be on the plane heading for home right now, maybe

getting ready to land at the Springfield airport. He'd want to take her to dinner tonight so they could catch up. He'd want to tell her how his presentation went, maybe bounce some ideas off of her. And he'd probably have something to say about how things went with Fiona. Julie possessed an uncanny peace about the situation. So, what had changed?

Then the truth struck her. What had changed was she'd learned to trust Mark. He hadn't changed. *She* had. It didn't matter what someone else said or did. She knew without a doubt, Mark would do the right thing.

She turned her attention back to Lakisha, who was fiddling with the TV remote. She smiled at Julie. "How about a soap opera?"

Julie squirmed. A soap opera? She hated them. They took precious hours out of a person's day. They dragged from one episode to the next. Problems weren't resolved for months, maybe even years. They kept women chained to their TV sets, wasting their days, and never getting anything of value done.

"A soap opera might be nice," she said. "Got any favorites?"

Julie settled into Greg's recliner a few feet away from Lakisha. Her friend flipped through the channels. Bold images flashed on the giant TV screen on the wall across the room. Julie snuck a look at her watch. 1:30. She'd given up an afternoon of work for a soap opera marathon.

They got through two soap operas and a game show. At one point, Lakisha drifted off to sleep. When she woke up, Julie went into the kitchen to fix an afternoon snack for the two of them. She rooted through the refrigerator and several cupboards and came up with a block of cheese and some crackers, a couple bananas, and two cups of herbal tea.

They spent the next hour checking out decorating ideas

in baby magazines, and they talked about Lakisha's plan to set up a home office.

"I'm not leaving my baby in someone else's care while I run off to work," she said. "I already checked with my boss. I can arrange my appointments from home, and if I have to do a showing, I'll put the baby in a car seat and take her along with me." She smiled at Julie. "My baby actually could be an ice breaker. Maybe I'll sell more properties having her along."

At that moment, Mark called and let her know he'd made it home.

"Dinner tonight?" he said.

"Of course." Julie had given up getting anymore work done today. She was already exhausted from doing nothing. Maybe all she needed was a relaxing dinner with Mark.

"Where to?" she said.

"How about the little dive by the river? No atmosphere but they serve good home-cooked food, and we can grab a quiet corner where we can talk."

"I'm not particular, Mark. Anyplace is fine with me. I can always find something on the menu."

"I can't wait to see you," he said.

A flush rose to Julie's cheeks—not from embarrassment or shame, but from a deep sense of being loved beyond anything she'd ever known. The guy had just spent two days with one of the most gorgeous women Julie had ever seen, but he couldn't wait to be with *her*. That had to mean something.

"See you at 7:00," he said.

She hung up and gave Lakisha one of their secret girlfriend smiles.

"Mark?" Lakisha said.

"Yeah. He said he can't wait to see me."

Lakisha frowned at her. "So? You look like you just won the lottery."

"He spent the weekend with Fiona."

"And?"

"And he wants to see *me*."

Lakisha let out a little laugh. "I'm not surprised, girl. The guy's in love with you. Remember how he dodged my flirtatious girlfriends at the wedding?"

Julie nodded. He'd broken away from the crowd and headed straight for her. "Forward women always turned him off," she said with a giggle. "Greg's the same way, isn't he?"

Lakisha laughed aloud and pressed her hand to her abdomen. "I made him chase me, too, before I caught him. For me, it was hard work, but you did it naturally."

Julie huffed. "I truly wasn't interested," she said laughing. "The thing is, I wasn't looking for romance or marriage."

"Listen, marriage isn't for everyone. But you and Mark belong together. He's easy-going, controlled, soft-spoken. He's got the right temperament to balance somebody like you. Believe me, you fit together like a puzzle."

Julie smiled. "Oh, so we're a puzzle, huh?"

"You know what I mean. You're not every guy's image of a stay-at-home mom. But differences can be good, Julie. You just have to embrace them."

"Well, you've given me lots to think about," Julie said.

Lakisha lifted the TV control and brought the screen back to life. "How about the Discovery Channel?" she said.

They were in the middle of a documentary about hobbled camels in the Sinai Desert when Howard and Mildred came through the door. It was 4:15. Howard gave Lakisha a hug, acknowledged Julie, and immediately said his good-bye, adding that he needed to get back to the farm before dark. Julie showed Mildred around the house and spent a decent amount of time getting her familiar with the kitchen. As she started to leave, she turned and caught sight of a vision that stirred her heart. Mildred had drawn a kitchen chair close to Lakisha's recliner. The older woman was holding her daughter-in-law's hand. They were staring into each other's eyes and talking softly. They didn't notice when Julie slipped out the door.

31

MONDAY EVENING

Julie barely had time to get ready for dinner. She quickly showered and dressed, ran a brush through her hair, and was putting on her shoes when Mark knocked. She hobbled into the living room and opened the front door.

Mark stood there looking flawless, from his gelled mop of hair to the unscuffed, pure white Adidas on his feet. His clothes—blue jeans and a tan polo shirt—had a freshly pressed look, like he'd just pulled them out of the store packaging or perhaps had taken an iron to them. He couldn't have had much more time than she did. He just spent two days in Chicago, flew home this afternoon, and probably stopped by the college to fill Melanie in on his trip, yet he looked like he'd just stepped off a GQ magazine cover.

Did she really want to spend the rest of her life with Mr. Perfect?

One look at his scintillating blue eyes and his endearing grin and she knew the answer. No one else balanced her so well. Just like handsome Norton and scruffy Marjorie. But their differences weren't merely physical. Mark kept his cool in every situation. So did Norton. Julie flared up like a Fourth of July firecracker at the slightest offense. So did Marjorie. Mark took time to evaluate everything. She scrambled around like a mad woman.

Yep, Norton and Marjorie come back from the grave, she thought.

Like Lakisha said, they were two pieces of a puzzle. Their differences blended together to make a beautiful picture.

She slipped her hand in the crook of his arm and walked out the door with him. She had a lot to tell him, and, she assumed, he had plenty to tell her.

Over a dinner of roast beef and mashed potatoes, Julie talked about Lakisha's improved condition and the arrival of her mother-in-law. With the older woman settling into her caregiver role, the level of stress went down. Greg returned to work without having to worry about his wife being alone in the house, and Julie would be able to work on her magazine story.

Julie moaned about having to sit as a captive audience to Lakisha's soap operas, and she confessed she actually had started getting interest in some of the plots. She'd gotten so wrapped up in the Forrester family they'd begun to seem like real people. Now she feared she'd be hooked like so many other women—and men.

Mark kept chuckling between bites, and his blue eyes danced with delight.

Her discourse took them through the entire main course. For desert, they ordered apple pie and coffee. Mark dug into his pie like a kid at a party. Julie took a few bites, then slid the plate aside.

"It sounds like you had quite a day with Lakisha," he said. "Did you get any work done on your article?"

She breathed a dejected sigh. "Barely," she said. "I want to work in as much material about the real Marjorie as possible. I was able to get a lot of personal information when I talked with my tour guide's Aunt Emma. And the university archives contained an overwhelming amount of unpublished writings. It would take months to go through all of the files, but I think I got enough for my story."

"Wow, Julie. That woman may have met an untimely death, but you're going to keep her alive, at least for her faithful readers. And think about all the people who visit Florida and only see the beaches and the theme parks. Your article will lure them to a part of Florida they never would have seen otherwise."

He nodded toward her dessert plate. "You gonna finish that?"

She smiled and slid her leftover pie in front of him. He didn't hesitate—took three hearty bites and scraped the plate clean.

The server refilled their coffee cups. Julie added a little cream to hers. She sat back and watched Mark doctor his with cream and several bags of sugar. She smiled with amusement.

He stared at her. "What? Haven't you seen me do this before? It's how my mother taught me to drink coffee when I was a kid." He shrugged. "So, it stuck."

She sipped her coffee and eyed him over the top of her cup. The truth was, she didn't want to change a thing about this man. Perfect or not, he was perfect for her.

"We never talked about what you were doing while I was away."

"I worked out and I put some time in on my PowerPoint project. Greg and I went to the retro theater for a replay of *Cross Creek.*"

Julie perked up. "Why did you do that?"

He gave a shy little shrug. "I wanted to know a little more about your work, so I could talk about it with some intelligence."

"And? What did you think?"

"I thought it was well-done and fairly authentic considering it was Hollywood."

"They made some mistakes most people don't catch," Julie said, trying not to sound smug.

"Like what?" He raised his eyebrows and stared at her like he was truly interested.

"Well, the casting was off. I mean, Peter Coyote was well-matched to Norton Baskin. They had the same humble, soft-spoken manner. And Rip Torn pulled off the moon-shine character like he'd grown up in the swamp himself. But Mary Steenburgen is a little too feminine and sweet to play Marjorie. Of course, this is my opinion, but I think Kathy Bates might have fit a lot better. Did you see her in *Misery*? She could switch personalities in a split second."

Mark chuckled. "I can picture it now. Sweet one minute, a tiger the next. Didn't Mary Steenburgen accomplish those changes?"

"Mildly. From what I've read about Marjorie, she could get a Marine sergeant to blush." Her description evoked more laughter from Mark.

"There's more," she said, egged on by his lighthearted response. "Some of the facts were incorrect, although they were insignificant enough for people to overlook them. For example, Charles was the one who first suggested buying the orange grove in Florida. His two brothers lived in Island Grove and ran a business there. In fact, they helped with the purchase, and Marjorie didn't get a chance to see it until the day they moved in. And that's another thing, they both moved in at first. Charles didn't leave until 1933, that was nearly five years after they bought the property."

She took a sip of her coffee, then continued. "I didn't read anywhere that Marjorie ever yelled at Max Perkins like she was shown to do in the movie. Their correspondence was polite at first, and, over time, it became more personal, friendly even, but never angry. It was obvious Marjorie respected and liked the man."

Julie shrugged. "Anyway, the real Norton Baskin served as an advisor on the set, so the movie couldn't have been too far off." She cocked her head. "By the way, did you happen to notice the guy in the wicker chair in front of the General Mercantile Store at the beginning of the film—the older gentleman who gave Marjorie directions to the hotel?"

Mark brightened. "Was that Norton Baskin?"

"In the flesh," Julie said with a nod. "They gave him a cameo role."

"Sweet. Guess I'll have to see it again and catch his scene."

They went back to their coffee in silence. It was time to ask Mark about Chicago. She took a deep breath and tried to appear nonchalant. "So, how was *your* trip?"

He hesitated—or was it her imagination? He drank some of his coffee, then coddled the cup between his hands. "My presentation went well," he said, nodding. "After I finished talking, several college students approached me and pummeled me with questions. I felt like a celebrity. Things got even better when two professors came up to me. They asked for my business card and told me they were going to recommend my presentation to their colleagues at other schools."

"What was it like, you know, to visit a major institution like Moody?"

Mark raised his eyebrows and blew out a long breath with a shake of his head, like he'd been overwhelmed. "Their massive complex puts my little workplace to shame. We have two buildings. Period. They have multiple centers and halls spread out over several acres, plus two outdoor recreational fields. We don't even have a volleyball court."

Julie frowned. "Hasn't Moody been around for decades?"

"Yeah, Dwight L. Moody founded it in 1886, so—more than 130 years."

"And how long has St. Paul Bible College been around?"

"It's about 40 years old."

"Give it time, Mark. Someday, if everything goes well, it will have a huge campus of buildings and sports fields, just like Moody." She reached across the table and took hold of his hand. "I'm proud of you. To be called from little ol' Springfield to the big city of Chicago to give your spiel has got to mean something."

He smiled at her and nodded. "You know? The professor at Moody was the first to respond to the emails I sent out to colleges all over the country."

"Maybe more will come in now."

He smiled at her. "Maybe."

Julie slid her hand away and their conversation dropped to an uncomfortable lull. Mark shuffled the empty sugar bags, folded and refolded his napkin, then he turned his attention to a nearby window like he was captivated by the sunset. They had to be thinking about the same thing. Fiona.

Julie could wait no longer. "Okay, how did the rest of your trip go?"

He snickered and gave her a half-smile. "You've been dying to ask me, haven't you?"

She pressed her lips together and glared at him.

He took another sip of his coffee. She slumped back in her chair. "Okay. Tell me. Or don't tell me." She crossed her arms. "I don't care."

He set down his cup and grew serious. "Nothing happened, Julie."

"Nothing?" She eyed him with incredulity.

"It's the truth. I took great pains to avoid Fiona during the entire trip. On the flight over I changed my seat on the airplane, and I switched to another room at the hotel."

"Okay..."

"This morning, I went for my usual ten-mile run. Early. Before the sun came up."

"And..."

"And, as soon as I got back to the hotel, I showered, dressed, and checked out, went straight to the college ahead of schedule. From the time we first got to the hotel, I didn't see Fiona until she walked into the assembly hall lugging her suitcase behind her. She caught the end of my presentation. But there's more, and here's the good part."

Julie listened with bated breath. So far he'd satisfied her concerns. She'd already decided to trust him, no matter what. So why was she suddenly nervous? And, what did he mean by "the good part?" She straightened her shoulders and cocked her head with interest.

"You may or may not understand what I did next," Mark said, his voice softly persuasive. "Just hear me out, and I think you'll agree this needed to be done. Don't say a word until I finish."

She frowned but nodded her ascent.

"During the flight home, I didn't change to another seat on the airplane. I didn't take out my paperwork or get busy on my iPad, didn't even ask the flight attendants for something to eat or drink. I put all of my attention on Fiona."

Julie tensed up but remained silent.

"You know what I did? I talked to her, Julie. I told her how her behavior was having an opposite effect than what she'd been expecting. I said, 'You're not going to attract the right kind of guy, Fiona. What you'll do is put yourself in compromising situations, maybe even in danger. A girl like you doesn't need to be flaunting herself. Men will pursue you. All you have to do is work hard at your job and develop a well-rounded lifestyle. Relationships aren't all about good looks and fun. You need to fill your life with other activities and hobbies. Groom your talents—art, music, whatever they may be.'"

He paused, like he was waiting for an emotional response. She remained rigid and kept her attention on him.

"Anyway," Mark said. "I told her, 'Do you know what I see when I look at you?' Of course, she shook her head. I said, 'I see a shallow, insecure person, an attractive young woman who hasn't tapped into her true potential. You don't want to be someone's trophy wife. You want to be more. You needed someone to push you in the right direction. That's what I'm trying to do.' Then, for some odd reason, she burst into tears, right there on the airplane. I mean, she literally fell apart. I looked around. Most of the other passengers were caught up in their own business. Only one guy across the aisle glanced in our direction. I stared back at him and he went back to his newspaper."

Julie was smiling now. "My fiancé has turned into a counselor."

Mark shook his head emphatically. "No way. After listening to Pastor Joe's sermon on Sunday, I was convicted about my own behavior. I had a good talk with myself, and I convinced myself that I needed to help out another human being. Anyway, after she finished her crying jag, she opened up to me. She talked about her dysfunctional home life, how her father runs off every morning to the office or for a golf game with his buddies, how her mother consumes herself with social activities, and Fiona has no one to talk to but the maid."

Julie never expected to feel any compassion for Fiona. She'd known women like her. They exuded the same shallow insecurity Mark just described. Most of them continued on a downhill path only to end up married to the wrong guy and then divorced. She recalled a similar girl she'd known in college. A school counselor took the girl under her wing, and miraculous changes happened. She went on to be a top student and a champion track star, and at graduation she was named valedictorian.

She looked across the table at Mark. "Does this mean you're gonna have to keep counseling her?"

He shook his head and smiled. "My girlfriend wouldn't allow it," he said. "No, I urged Fiona to seek counseling from a woman. I'm sure Melanie will be able to recommend someone."

"So, that's it?"

He nodded. "Yep. I'm pretty sure there will be no more late-night phone calls, no more interruptions at my office, and no more notes."

"How can you be sure?"

He shrugged. "Just a feeling. By the time we got off the plane, Fiona had gone through a definite change. She made no more advances, no suggestive comments. She stared out the window for the rest of the flight, like maybe she was thinking about what I had said. Everything was different, Julie. Completely different."

She breathed a long sigh. Up until then, she'd been taking shallow breaths. She could have passed out from lack of oxygen. She had to laugh at herself. Like always, Mark did the right thing. She stared at him, and her heart surged with admiration.

So, Fiona was on her way to healing. If Fiona could get help, maybe she could too. Maybe her own path to healing lay just around the next corner.

On Tuesday, Julie worked on her magazine piece all day, but took two breaks to visit Lakisha. Mark also had a full schedule. They talked on the phone once, then got back to their individual jobs.

The biggest challenge Julie faced was how to pare down the ton of information she'd collected on Marjorie. She cut, pasted, and cut again, and brought the text down to about 4,000 words—still a tad too long for the space she was allowed.

She went over the piece several times more, did more cutting and grooming and tweaking. She selected photos from her cache, taking care to include images of Marjorie's Cross Creek property—the big, imposing barn, the stately orange grove, a panorama of the house and front lawn, even the tumbledown outhouse—plus several interesting photos from inside the home—the dining room with its antique furnishings, Marjorie's bedroom and the old, four-poster bed, and the wood-burning stove in the kitchen. And, most importantly, the screened-in front porch where a lifeless Remington typewriter marked the place where Marjorie once wrote her stories.

She still needed to create a sidebar highlighting places to stay—the gorgeous Herlong Mansion bed-and-breakfast in Micanopy, The Yearling cabins, of course, and several hotels in nearby Gainesville and Ocala. She recommended dinner at The Yearling, and for travelers who planned to stay longer than a couple of days, she made a list of other sites of interest, such as Ocala's Silver Springs State Park, the beaches on both coasts, and Orlando's many theme parks, only a two-hour drive away.

The story was set to run in the October issue, appropriately in time for the influx of retired snowbirds. There was no doubt, Ian knew how to plan each issue for exactly the right audience.

Once she filed the package to Ian, she needed to concentrate on the other assignments he'd given her. Already the magazine's fan mail had started coming in, and Ian had quickly forwarded the emails to her. She was expecting a bunch more by U.S. mail. Once her story ran, perhaps the fans would direct their letters to her attention.

No question about it, Julie was on a high. She expected to get higher still, once she met with Doctor Balser on Wednesday. If her therapist agreed with her sister's amateur diagnosis, her problem finally would have a name—PTSD. Then there'd be one more step—to find a cure.

32

WEDNESDAY

Wednesday afternoon, Julie wrapped up her work at 2 p.m. She left her desk and pulled out the questionnaire Doctor Balser had given to her and Mark. She scanned through the list, jotted notes beside his questions on *Finances, Family Connections*, and *Job-Related Issues*. Those topics were easy. *Finances?* If she got married, she wanted to keep her salary separate from her husband's. They could share expenses and whatever was left over would be up to each individual person to use. She didn't want to depend on anyone. She couldn't stand the thought of having to ask for $50 to buy a new outfit or to get her hair done. She needed to have some control of her own income.

She returned her attention to Balser's questionnaire and moved on to *Family Connections*. Except for her sister, Rita, she'd kept her family at a distance. After six years of estrangement, she visited her parents after returning from Patmos. It was all part of Yanno's plan to help her forgive people who'd hurt her. The visit proved cathartic for her as well.

As for Mark's family, his mother died when he was 12, and his father now lived in Florida and was busy with his senior activities, whatever they were. She'd met the man and had liked him instantly. Mark was an only child. She didn't expect any family drama for either of them.

The third item on the list—*Job Related Issues*—also posed

no problems for Julie. She did her job, and Mark did his. They were kind of like Marjorie and her second husband, Norton. Marjorie stayed at the Creek most of the time working on her books, and Norton ran his hotels and restaurants in other parts of Florida. He spent most of his time at their Crescent Beach cottage, or he stayed in a hotel suite. They got together when it was convenient for Marjorie.

Julie could settle for the same kind of arrangement, to a certain degree. She didn't know if Mark could. She'd have to agree to a certain amount of give-and-take.

Last of all, Julie got to Balser's question on *Intimacy*, the only point that made her want to run for her life. What business was it of his to address such a personal topic? For years, she'd avoided the subject, hadn't thought much about it until now.

The attack had affected her in such a powerful way, she felt ashamed, disgusted, and fearful of reliving the horror. The truth was, she'd doubted she could be intimate with any man, even Mark. If she wanted to marry him, she was going to have to talk openly about her fears.

Up until today, she'd left that part of the questionnaire blank. Things were different now. She felt ready to address the worst event of her life and put it away for good. Like her sister had said, she may be suffering from Post Traumatic Stress Disorder. Her behavior over the past six years certainly confirmed it. The question was, could Doctor Balser help?

At three o'clock, she heard Mark's gentle rapping. She quickly stuffed the list of questions in her purse and opened the door.

"We have a few minutes," she said. "Will you take a quick look at the rough draft of my article?" She gestured toward her computer. "I left it up on the screen for you to read."

"Sure." Mark went straight to her desk and drew up her chair.

She held her breath as he scrolled through the file. His opinion meant the world to her. She stood at a distance, her eyes on his back. He kept nodding his head. The wait was excruciating.

"Wow, Julie," he said at last. "This is good. Real good." He kept reading to the end, muttered a few more praises, and scanned through her spread of photos. He glanced up at her. "Your descriptions are fascinating. And these pictures put me right there." He swiveled around to face her. "I'm proud of you, Julie. You're every bit as good as the best travel writers I've ever read. Even better than some."

"Sure," she said with a snicker. "But I think you're prejudiced." She checked her watch. "We'd better go. Doctor Balser's office is a half-hour away."

They drove across town and went inside Balser's waiting room. His office door was shut. A few minutes passed. Julie grabbed a medical magazine off the rack. Mark checked a few text messages on his phone.

Then the door to Balser's office opened. He finished up with his other patient and invited the two of them inside. She'd already grown comfortable with this kind man she'd met on the flight to Izmir a little over a month ago. As it turned out, his office was located a half-hour from her condo. She thought it was a coincidence. He said he didn't believe in coincidences.

Mark and Julie settled on the sofa together. With a notebook in one hand and a pen in the other, Balser grabbed his rolling desk chair and positioned it across from them, just like before. He started the session by inviting Julie to share her thoughts.

She took a deep breath, and pulled the list he'd given her

out of her purse. "I answered nearly every question," she said, unfolding the paper. She read her responses aloud.

Balser nodded in acknowledgement. "Terrific, Julie."

"There's more," she said. "When I got to the question on intimacy, I froze up. I'm afraid I left it blank."

She shot a quick glance at Mark. He responded with a compassionate smile.

She turned her attention back to Balser. "The assault damaged me, Doctor Balser. In more ways than anyone could imagine."

The doctor sat still, one leg crossed over the other, his head tilted to one side, silently prompting her to go on.

Slowly she dared to draw up the past. "Before the assault, I was an outgoing teenager, like any other. I hung out with lots of friends. I established some goals for my future. In one afternoon, my whole world came crashing down. I felt soiled, dirty, ashamed. I crawled into a shell. I was still going to school, but I walked around like a zombie, like the real me had died and come back from the grave, but lifeless. I avoided my friends—or maybe they avoided me." She looked down at the list, now crumpled in her hand. "Anyway, I did my schoolwork, but I let everything else go. No more parties, no more sports." She raised her head and locked eyes with Balser. "Did I ever tell you I once played soccer?"

The doctor shook his head. A hint of sadness clouded his gray eyes. Still, he said nothing.

"Doctor Balser, I want to get back to what I was before the attack, but I don't know how," Julie went on. "I concentrated on getting good grades, so I could earn a scholarship and get out of there. It was my only escape from those people who'd turned against me."

281

"You told me they didn't believe you, that they'd sided with the man who attacked you," Balser said, his brow wrinkled in concern.

"That's right." She let out a long sigh. "I'm afraid I wasn't the best behaved teenager. I'd already disappointed a lot of people."

Balser nodded. "Few teenagers live up to the expectations of adults. But you said the guy was caught with another young girl and is now paying for his crimes. Didn't the truth vindicate you with them?"

She raised one shoulder. "I didn't stick around to find out."

"So, how did you move on after high school?" Balser spoke in soft tones, his voice steady, comforting.

"I focused on my courses, worked on the college newspaper, and I lived on tips from a part-time job in a coffee shop. After graduation, the school counselor found me a job with the Springfield Daily Press, and I was on my way to complete independence."

"No dating?"

"Once in a while I accepted an invitation out, but I kept my relationships with men on a friends-only basis. One thing was certain, I needed to be in control."

"Not all men are like your attacker."

"I know—at least, I'd like to believe that."

"You trusted Mark."

She looked at Mark. He'd remained quiet, but tenderness emanated from the deep blue of his eyes, and he had a faint smile on his lips.

"I still do," she said, patting his hand. "Mark never wavered, never gave me any reason to mistrust him."

"But the trauma was still there, wasn't it?" the doctor said, his voice tender.

His question set her back. She could feel herself drifting into that lonely, troubled place again. It was time to bring it all out in the open.

"I–I kept reliving that terrible afternoon," she said, her voice breaking. "Those memories never went away. They were always there. I merely succeeded in covering them up for a while. And—" Here came the hardest admission of all. "I hated myself for not being more careful, for allowing myself to get into an unsafe situation. I tortured myself with questions. Was it the way I dressed? Did I unintentionally flirt with that man? Why did I let myself be alone with him? I should have known better."

Balser uncrossed his leg and leaned toward her. "You did *not* cause what happened to you. That man took something precious from you. He robbed you of your innocence. He stole your youth." The doctor cocked his head, his steel gray eyes filled with compassion. "Don't you want to take back what rightfully belongs to you?"

"I–I guess so." Tears blurred her vision. "I know I don't want to keep living the way I have been over the past six years. Dr. Balser, is there any way I can get back to what I used to be? Or is that girl gone forever?"

He folded his arms across his chest.

"What do *you* think, Julie?"

She paused for a couple of seconds, cast a sideways glance at Mark.

He leaned toward her. "Tell him what your sister, Rita, said."

She nodded and looked at Balser with a critical eye, trying to determine if he might be ready to hear Rita's amateur diagnosis. Her shoulders sagged as she gave in to the impulse. "My sister thinks I have PTSD."

Balser's eyebrows shot up. "Why do you think she believes that?"

"She's a nursing student. Did I ever tell you that?"

He nodded. "You did."

"Anyway, I checked it out online. I have many of the symptoms. The nightmares. The mood swings. Shutting people out of my life. My obsession with work and nothing else. The repulsion I feel when I think about marriage and intimacy. For a while I struggled with an eating disorder."

The man smiled. "When we met, you did look awfully thin, Julie. You seem to be doing better."

She blushed then. "Thanks, I don't recall how I overcame it, but the healing started before I left Patmos. Maybe it was the tropical setting and fresh air. Maybe it was the old man I met there and his words of encouragement. In any case, I developed an appetite. Now I need to get past all of my other self-destructive behaviors." Tears spilled from her eyes. "I think my sister is right. I believe I have PTSD."

Balser's smile broadened, as though he was about to reveal a secret. She didn't take her eyes off of him.

"You've just made two steps in the right direction, Julie. One, you admitted you may have PTSD. I've suspected it all along, but I needed you to say it. And two, you asked for help. Those two elements—admission and a cry for help—have to be present in order to begin the healing process. You've reached a plateau, Julie. From here, everything has to get better."

She grabbed a tissue from the side table next to her chair and mopped the moisture from her cheeks. "I always thought PTSD was a military sickness."

"That's a common misunderstanding," Balser said. "The truth is, PTSD can strike anyone, even children who've been the victims of a traumatic incident. More women than men suffer with PTSD, and rape is at the top of the list of causes." He leaned back in his chair. "You've described the typical symptoms. Nightmares, flashbacks, your own feelings of guilt."

"But, it's been six years. Shouldn't I have gotten past it all?"

He shook his head, and a sadness turned his gray eyes darker. "I have a 60-year-old patient who was raped when she was 25 and only recently came to me for help. It took her 35 years to realize she needed therapy. She suffered from more than nightmares and flashbacks. She developed some serious health problems. Believe it or not, they're starting to go away now."

He leaned toward her. "The same thing could have happened to you, Julie, if you hadn't come for help. In the beginning, you suffered rape trauma syndrome, but because you didn't seek treatment right away, your condition escalated over the next six years and gradually developed into full-fledged PTSD. If you were to continue along the same path, you too might eventually experience health issues. Some victims even try to numb their pain with drugs or alcohol. It's not too late, Julie. We can treat the psychological aspect of your trauma and help you get your life back."

She perked up. "So, what's the next step?"

Balser laughed heartily. "You are truly ready, young lady." His eyes crinkled at the corners. "Several methods are available, depending on your personal preferences. If you want to take medication, I can send you to someone who can prescribe an antidepressant, possibly Prozac or Zoloft. As a family counselor, I don't have—"

Julie shook her head adamantly and cut him off. "No. No drugs. The side effects can be worse than the illness."

"Not always. Medications work fine for some people, but they're not for everyone. There are other methods."

"Like what?"

"Like EMDR therapy."

Julie tilted her head. "EMDR?"

"Eye Movement Desensitization and Reprocessing. I've had great success using it with other clients. It was developed in the 1980s and has proved successful with military personnel and other individuals who suffer with PTSD. It's different from the usual 'talk therapy,' which requires the patient to relive the traumatic event multiple times in detail. Such an approach can take months or even years. But with EMDR, the patient needs only focus on one specific aspect of the traumatic incident at a time."

"You say it's been proven successful?" Julie said, still doubtful.

Balser nodded. "They used it with the first responders and victims of the attack on 9/11 and with some of the survivors and families in New Town, Connecticut. Those were more severe cases, of course. Their trauma was multiplied many times over. The point is, it worked."

"So, how will you use it to help me?"

"We'll schedule several meetings a week apart. Through the use of sensory stimuli, I'll work with you to draw energy from different parts of your brain. In short, we'll desensitize those negative memories and replace them with positive emotions. Eventually you'll come to understand how strong and capable you are. As the saying goes, we'll help you survive, and then we'll help you thrive."

"How many sessions will it take?" she said. "I don't want to spend my entire life in therapy."

"The process starts working almost immediately. In your

case, I suspect we probably will need no more than six sessions. Once you learn the technique, you should be able to use it whenever you feel a need."

Julie turned to Mark. "What do you think?"

Until that moment, he'd practically faded into the wallpaper, which was another of his qualities. He knew when to be a part of the conversation and when to observe from a distance.

Now he came to life. "I'm in favor of anything that might help you, Julie." He faced Doctor Balser, then. "This method— could it also help me get past the loss of my mother? It's been 15 years, but ever since her death, I've avoided funerals like the plague. I even stay away from people who could be on the brink of death." He snickered. "I guess nearly everyone has *some* debilitating issue. For Julie, it's the assault, something that was totally out of her control. For me, it's losing the most important person in my life at such a young age."

Julie stared at him as though seeing him for the first time. Mark never talked much about his mother's death. He'd appeared to be the epitome of strength, both physically and psychologically. She'd been so consumed with her own problems she'd never considered that he, too, might have issues. Didn't Balser say PTSD can strike anyone of any age, even children? Mark may have been carrying his trauma for 15 years, but he never told anyone.

She gazed at his sky-blue eyes, now moist with emotion. Overwhelmed with love for him, she reached out and placed her hand on his. He didn't flinch, didn't try to slip his hand away. Instead, he placed his other hand on top of hers.

The doctor gave them an encouraging smile. "This is good, really good—for both of you." He grabbed his iPad off the desk, and punched at the screen. "We need to put your premarital counseling on hold for now. Let's go ahead and schedule your individual sessions. I want you each to come in alone for your therapy. Julie, I'm scheduling you for next Wednesday at two o'clock. Mark, I'll put you down for 4:00. Afterward, we'll meet every Wednesday at those times. We'll space your sessions out until you only need to come back when you want another meeting. Perhaps by that time, the two of you will be able to come here together, and we can get going with your premarital counseling."

Balser's plan instilled fresh confidence in Julie. Six private sessions would take them to the end of September. Then, premarital counseling. She could do this.

She left Balser's office with a spring in her step. As they got to the street, Mark reached for her hand. "So, what do you think?" he said. "Do you feel comfortable with Balser's plan?"

She nodded slowly, pensively. "I have to admit, EMDR sounds a little different, but he did say he's had success using it with other clients."

As he usually did, Mark held the car door open for her and waited while she slid into the front seat. After getting her settled, he jogged around to the driver's side and got in. He held the key in his hand, but he didn't start the car.

He eyed her with suspicion. "You look like the cat who swallowed the canary, Julie. What's the matter?"

"Nothing. I've been thinking about Marjorie. How she lived alone most of the time. How she never had children of her own; never had the kind of life most women seek. She worked hard and made a name for herself in the literary arts. But she also made sacrifices. She spent little time with her husband, though she loved him dearly. It had to be a painful way to exist."

She grew even more serious. "I'm not sure I want that kind of life, Mark. I like my job, but I also like being with you, and I can't imagine what my life would be without you, even for a little while." She gazed into his eyes. "I don't see any reason why I can't have the best of both worlds. I may never be famous like Marjorie, but I can find a decent balance between work and home life. Together, we can figure out a system that will work for us. We shouldn't have to compromise, shouldn't have to live apart for long stretches at a time."

"What are you saying, Julie?" He shifted his upper body toward her.

She smiled again. "I don't see any reason why we shouldn't set a date. For real, this time."

Mark's eyes grew wide, and his eyebrows went up. "Are you kidding? Do you think you're ready?"

"Doctor Balser said my therapy will take up to six weeks. If he's right, I can expect to reach another level of healing by the end of September. In fact, now that I know there's a label for what's wrong with me and a method to cure it, I feel better already. Soooo—what do you think about a Christmas wedding? You've mentioned it before."

He stared out the front window, like he was deep in thought.

"Christmas, huh?" He faced her and broke into a big grin. "Sounds great. The timing is far better than what we originally planned."

She nodded. "Lakisha is supposed to deliver in October. She should be back in a size 10 dress by the time the wedding comes around. She'll make a beautiful matron of honor. You'll be on Christmas break from the college. So will Rita, my maid of honor."

For the first time in years, a surge of excitement stirred Julie's heart. "We can start making the arrangements tomorrow," she said. "This time, I won't delay. We can order our invitations. Lakisha promised to help me send them out. It's perfect. She'll need something to do while she's on bed rest. I'll call my parents to arrange for the church and fellowship hall."

Then a thought struck her like a time bomb. "Do you realize, we'll have our reception in the exact location where I was attacked?" She pressed her fingers to her lips.

Mark reached out and took one of her hands in his. "Do you think you can handle it?"

"I've been there twice since we came home from Patmos. If I get married there, I'll create a whole different set of memories in that church. Better ones. Maybe that's how EMDR works. Through substitution."

He kissed her fingers, then slowly released her hand.

"You know," Julie said. "When I was a teenager my grampa said something that stayed with me for a long time after he died. He told me, at some point I'd reach a fork in the road, and I'd have to make a decision that would affect the rest of my life. Well, I've reached that fork. I could keep on doing what I've been doing for the past six years. Or I could choose another path, even though I don't know for sure where it will lead. I'm choosing that other path, the fork in the road, as my grampa would say. I choose therapy. I choose to heal. And I choose you, Mark. I want to spend the rest of my life with you."

He slid his arm around her shoulder and drew her close. "You're gonna make it, Julie. You're a survivor. You always have been, and I suspect you always will be."

She smiled. "You've been great, Mark. In spite of all my ridiculous outbursts, you always stuck by me." She shook her head and giggled. "Most men would have run for the hills by now."

He gave her a little squeeze and then started the car. "Don't worry, honey. I'm not going anywhere."

She tilted her head. "Speaking of going anywhere, we haven't talked about where we might go for a honeymoon."

He let out a little laugh. "I know *exactly* where I want to go."

She eyed him with anticipation. "And where's that?"

"Well, when I read through your article this afternoon, I felt a sudden urge to visit Cross Creek." He pulled away from the curb and headed down the street. "Your descriptions of the place make me want to tour Marjorie's house. I want to peek inside the old barn. I want to walk the trail around her property, maybe pluck an orange off of one of her trees, peel it, and eat it right there on the front lawn. I want to stay overnight in one of the cabins, sample fried gator tail at The Yearling Restaurant, sit back and listen to Willie 'Big Toe' Green play his guitar and harmonica. And I want to meet the tour guide you told me about—Lucy, and her Aunt Emma." He shot her a sideways glance. "The truth is, I want to immerse myself in everything you experienced in Florida. Does that sound silly to you?"

Julie laughed out loud. "Not at all. I'd love to go back there and reconnect with Lucy and Aunt Emma. And I want to find Marjorie again, if only in spirit."

"Then it's settled," Mark said. "We're going to Florida for our honeymoon. Afterward, we'll go lots of other places together, for the rest of our lives. Heck, I'll even go on some of your work assignments with you."

Julie smiled at the thought of being Mrs. Julie Bensen, a member of the traveling duo of Bensen and Bensen, programmed to take on the world, one state at a time and maybe one country at a time. Together, in search of another story. This time, she'd titled the article, "In Search of Felicity." Next time it would be "In Search of..." something else.

The funny thing was, while searching for Marjorie's *Felicity*, Julie had discovered an "intense happiness" of her own. Marjorie had found her felicity in the solitude of Cross Creek, the place she ultimately called home. Julie found hers by stepping out of her reclusive shell and into a full life with Mark.

At that moment, she knew the truth. It hit her like the bolt of lightning that had split that old oak tree in half at the edge of the creek. She recalled how tall and straight it stood. It didn't fall. It survived, maybe for many years to come. She'd been damaged too, but she was still standing. And she had a wonderful support system—Mark and Lakisha and Greg and Doctor Balser and Rita, maybe even Marjorie herself. There was no longer any doubt in Julie's mind. Her healing had already begun.

ACKNOWLEDGEMENTS

Many thanks to Florence Turcotte, literary archivist in the Smathers Library at the University of Florida. Special thanks to Geoffrey Gates, a Florida State Parks ranger who gave me a private tour of the grounds and house and verified details in the story. Also thanks to Rick Mulligan, a staff volunteer at the historic park, for his illuminating comments. Much appreciation also to Clarice Ruttenber, certified EMDRIA therapist. And thanks to my many readers whose feedback was invaluable to the completion of this work.

Much appreciation to my daughter, Joanna Jones, for contributing her painting, *Marjorie Kinnan Rawlings' Barn* (oil on canvas) for the back cover. Visit www.joannajonesart. simplesite.com for more of Joanna's artwork.

Much appreciation to my publisher, Mike Parker, my personal "Maxwell Perkins," Marjorie's editor who wrote these words: "A book must be done according to the writer's conception of it as nearly perfectly as possible...the publisher must not try to get a writer to fit the book to the conditions of the trade. It must be the other way round." That sounds exactly like Mike.

Quoted materials were used with permission from Marjorie Kinnan Rawlings' Special and Area Studies Collections, George A. Smathers Libraries, University of Florida, Gainesville, Florida.

Quotes from *Max & Marjorie: The Correspondence between Maxwell E. Perkins and Marjorie Kinnan Rawlings*, edited by Rodger L. Tarr. Gainesville: University Press of Florida, 1999, selected quotations.

Quotes from *The Private Marjorie, The Love Letters of Marjorie Kinnan Rawlings to Norton S. Baskin*, by Rodger L. Tarr. Gainesville: University Press of Florida, 2004, selected quotations.

Ultimately: To God be the Glory for all He has done in my work, in my salvation, and in my life.

ABOUT THE AUTHOR

Pulitzer Prize nominee Marian Rizzo has written four contemporary novels and two biblical era novels. She's been a journalist for twenty-five years with the Ocala Star-Banner Newspaper, part of the Gatehouse Media Group. Now retired, Marian has continued to work with the Star-Banner as a correspondent. She's won numerous awards in journalism, including the New York Times Chairman's Award and first place in the annual Amy Foundation Writing Awards.

Marian lives in Ocala, Florida, with her daughter Vicki who has Down Syndrome. Her other daughter, Joanna, is the mother of three children. Grandparenting has added another element of joy to Marian's busy schedule, which includes workouts five times a week, lots of reading, and lunches with the girls.

Visit her online at Marianscorner.com

Also Available From

WordCrafts Press

A Purpose True
by Gail Kittleson

End of Summer
by Michael Potts

Odd Man Outlaw
by K.M. Zahrt

Maggie's Song
by Marcia Ware

The Pruning
by Jan Cline

White Squirrels and Other Monsters
By Gerry Brown

www.WordCrafts.net

Made in the USA
Las Vegas, NV
18 July 2021

26669851R00177